painting the taj mahal

David I Brown

Sorrell Books

A Sorrell Books Production

ISBN: 9798569427079

painting the taj mahal

acknowledgements

This is a book of passions and emotions, of painting and murder. Set mainly in India, it richly exposes both the poverty and beauty of its people and cultures. Drawing on the writer's own experiences whilst travelling there, he also must thank great writers, like Paul Torday, Dan Brown and Gregory Roberts for their amazing use of words that enhanced his work.

also by david i brown

Cancer Was My Companion: A Memoir
Jab Jab Molassi at the Break Point Hotel (Illustrated)
Break Point Hotel (Revised)

Chapter 1

The sea breeze felt warm against my face, even though it was quite a strong westerly wind and the sound of the waves hurtling up the shingle beach soothed me as I struggled to hold the paper in my sketch book flat enough to daub another deeper blue grey wash across it. Although the sun was beginning to set, the light was glorious, and the ever-changing colours made the sea look wine red before I finally laid my brush back in its box and put down my pallet and folded over the sketch pad cover.

I had found a sheltered spot on the other side of a breaker that allowed me to be sheltered from the south westerly winds that were incessant on the West Sussex beaches especially around Elmer Sands and also allowed me to paint with my water colours, a scene across the beach to a big old house that sat precariously on a promontory as the sea defences were slowly being eroded annually. It wouldn't be long before it might end up being on an island of its own.

It had once belonged to a famous family, I had been told, but having been recently sold to a young city broker, was now having a million pound make over.

I had done a few sketches and using sea water, not ideal but it did the job, had tried to capture the sea greens and blood orange sky as the sun moved ever lower. These would be my base for an intended oil painting once I got back to my one roomed studio. A final image captured on my iphone completed the collection of ideas and colours.

I was ready to go home and struggled to get up from my little folding painting stool, stumbling as I did through the deep shingle. The steep slope didn't help, and I staggered back a step and into the incoming tide. Cursing and shaking a dripping foot I stomped my way up to the top of the beach, turning just once to see the oyster catchers feeding ravenously at the water's edge as each wave washed further up the stones, changing and darkening their colour as it did so.

The walk back along the beach, as the tide ebbed, wasn't easy. Well it never was because the deep shingle moved sideways with every step. It wasn't made any easier either, as I was carrying a rucksack of paints and pencils, paper and pictures.

Half an hour later I finally got back home and was glad to get inside, dumping everything on the kitchen floor to put the kettle on and make a cuppa.

I sipped my hot tea in between delving into my rucksack and pulling out the various pieces of half crumpled cartridge papers that were still a little damp from my over exuberant brush strokes. Spreading them across the table I had to move the post that I had picked up as I swung open the front door. Most of the post was either junk or bills or reminders of unpaid bills, but amongst today's pile I noticed a cream envelope with my name and address handwritten in black ink on it in a sweeping calligraphic style that immediately caught my eye. The postage suggested it was from India. I didn't know anyone in India.

Not having a letter opener handy, I grabbed a knife from the kitchen draw a slit it open, peered inside and pulled out the two sheets of note paper, similarly scribed in black ink in the same hand as the envelope.

I finished my tea and read the letter.

Dr Satwinder Singh
Mango Villa
Chennai Road
Mumbai, India

20th September 2020

Dear Mr Ianson,

I send you my greetings from the shores of the Indian Ocean where our home overlooks the sea a few miles north of the ever-expanding metropolis of Mumbai.

Although our most glorious country of India continues to grow extremely well, we are still not as blessed as your country where civilisation is so much more advanced.

We still have so many problems with poverty and malfunctions that I wonder if we will ever be as great as Britain is.

The reason why it is that I write to you, concerns the fact that I have been referred to you by a colleague of mine that has seen your website and the wonderful paintings that you produce.

As a reasonably wealthy doctor, I have enough funds to sponsor a painting commission of my two sons and dear wife, in front of the Taj Mahal in the north of India in Agra.

I recognise the possible challenge in you coming out to India but have been so impressed with your work that I would genuinely appreciate your consideration of this project.

I will be more than happy to provide you with ample compensation, as well as your actual fee for the painting.

Without going into any further details, I would endeavour to seek a telephone conversation with you at your convenience to determine whether you would indeed be interested.

Yours most sincerely,

Dr Singh

It was quite a while and another several reads before I could sit back in my chair.

"Blimey. Well I never!"

Talking to myself seemed to be a trait that my friends had recently started to comment on despite the fact I seemed to have been doing it for years without a single comment before.

I didn't know what to think really. Initially, it seemed so preposterous that I assumed it was a joke. A prank played on me by one of my old pals. Most of my old friends had stopped buying any of my work years ago, for many obvious reasons. Unless I was giving stuff away, they weren't interested.

"Not enough room left on the walls, Peter," they would often bleat.

A card had been slipped into the envelope with Dr Singh's telephone number and email address, so I thought, well why not. Can't do any harm. Worse case would be an embarrassing – thanks but no thanks.

I decided to email him the following morning having worked out that Mumbai was probably some four and a half hours ahead and as it was early evening now, he might not want to read my response this late.

chapter 2

The following morning as the late summer sun cut through the old velvet curtains, it caught me across my face waking me up with a start. The words in the letter from Dr Singh circled through my brain almost immediately. Sliding out from under the duvet, I picked up the letter again that I had left on the dressing table and re read it.

Slippers and dressing gown on, I managed to trip down the stairs before flip-flopping into the kitchen to fill the kettle and switch it on. Reaching up to the cupboard to get a mug with one hand I grabbed a tea bag with the other before tossing it into the mug and pouring just a little skimmed milk on top. Not a typical cup of Indian char, I thought. Indian tea is always very milky and far too sweet. The steaming kettle clicked off and I filled the mug and leaving the tea bag in, flip flopped across the hall into my studio. The northern light was perfect for painting in, but I couldn't see the sea from there. My so-called study was on the other side of the house, overlooking the long shingle beaches in both directions. The south westerly breezes were still warm at this time of year, but I knew it wouldn't be long before the bitter cold wind and at times horizontal rain would soon take its place.

Swinging round in my old, well used leather chair, I sat and plugged in the laptop, switched it on and called up my emails. I sat in front of the pale blue lit screen for a moment before writing my response to Dr Singh.

I made up my mind there and then - I was going to do it. I was going to take on the commission and go to India.

Peter Ianson
Sorrell Cottage
Elmer Sands
West Sussex
England

28th September 2020

Dear Dr Singh,

It was wonderful to receive your letter requesting me to undertake a commission by your good self to paint a portrait of your family in front of the Taj Mahal.

I must admit at first, I wasn't sure if the letter were genuine, but soon realised that it was and that it was an opportunity that I would most gratefully accept.

I am sure there is a lot to discuss, plans to be made regarding timings, understandings and expectations and as you have already suggested, we should set up a telephone conversation once you have received this email.

I have attached a file link with both my mobile and land line numbers and eagerly await your call.

Yours most graciously,

Peter Ianson

I sent off the email, sat back putting my hands behind my head and smiled. This felt like it was going to be a good day.

It took no longer than shaving, showering and soft boiling my egg before I heard a ping on my laptop. It was Dr Singh. His email was full of exuberance and joy and finished off with a promise to call me within the hour to discuss the details.

It was just before 9-30 when my mobile vibrated across the table whilst playing the first three bars of "O Sole Mio".

"I really must change that ring tone," I thought.

It was Dr Singh.

I listened to his excited voice. He was almost squealing with excitement and praise while we discussed the proposal, sorted through the detail of the commission and briefly discussed the final but most important issue of money.

Until today, my life had for the most part been spent painting, appointments with potential buyers and more painting or other pointless engagements. But for the past few months I had felt the need to branch out more, see the world maybe and satisfy some of the increasing sense of emotional and artistic restlessness which had grown in me. Today's date marked a turning point I thought. Although I had been in a relationship, Elizabeth and I had just decided to have a break. It seemed right, somehow, to change the pattern of my daily existence. Perhaps going to India to work on this commission would help me find a new perspective to my life and create new value in what I believed in and wanted to become.

Elizabeth and I had initially settled into a calm and rational relationship. She was career minded, a professional and a scientist, supporting the richness that drives our expanding population, with food. She has authored papers, given many lectures and enjoyed the academic world. She was prospering in a well-paid job and was highly respected and will no doubt go far. The only disadvantage was that I was seeing less of her as she travelled a great deal. That is why in the end we decided to have some time apart.

I though, only made my name, such as it is, selling my paintings. My career had developed too but so far, I hadn't made much money and certainly not as well remunerated as Elizabeth, but my painting gave me satisfaction and I believe I am sort of well regarded in the art world, having won a few prizes and produced several paintings through commissions that have been well thought of by my peers as well as my clients.

My life is relatively unruffled, and I am still young enough to remain selfish and therefore explore new horizons. Unpaid teaching in my local school provoked interest in some students that had made me happy, although regrettably, their interest in art didn't seem to continue beyond the class lessons.

It has only taken something like this Indian commission to raise its head to remind me that there is a wonderful world of opportunity and beauty in this world, an unknown that will be full of excitement and challenges – the things my soul needs and my heart yearns for.

Dr Singh's praise on the phone was highly encouraging and we agreed quite quickly the travel arrangements, timings and my expenses and fee. Dr Singh went so far as to say that, following the completion of the painting, there could be an extra bonus. Praise indeed. I know that money isn't the most important thing, but it does rather help! Elizabeth used to complain that I was never paid enough for my pieces at the best of times.

The day slipped by quite quickly as I busied myself, finding my passport, sending off for my Indian visa, looking up flight details and generally learning so much more about Agra. Finding that I had little in the fridge for supper, I had decided to walk down the street to the

Indian Restaurant to buy a takeaway. Might as well start getting used to some Indian cuisine. Continuing with my Agra research and mopping up Chicken Vindaloo from my lap after some of it slipped off my spoon, was not a good start. A glass of Cobra beer helped sooth my heated throat though. I sat back, glass still in hand and smiled a little triumphant smile. At last a chance, perhaps, to make a real statement.

My bowel movements the following morning were not surprisingly, a little easier than usual, having been affected somewhat by the vindaloo. However, it didn't stop me from going for a quick run along the beach and then to the local shop for a pint of milk and a paper. I arrived back home and immediately set about checking my oil paints and brushes, but I gave the morning café longo a miss. My trip was planned for two weeks' time, assuming my visa came back in time, so I needed to start organising things. Canvases were to be provided on my arrival, all pre-prepared and ready.

It is strange how quickly things can change in your life I thought. For the last month, since Elizabeth moved out, I had been contemplating the newfound tranquil, albeit silent and lonely nature of my new-found existence and then suddenly I am basking in the intense rewards of an exciting commission in Asia.

I inspected each brush, holding them in front of me in the light to decide if they needed replacing or not. Should I buy some new tubes of oil paints? Did I have all the right tones and colours? I certainly needed more Zinc White and maybe another tube of Burnt Sienna. I went online to my usual supplier and ordered one of each and then I got carried away and bought some new expensive brushes, extra colours and a new HB pencil set.

I had been excited when I logged off. Like a kid in a candy shop, until I saw the bill. The previous night's takeaway helped take my mind off the invoice. I reflected, sitting on the loo, that it would have been nice if Elizabeth had been at home. We could have talked things over. I could phone her I thought, but she doesn't like long phone calls. She used to tell me that phone calls were for information. The trouble was, that she wasn't at home to have the conversation and I am sure she would want to have it over the phone, even less. I was proud of what I was about to do and hoped she would have been proud of me too. I missed her.

Looking through my wardrobe I saw that I had nothing suitable to wear in India. It was going to be hot and humid during the day, but I did think I needed a new pair of pyjama bottoms, as the elastic had gone in my present pair. The nights in Northern India might be a little cooler than people imagined. I had no short sleeve shirts and only a few well used and mainly paint daubed T shirts. My shorts were somewhat faded and various things like socks had holes in the heels and as for a dusty pair of sandals. They weren't even fit for a dog to chew. I was getting a little despondent as I was detecting a steady and disparaging downward trend in the condition of most of my so-called summer clothes. Having decided a shopping spree was in order, I suddenly realised that T shirts and shorts might be in short supply in Tesco in September. Perhaps on-line catalogues might be more reliable.

Several days later, having had my Passport mailed back to me that included my new Indian visa, I received a phone call. It was a disjointed call but there was a Neelu Someone on the line from Mumbai and could I talk right now? I so nearly said no as I often got call centres based in India cold calling me, usually pretending they were in Bognor Regis and wondered whether I wanted to buy solar panels at half price. But instead I decided to continue with the call as her voice was warm and refined. With the hint of an Indian accent, she asked if she was speaking to Mr Ianson.

She was very polite, and she apologised for disturbing me, told me she understood that I was about to come out to India to carry out an important painting commission and said that she would not have disturbed me except that Dr Singh was being very pressing. She introduced herself as Dr Singh's personal secretary and asked if I had a date for my pending arrival into Mumbai.

I was a little taken aback as I hadn't expected a phone call, because I had been waiting for an email or letter of formal invitation to arrive.

I made an assenting sound in my throat not daring to speak initially. She took this to mean yes and asked for my flight dates and times. For a moment I was stunned into silence before I finally cleared my throat and quietly informed her that I hadn't yet booked flights.

"Will you be doing so today, or shall I be doing this for you?" she asked.

I found myself asking her to book the appropriate flights at a time to suit her and the doctor.

"It will mean that you arrive in Mumbai about midnight local time if that is alright, Mr Ianson. You will be met at the airport and taken to the Intercontinental Hotel for the night," she continued.

"Will Dr Singh be there?" I asked.

"Dr Singh will meet you there the following morning," she quietly assured me.

"He is very anxious to meet you as soon as possible. That is, if you agree to meeting the following morning."

I agreed immediately on a day and time and I put the phone down, poured myself a glass of cheap red wine and sat on the sofa, totally content with my life. It would have been nice if I had been able to talk to someone about my pending trip, but as I lounged across the cushions, I just had to smile even though I knew I was being selfish.

Chapter 3

A week later I was standing in the front room of my little cottage, with a small suitcase containing all my new clothes and another, larger suitcase packed to the maximum weight with all my painting paraphernalia. A large black car pulled up outside. As I dragged my suitcases out to the car the driver opened the rear door for me having sprung the boot.

"The airport, sir?" he said, without looking at me.

The car purred off up the road. A newspaper sat folded next to me. I sat back in the comfortable black leather seat, read the paper and enjoyed the unaccustomed luxury. We drove up the motorway, into the airport terminal and stopped.

The driver took off his spectacles, turned his head from the front seat and gave me a smile.

"Here we are, sir. The check-in desks are just through these doors," he said, quietly and nodded towards the terminal entrance.

It was midnight, local time, when the plane finally touched down at the Chhatrapati Shivaji Maharaj International Airport. As I disembarked from the plane along the narrow corridor, the first thing I noticed was the smell of the air. I could smell it before I saw anything of India. I was excited and delighted by it, but I couldn't recognise it. It was a mixture of sweet smelling, hot steaming vegetation. The smell of hope and yet it also smelt of sour, stifling sweat and the smell of greed and demons and a crumbling empire and civilisations in resurrection and decay. As I negotiated passport control and made my way through the huge throng of people, the smell of diesel and the blood metal smell of machinery struck me, along with that of the waste of tens of millions of animals, more than half of them humans and rats. It also smelt of heartbreak and the struggle to live and survive. I could smell the perfumes from the temples and shrines, and also the spices and freshly cut flowers.

In some ways it the worst good smell in the world. It is a smell that I would never forget and one that to this day, always reminds me of Mumbai. I was happy to be there, that was until I stepped out of the airconditioned airport and into the heat. A mosquito immediately buzzed around my forehead. I had been standing for no more than a few minutes, looking for a driver with a sign that would have my name written on it. Within those few minutes as I scoured the faces of several tens of similar drivers, the first beads of sweat ran down my forehead and neck. My clothes clung to me as if I had stepped fully clothed into a sauna. My heart beat heavily, under the command of the new climate and my increasing concern at not being able to locate my name on any of the numerous handwritten boards. Each breathe became a little more laboured. I came to understand that it never stops, the jungle sweat, because the heat that makes it, day and night, is a wet sticking heat.

Then there were all the people, Punjabis, people from Bengal and Rajasthan and Cochin and of course the untouchables. All the different religions from Hindus to Muslims, Christians and Buddhists. Dark skinned and fair, green eyes, golden brown and black eyes. Different faces old and young. All that makes up the incomparable beauty that is India. To add to this there were camels, mules, goats, oxen and feral dogs and of course the sacred cows. These all just roamed the streets, some working most of them not. I continued to hunt for my name, pushing through the growing throng of humanity. The hot night air outside the airport canopy was fierce but I was intoxicated with the exhilaration of my escape.

"Sir, sir!" a voice called from somewhere in amongst the signs and name plaques. A hand grabbed at my arm. I stopped and tensed. I turned around to see a small man, dressed in a greasy brown uniform.

"Taxi? Taxi? You want taxi?" he smiled at me and shook his head from side to side and opened both his hands pleading.

"No, err, thank you. I have a car," I said, not really knowing if that were true or not.

At that moment I saw my name, handwritten in thick black marker pen on a white card. I smiled at the holder and waved, dropping both suitcases. A tall good-looking man dressed in a black suit and crisp white shirt, forced his way through the waiting crowd of other drivers.

"Your driver, sir. I will be taking your cases, isn't it?" he said through a row of bright white teeth.

When I smiled my relief and surprise, the man grinned back even more with that perfect sincerity we fear in case we are wrong. We walked in the sticky night heat. I followed him through an endless mass of people and cars, weaving in and out trying to keep close to him. I watched when we stopped as my suitcases were lifted into the boot of a shiny new Toyota. I took my place in the back seat, the driver closed the door and slipped into his seat. I looked through window as he turned on the engine and felt the cool air-conditioned darkened space envelop me. A passing porter scowled at me, spat a vivid jet of red betel juice by the car door. The engine roared and gears meshed, and we sped off through the crowds and pedestrians, who nimbly seemed to always just step out of the way with millimetres to spare.

The journey from the airport to the hotel began on a wide, modern motorway, lined with trees and pink flowering shrubs that the dim yellow headlamps occasionally picked out. It was neat and clean and green and colourful, and the traffic flowed so well. It wasn't long however before, having been lulled into a false sense of wellbeing, that image was shattered, as the first narrowing of the road, showed me the contrast and its effect that were India. The first sight of the slums as the three lanes of the motorway became one potholed mud lined one and the disappearance of the trees, grasped at my heart with a feeling of shock and shame. We were in the centre of Mumbai, with big, gated houses behind high walls, but in-front were the miserable shelters patched together with corrugated iron, plastic and string. Cardboard and reed mats were all that covered the floor, except for a charcoal brazier here and there and plenty of bamboo sticks supporting the walls and roofs. Each dwelling seemed to support the next. All attached to one another and with an occasional narrow lane winding between them.

It seemed impossible that a modern Indian city, so close to the airport, sitting nestled between magnificent houses and posh hotels full of prosperous and intelligent travellers and workers, was awash with a totally opposite view of human existence.

The continuing mass of slums rolled on as we drove past them meeting the horizon like a dirty heat haze mirage. People had come to the city in their tens of thousands to seek work and money. I had been defiled as my spirit withered. The guilt I felt knowing my own wealth as I felt my thick wallet in my jacket pocket. I watched their terrible lives as we drove on. That first encounter with the ragged misery of the slum, heartbreak all the way along the roads, cut into my eyes and soul. Those smoulderings of shame and guilt flamed into anger at the unfairness of it all. What kind of government and system and people allows suffering like this? The awful contrast was the shining hotels for the tourists and travellers – like me. Only occasionally the crumbling moss-covered apartments of the comparatively affluent broke the comparison.

I began to see the people who inhabited the slums. Women washing in a bowl or cooking on a charcoal fire. One stooping to brush her black mane of hair, another bathing her children from an aluminium churn, and all this was in the middle of the night a few hours before dawn!

A man led two goats with blue nylon ropes tied to the collars at their throats, while another struggled to shave himself as he gazed into a cracked piece of mirror and little light. Women carried water on their heads as children played with sticks, but everywhere I looked these people were smiling and laughing. What was there to be happy about I thought?

The car had stopped in the traffic and two small brown faces appeared. Dawn was breaking. They knocked quietly on the window. Their sad eyes stared at me as their dirty begging hands made feeding gestures to their open mouths. They looked strange and remote. The car moved on and their faces disappeared. I continued to look at the people as we passed. They all seemed so busy. Where were they all going to? What were they all doing? How much industry and energy described their lives?

As we sped on, I caught glimpses of inside their houses. Despite the poverty, their single rooms were spotless. The metal pots shone, stacked in neat piles. I saw how beautiful they were; the women wrapped in saris of so many different colours. Purples, ochre, deep blues and gold. All of them were barefoot, walking through the tangled shabbiness of the narrow muddy streets, wet with washing water and food waste. They looked so proud and upright, so graceful and calm. All seemed to have white teeth and beautiful almond eyes. The men were handsome and there was the affectionate friendliness of the slim and fine limbed children. Slender-hipped girls and tall boys with cricket bats and for the first time since getting in the car, I smiled.

As we neared the hotel, the car moved at a crawl passed three storey houses and down narrow streets lined with trees. The traffic churned on, smoke and fumes pouring endlessly out of every vehicle. Cars and bikes weaved mysteriously round each other in organised chaos and efficiency. It was a manic ballistic dance of buses, bikes, cars and trucks. Ox drawn carts made the passage even slower and then there were people - everywhere, darting dangerously in and out of the traffic. I opened the window a little as I could see the sun now rising after dawn. The diesel smoke was mixed with spices, perfumes and camel manure. Voices rose everywhere although most were drowned out by the constant and never-ending cacophony of the sound of car horns. Every truck had a sign on the back asking you to "sound your horn" and they did, everyone did, all the time. Unfamiliar music escaped from a shop door and every corner carried gigantic posters, advertising the latest Bollywood films and their stars. Mumbai was waking up.

We suddenly turned into a neat driveway bedecked with lush vegetation and flowers. Standing at the entrance was a liveried doorman beneath a shiny steel and glass awning. The automatic doors where garlanded with fuchsia coloured flowers. The morning sunlight flashed on the polished glass. On the corner was a small Indian man setting out his stall for the long day ahead, putting up his umbrella to shelter him from what would be another scorching hot day no doubt. Indian men walked out of the hotel and they were dressed in hard shoes and western business suits. A woman entered the hotel as we drew up, wearing an expensive crimson silk sari and long beautiful gold earrings and necklace. They all looked purposeful and sober, their expressions stern as they bustled into the hotel foyer.

The contrast between this and what I had just experienced on the drive here was exceptional and still it persisted. As the driver opened my car door, I noticed a bullock cart that had drawn up on the road next to an expensive sports car. Behind the hotel driveway entrance, a man squatted to relieve himself. An LGP fork-truck was unloading boxes from an ancient wooden cart with wooden spoked wheels. The vision was of a slow distant past that had crashed intact, through the barriers of time and into its future. It was appallingly wonderful, and I had to admit, I liked it and smiled again.

The automatic doors swished open as I gave the driver what I thought was a reasonable tip. He took my two suitcases into the foyer and across to the reception check in desk, then disappeared quickly.

I had a lovely room at the end of a corridor on the tenth floor. It was a large room, with a large king-size bed covered in clean perfectly ironed white sheets, one window that overlooked yet another slum and another window that looked down upon the street that was now becoming busier as the sun warmed the city and the morning activities of the hoards began. The walls were painted pale headache green.

An envelope was on the white sheets addressed to me. I opened it. It was from Miss Prabaktar.

Peter Ianson
c/o International Hotel
Mumbai, India

Dear Mr Ianson,

Dr Singh has asked me to thank you for coming out to India and to welcome you to our great commercial city of Mumbai.

I hope that your journey and driver were to your liking and the hotel is to your satisfaction and that everything meets with your expectations.

Knowing that you will have only arrived in the early morning, I have been instructed to allow you to rest until midday when I should like to be making your acquaintance in the foyer of your hotel.

Dr Singh will be meeting with you for dinner, providing that you will not be too tired from your journey still.

Have a good rest and see you, if convenient, later.

Yours most sincerely,

Ms N Prabaktar

I put down the letter, opened a bottle of sparkling water and poured a glassful, drank it all and flopped onto the bed and fell asleep almost immediately.

It was just after 11 am when I woke with a start. Realising the time, I took a warm shower, unpacked and found a new crumpled short sleeved shirt and chinos and dressed to be meet Ms Prabaktar for noon.

She was waiting in the foyer. As the doors of the lift opened, I saw a slim tall young woman standing by the reception desk, swinging a black leather brief case gently from side to side, her body swaying too as she did so. The gentle swish of her white and fuchsia pink sari moved as she did. As there was no other woman around, I assumed it was her and walked up to her and stretched out my open-handed arm to shake hands expecting her to reciprocate. She stopped swaying and looked straight into my eyes. Hers were coal black and shining. Her red lips curled just a little at the edges suggesting a smile, but she kept hold of her brief case with both hands and bowed ever so slightly. I dropped my arm and closed my hand into a fist a little embarrassed.

"Hello, you must be Miss Prabaktar?" I enquired.

"I am, yes, but please call me Neelu. Everybody does," she said quietly and smiled. Her white teeth shone, and her eyes twinkled.

"I will be taking you to meet Dr Singh," she said.

I smiled back a little longer than was necessary and she lowered her eyelids over her beautiful almond eyes and dropped her head slightly as before.

She led me out into the searing sun, and we slipped into a waiting Range Rover. We drove onto the motorway and headed north for thirty minutes or so and then turned off down a single unmade track towards a distant, walled villa. A sign read, "Mango Villa. Private". The gates opened, and a large white villa came into sight. There were lush green lawns and a mass of exotic flowers. Sprinklers fed the coarse grassed spaces with jets of water that sparkled in the sunlight. There was a sweeping drive that led to a wide staircase and a central portico with pillars surrounding the massive front door. The car stopped with a crunch as it pulled up on the gravel by the steps.

For a moment I thought it was Dr Singh, but as we got out of the air-conditioned car, I heard him say. "Welcome to Mango Villa, Mr Peter, and to you, Miss Neelu."

Neelu said, "How are you, Vijay?"

Vijay bowed his head in answer to the enquiry, made another murmur of welcome and then asked us to follow him inside. We entered the house, and I was greeted by a small dark woman who slipped a garland of marigolds around my neck, clasped her hands together and bowed moving backwards into the shadow of the great hallway. In the centre of the hall was a round gold painted table with a large bowl containing freshly cut Chromatella waterlilies. A few dark pictures of men in traditional dress hung on the walls and a large intimidating Indian rug occupied the space between them.

"Dr Singh is dressing," Vijay said to me, "and he will join you shortly. If you would both very much like to go to his office. He will join you there very soon indeed."

Vijay led us along a corridor to a study. He looked more like a butler as he handed us both a glass of fresh orange and mango juice that he had balanced on a silver tray. Vijay wore a white cotton suit and a white open necked collarless shirt. He looked sombre and discreet and moved noiselessly around the room. We were offered small vegetarian samosas to go with our iced drinks.

As we stood waiting, I had time to study Neelu once more. She was wearing small gold earrings that I hadn't noticed before and a delicate, matching chain around her neck. I had to admit she looked incredibly glamorous. She could have been a Bollywood actor.

She saw me looking, smiled and said, "A present from a very dear friend."

I bent my head and blushed a little at being caught out. I no longer minded having to wait there with her though. I felt curious and expectant, as if some important secret were about to be revealed to me and was looking forward to meeting Dr Singh.

We stood close together, waiting. Neelu was wearing a perfume which, although faint, reminded me of the smell in an English garden on a summer evening after rain. I found myself inhaling it as we stood together.

Suddenly the door opened and in walked a small man in a long crisp white linen jacket and charcoal grey trousers. The jacket lapels were lightly trimmed with gold. His face was dark-skinned with a grey moustache and beard beneath a long nose and small, deep-set brown eyes. He had an air of stillness about him and stood very straight backed and upright so that I forgot his small stature.

"Welcome to my house, Mr Ianson," he said, extending a hand.

I went forward to take it, the garland of flowers round my neck getting in the way. As I did so, Neelu said, "May I present Dr Singh?"

I shook his hand and then we all stood and looked at each other until Vijay arrived back with the silver tray and three flutes of sparkling wine.

"Indian champagne. From Pune. Well, we call it champagne," Dr Singh informed me and smiled gently, with a twinkle in his eye that I liked.

We are going to get on very well I thought and took a sip. The "champagne" was cold, extremely dry and not particularly delicious, reminding me of some of the poorer quality sparkling white wines produced in southern England!

"You are surprised," said Dr Singh, in a rather refined English accent, "that our champagne is so good I can see. We employ French wine growers up in Pune to help with the vineyards and production," he continued.

"My friends are kind enough to say it is palatable," he motioned us to sit down and Neelu and I settled side by side on one small leather sofa, whilst he sat opposite us. Then he began to speak about, to my surprise, the Taj Mahal.

"I should like very much, Mr Ianson, to tell you a little about one of India's greatest monuments," he said, sitting back in his armchair, crossing his legs and holding the flute on his stomach.

"Over the past three decades, the Taj Mahal has become darker. Cracks have appeared in places and the marble is decaying. The Taj was built in the city of Agra in the 17th century by the Emperor Shah Jahan. It was a mausoleum for his favourite queen, Mumtaz Mahal who died giving birth to their 14th child. The emperor used marble from Rajasthan as it has unique features – it looks pink in the morning and milky white in the evening. A famous Indian poet, Rabindranath Tagore, described the Taj Mahal as 'a tear of marble, on the cheek of time'.

"Photographed and visited over a million times a year it is now beginning to lose its shine. As its foundations weaken and the cracks get larger and deeper in its marble dome, it is in grave danger. The upper parts of the minarets are said to be on the verge of collapse and only recently, this year due to the high winds, two pillars on the outer buildings fell to the ground. It must be protected, or it should be demolished, which would be sacrilege. Air pollution around Agra is the main cause with sulphur dioxide levels over 300 micrograms per cubic meter. Its acid rain that is eating away the marble and turning it yellow, even know as we speak. Manufactures have been ordered to use only natural gas and a ban was put on diesel vehicles. Even tanneries were moved from the area and an order passed in government to stop buffalo going into the Yamuna, the river on whose banks the Taj Mahal stands. Unfortunately, nothing seems to have changed. The threat is not just from the air but from the river too, as it is so polluted.

"Did you know, it is one of the most polluted rivers in the world! From Delhi to Agra, industries pour chemicals and waste directly into the river. Fish cannot survive in those conditions and in their absence, flies and mosquitoes swarm around the Taj Mahal and their droppings add to the discolouration.

"The foundations are wooden, requiring water all year round and sit on 180 wells so without water the wood will eventually dry up, break and rot," he stopped abruptly and took a sip from his flute. Vijay appeared from nowhere with small tables to put our drinks on, then faded away to some corner of the room out of the light. The room was cool, and a large rotating fan hummed above us.

Dr Singh seemed to have completed his sad rendition of the state of the Taj Mahal and had moved the conversation on.

"I have observed," said the doctor, "over the many years of seeing foreigners in India, a curious thing. Will you forgive me if I speak openly about your countrymen?" I nodded in agreement.

"The British are still very snobbish, but in our country, we too have many different classes, but everyone accepts their rank without question, even down to the untouchables," he continued." I am a doctor but most of my staff are of a much lower class. Some are well educated, like Neelu here, but many others cannot read nor write." He paused for a while to reflect, then continued.

"They talk to each other without fear of ridicule, but in Britain there is no class system anymore. They no longer know their class and role in the world and so they want to appear as if they are from another. Your educated working class put on the same accent as a taxi driver in London and I never know if I am speaking to a Lord or a butcher. Yet your country is riddled with class and prejudices. Is this not the case, Mr Ianson?"

Neelu smiled and inclined her head ambiguously but refrained from saying anything.

He sipped at his champagne again as Vijay arrived from the shadows to top it up.

"My own Indian people have some faults too. We do not always treat our people with respect and there is often violence, particularly against women, especially in the countryside. The divisions across our country are wide and have existed for centuries, but as India gets richer, sadly these divisions are still remaining."

Neelu sat very still, not daring to look at either of us.

Dr Singh's voice became a little gentler. He had the gift of compelling attention and respect. I said nothing, not wishing nor daring to break his chain of thought.

"However, there seems to be one group for whom patience and tolerance have some virtues. I speak of painters and artists, Mr Ianson, and perhaps all artists in general."

"This is the time to discuss my project, Mr Ianson, or may I call you Peter?" Dr Singh said quietly.

"I would like you to paint my wife and children sitting in front of the Taj Mahal. You may of course have to paint the two scenes separately as I don't think even I can get them together long enough to sit still and quiet for you, in front of that magnificent building."

There was a slight pause and Dr Singh looked at me with a sideways glance and a smile.

"You will need all your patience and tolerance to paint my children I can assure you," said Dr Singh. "In fact, it will be a miracle of God if it happens, I know it," he laughed out loud and Neelu did too.

I smiled at them both but wondered why it would seem to be so difficult.

"My money and your painting skills, Peter, will not alone achieve this thing, but just as elephants live in India, if God wills it and we can get you to paint the Taj Mahal and then paint my family on the canvas sitting in front of it, the picture of my family and the monument of all monuments, will happen."

He sipped the last of his champagne as Neelu and I did, and he said: "Let us arise and go and eat lunch."

What we ate and drank I cannot remember, except that it was all spicy and delicious. Neelu and Dr Singh talked about their country with deep affection and we all discussed this and that for the rest of the afternoon.

At the end of lunch, when Dr Singh put his coffee cup down and smiled at me, something made me say, "This will be a wonderful painting and I am sure that it will meet all your expectations, Doctor."

I hesitated, so there was a slight pause before I continued.

"I suggest that perhaps we take photographs of all the family sitting in front of the Taj Mahal first. I can then start the painting of the monument and then perhaps you could bring all the family here, to your wonderful garden, where I will paint them onto the canvas with the Taj Mahal as the backdrop," I said with a little hesitation.

The smile had suddenly disappeared from Dr Singh's face and I found myself being scrutinised as he looked deep into my eyes.

"I will consider the best way of managing this portraiture, Mr Ianson, but I shall give your idea some thought," he said. And with that he stood up. Neelu and I followed suit and waited.

chapter 4

The good doctor had bowed ever so slightly and then had disappeared into an anti-room. Vijay had reappeared at the same time and with a smile, raised his hand in a gesture towards the door. I suddenly found myself back out in the searing heat and watched as the car that brought Neelu and me here draw up beside me. This time I was to be taken back into the city, alone.

I climbed into the back seat and the Range Rover sped away down the drive and passed through the opened gates. Once more I was being driven through the puzzle of alleyways, passing a group of men on bicycles and then passed dilapidated buildings whose once splendid facades were now left crumbling, grimed and patched with haphazard necessity. I looked up to a balcony that jutted out overhead. A woman was chatting with another on the other side of the road. They were that close. Glimpses inside the houses showed unpainted walls and sagging ceilings. Ground floor windows were propped up with sticks revealing makeshift shops selling cigarettes, groceries, sweets and utensils. We passed a group of women and children huddled round a water pump. It was clear the plumbing was rudimentary. Most did not have running water and if they did the sewage never seemed to be connected as large disgusting pools often sat stagnating by the side of the roads, breeding grounds for my favourite blood sucking mosquitos. The group by the water pump had shiny pots that glinted in the sunlight. They were filling them with water from the gushing spout as a young boy was vigorously pumping the handle. Overhead and skeined over the buildings like metal cobwebs were complicated traceries of electrical conduits and wires. In a modern India with all its IT power, these constantly demonstrated the fragile and temporary net of modernity.

Every contracted lane seemed to belong to another age. There were men, dressed in long silk or cotton shirts with pearl buttons that descended to their knees and baggy trousers tied up with string; kaftan robes in bright plain colours, hooded cloaks resembling that of monks. There were sheiks in turbans of red, yellow and electric blue, sporting long beards. The women were more conspicuously bejewelled, despite the indigence of the area and what those jewels lacked in money's worth was found in the extravagance of their design. All wore traditional saris that were every colour and pattern imaginable. Some wore the caste marks on their foreheads and hands and many a bare feminine foot was graced by ankles of silver bells and coiled brass toe-rings.

Despite the buildings, cracked and smeared and the piles of stinking putrid rubbish in the gutters, these people were costumed with pride and beauty. Although the streets were crowed with goats, chickens, wild dogs and people, each thin human face showing the hollows of penury, the people were stainless and scrupulously clean.

I fell asleep in the soft rear seats and only awoke as we were pulling into the entrance to my hotel. It was early evening by now and I realised how tired I was as I crossed the hotel foyer to the lifts. I also realised that I had just been dismissed from Dr Singh's villa with extraordinarily little information about how things were really going to progress.

I reached my room, ordered room service and after a delightful, curried chicken dish with a nan and lentils, fell into a deep sleep.

The following morning, Neelu called me from reception, asking to meet me in the foyer as soon as possible. I was showered and dressed so left straight away. As the doors to the lift opened, she waved at me and pointed to two chairs near a cool waterfall. She was beaming: "You seem to have worked your charms on Dr Singh."

"Have I?"

She nodded and handed me a sheaf of documents.

"He gave me these instructions and an agreement to sign this morning. They are sort of a legal set of papers, but really only a formality," she tapped the top page with her forefinger. "Oh! and the fee for the work is right there."

I looked at the figure and must have shown my delighted surprise as Neelu smiled.

"Yes, $50,000 is a rather handsome sum, I think you will agree, Mr Ianson."

"Please call me Peter," I stumbled. I was taken aback by the amount. It seemed extravagantly generous for a family portrait.

"Did you pick these up this morning Neelu?" I asked, wondering how she had managed to get them to me so quickly.

Neelu suddenly threw me a dark stare with her left eyebrow raised. I thought a slight flush reddened her cheeks.

"I, I stayed the night at the villa. I often do as Dr Singh prefers it. It's easier sometimes," the tone in her voice was a little harsher than I had expected. She turned away slightly. It was an unexpected response.

"It's all there," said Neelu, her voice not softening. "Dr Singh's legal people drew this up and it has everything you should require in it. No fault clause. Payment no matter what happens and a first instalment payment when you reach an agreed stage."

I rolled my eyes to the ceiling. "Wow, manna from heaven. If I cannot paint something decent for this fee, then I've lost my artistic touch."

I said that I hoped I would not be taking Dr Singh's money under false pretences and laughed.

Neelu did not.

The day before, when I had left Dr Singh's villa, Neelu and he, having watch the Range Rover disappear in a cloud of dust as it sped away, settled back into the velvet covered sofa in his garden room and smiled at one another. He took her hand gently as they clinked their champagne flutes together.

"Now we need to plan the really difficult part, my darling," he whispered hoarsely into her diamond studded ear. She blushed a little as her eyes closed and he kissed her warming cheek.

"Getting rid of my wife and blaming it on poor Mr Ianson shouldn't be too difficult. I don't think he will cause us any problems, do you?"

Neelu did not answer. She did not need to as she too was sure that all would be well. She smiled again and the dark twinkle in her eyes confirmed to Dr Singh that she would be a welcome and compliant accomplice.

"Now let's talk about the details," said Dr Singh. "I'm going to talk to Vijay. He can head up our little project and take the responsibility for getting rid of her and the children..."

"The children as well, Satwinder?" Neelu suddenly sat up straight. She had not realised that they would be part of the murder plot.

Dr Singh tapped the side of his nose with his forefinger in a stagey gesture. "The children will have to be dealt with as they are involved with all this. How can you and I have a future together with them around? Vijay will be very discreet about all this and you both must keep your mouth buttoned up too," he laughed cruelly to show that he was deadly serious.

"Now then, where was I? Yes. Vijay will oversee carrying out the deed and report to me, and you, my darling, will keep that Ianson chap, both occupied and focused on his task of painting the backdrop of the Taj Mahal in readiness."

He turned around and shouted for his trusted servant to enter.

"He will take all the credit and Mr Ianson all the blame, if there is to be blame, of course," his lips curled nastily as he spoke the last few words.

"Dear Mr Ianson has no concept of how difficult it is going to be to at least avoid suspicion, if not worse. My head feels like it will explode when I think of the wonderful future we will then have together. I think about the complexity of it all, but here is this idiot artist about to help it all become possible."

Vijay, hearing his master's voice, rose from his creaking wooden stool and crossed the room, opened the door and trudged his way to the lounge. Although he disliked the menial filth of servitude, he had learned to endure the demeaning life along this new road to glory. He left the little grungy room, knowing that Dr Singh expected punctuality and how touchy he was about being served promptly. Dr Singh had promised to, *set him free* and Vijay had not gotten to where he was by being careless and ungrateful. As Vijay moved towards the seated couple, he felt the familiar edginess that he always experienced before standing in front of the doctor.

Forcing himself to relax his shoulders, he arrived and stood upright to Dr Singh's left. His master looked up but did not smile, but then he never did. Vijay looked at the deep brown leathery complexion and the ruthless gaze.

"Close the door and sit over there," the doctor said, his voice callous. Vijay obeyed, tolerating the gruffness graciously. After all, this man represented an awful lot of power over him as well as his freedom.

"I assume you know why I have called for you, Vijay?" said the doctor, without averting his gaze.

"I do and, as usual sir, I am ready to carry out your command."

"As I mentioned to you this morning," the old man said, "I have a particularly important project that I need you to undertake."

Without waiting for a reply, the old doctor handed him a folder.

"Here is the information on… the project. Study it. I want to know that you fully understand what is needed, what commitment is required and the consequences of failure. I suggest we meet privately tomorrow in the garden."

Vijay gave a quick nod. "Of course, sir. Total privacy."

Vijay turned to leave.

"And you know I expect absolute confidentiality."

Vijay trudged out of the room again as Dr Singh turned back to Neelu, finishing the last of his champagne. She tried to smile but all she could manage was a slight grimace.

Chapter 5

Dr Singh's wife, Mahima, came back from Mumbai that evening. She had gone to a spare room for a sleep. Dr Singh found her there a couple of hours later and they had a row. She had tried to tell him about her shopping expedition and the wonderful new handbag she had bought. He dismissed it by saying, "You must be insane, woman. Are you sure you wanted yet another bag?"

"But you told me to go shopping," she said.

"I told you to go shopping, but not to waste money on trinkets. I didn't tell you to buy yet another handbag when you have so many already."

There was a long silence and then she said she was sorry. It had been a long day.

Mahima often had long days. Most of her life was spent having long, lonely days. The boys had been sent away to school and so she spent many tedious hours resisting the temptation to doodle over some sowing or just looking out over the sea. Vijay provided her with meals and drinks and her husband was never there if he was downtown at his surgery, or busy locked away in the library with his secretary, Neelu.

Her husband was not interested in her and any excitement about an event or day out that she had, had become buried deep within her, as if nothing that she did was of any importance. He just did not want to know and so she had generally stopped telling him.

Later over supper that evening, she asked him what was on his mind as he appeared more distant than usual after the earlier row. Vijay was standing by the table as usual, and beads of sweat formed on his brow. He did not dare look at either of them. Dr Singh noticed his agitation and asked him to leave them so he could talk to his wife, alone.

"I want you and the children to have your portraits painted, and I have instructed a young artist from England to carry out my wishes," he said coldly.

She did not look at him when he spoke but concentrated on dipping her samosa in a dish of lime chutney.

"Portrait?" She asked, putting down her food, but not looking up.

"Portrait, yes, as in a picture."

"Why?"

"Because I would like to have a portrait of you all in front of the Taj Mahal as a remembrance."

She considered this for a moment.

"A remembrance? How is this going to be possible and why can't we all just go to Agra and you just take a photograph? That would be a day of remembrance, and a chance for you to spend some precious time with the boys."

"That's not what I want," her husband said, fixing her with a level stare and sitting upright in his chair.

"Well, I mean how can we, with the children at school...? And it's such a long way. Can't he just paint you here, in the villa, by the sea? He can paint it on the canvas with the Taj behind already painted."

Dr Singh sat silently and ate a spoonful of lentils. Finally, he said, "Anyway, I've already sorted it all out. I have arranged for the boys to come home, just for a weekend, to be painted. It will be done as I have suggested."

Mahima burst into tears and left the room. She went back to the spare bedroom and lay on the bed with her eyes tightly closed and cried herself to sleep.

It was the response that Dr Singh expected but did not care one way or the other about.

It was early the next morning when Vijay was summoned to the garden. The doctor was gazing out, arms folded and a little agitated, across the sea as Vijay approached, trudging along in his usual way. Dr Singh heard his shuffling feet on the gravelled pathway behind him and turned to meet the man's slumped shoulders and cowed head. The doctor nodded, clearly displeased that he had had to wait. Vijay arrived and stood silently next to his master.

"Have you read the *project* I gave you?"

He nodded, swaying his head from side to side in typical Indian fashion showing agreement.

The doctor stepped closer.

"Follow me. We will walk and talk," he said, moving away and walking slowly under the shade of the arbour.

Today was going to be the beginning of the doctor's salvation. Five months ago, the doctor had returned from a weekend away with Neelu and had looked disgustedly at his wife. He had learned something that left him deeply changed. He realised he was in love with her. Depressed for weeks, the doctor had finally decided to get rid of his wife.

"This is not possible!" Vijay had suddenly cried out. "I cannot accept this *project,* as you are calling this thing."

"You will accept it. Unthinkable as you might believe, but possible, it is," the doctor said. "You will carry it out, and soon."

The man's words terrified Vijay, but he knew, his freedom or indeed if he failed, his possible imprisonment and hanging, depended on fulfilling the doctor's dastardly orders. He had prayed the night before for deliverance as his trust in the doctor had wavered. Divine justice, the doctor had called it in the written briefing he had handed to Vijay the previous evening.

The doctor had seemed hopeful for the first time now that his plan had been revealed.

"Vijay," he whispered, "God has bestowed upon us an opportunity for happiness and freedom, for us both. Our freedom will take sacrifice. Will you be my freeing soldier?"

Vijay suddenly stopped and fell to his knees before the doctor and said, "I am your servant. Direct me as your heart commands. I will do as you command."

The doctor described the way he wanted the deed to be carried out, Vijay knew that he had no alternative but to carry out the plan and do the doctor's bidding.

Things had been worked out in detail by the doctor who seemed to know all and had finally decided to place his entire trust in him.

"Do as I command of you," the doctor told him, "and we will be victorious."

"I will call upon you soon. Our work has just begun."

Chapter 6

I had decided to explore a little, early the next morning. On leaving the hotel and crossing the street, I turned into a narrow lane and came across a stall where a man was already cooking breakfasts for the busy morning rush. He had a sweat stained white cotton vest on and was gently stirring battered samosas in a shallow dish of hot, bubbling oil. The blue flames from his kerosene stove hissed as they heated the dish. I moved past him as he smiled and offered me one. He nodded his head from side to side and a row of white teeth and dark brown eyes shouted at me. The back street, fried food cook, stared at me pleadingly. In my own eyes there were words as well. I am sorry, they said. I am sorry that you must do this hot hard work. I am sorry that I do not want one of your samosas though,

I reached into my pocket and handed him a few rupees. He continued to smile and gave me two, fresh and hot triangles of battered and fried vegetables. It wasn't what I had intended, but embarrassed, I took them. A couple of steps further whilst trying to eat and handle them both, I stumbled as my foot got caught in a crack in the path. I fell onto an old thin frail man. I could feel his thin bones through his coarse tunic. We both fell heavily into an open entrance of a house. I scrambled to my feet and tried to help the old man up. An elderly woman swatted me away. I apologised in English and then in Hindi. "Mujhako afsos hain," I muttered the words, repeating them louder. I suddenly thrust the two samosas into his hands and scurried on quickly as I heard the old man moan, slouched in the doorway and the elderly woman curse me. I looked back through the crowd as she wiped a little blood off his face with the corner of her head scarf. There was a frown of contempt as she gestured to me holding the corner of her scarf.

I don't think he was badly hurt, but I was choked by the heat and what had just happened. Suddenly a hand grasped my shoulder. It was a gentle touch, but it made me jump sideways, beads of sweat forming on my brow.

"This way mister sir," a determined looking young man said, laughing quietly.

"Where are you taking me?" I found myself saying as he grasped my arm and pulled me along.

"This way only. Along this passage now please and you must be keeping your feets to the outside because too much dirty it is here, okay?"

As we continued, half running, my right foot strayed into the middle and my shoe squelched into a muddy slime, a foul smell emanating upwards from the viscous mess. He suddenly stopped and I bumped into him as two big rats scurried across our path.

"No problem with big rats as they are friendly fellows, not making the mischief for people. If you don't attack them with the sticks. Only then they could bite, and you get sick maybe and things," he scowled a bit and then smiled as he grabbed my arm again and pressed me onwards.

Finally, we stopped by an old, panelled door.

"We are here," he whispered, reaching out to twist the grimy knob of the door. He swung the door open and stretched out a hand to signal me in.

"Quickly, mister sir. No big rats must get in!"

We both stepped into the small room, hemmed in by blank beige walls and lit from a small window higher up. Here, in the half-light I had a chance to look at the man as he shook his head repeatedly and smiled. I was standing so close to him I could feel his breath on my face. He was a little shorter than I and his hair was noticeably short, exposing large ears. He had bushy eyebrows, a deep frown and big brown eyes. A fine dagger line of a moustache accentuated his smile as he looked at me.

"Why did you bring me here and who are you?" I managed to say, a little out of breath and still shaken from the incident in the street.

The man in front of me in his khaki tunic and short black hair, folded his arms.

"You now are safe as houses," he said.

"I don't think this was such a good idea," I mumbled, under a tight smile.

"Certainly, it is!" the man insisted. "Tourists are not welcome very well in the alleyways, but at least you know a little of Indian language. Just make a begin. Tell me your name."

"My name?"

"Yes, like you need to be introducing yourself.

"Ah! Maza nao Peter ahey," I muttered, uncertainly. *My name is Peter.*

Encouraged by his silence, I tried another of the phrases that I had learnt from my tourist booklet.

"Maza desh England ahey."

"Kai garam mad'chud!" he roared out loud and laughed, bending over. The phrase he said is a rude one, I learnt later.

"My name is Sidharth, but you are able to call me Sid," he said.

"Also, you are not speaking Hindi but Marathi," he continued, swiftly gesturing expressively with his hands.

"I am happy to be meeting you and I come from Pune. We speak very pure Marathi in Pune and I am incredibly happy you are now my friend so we can eat foods. That will be five hundred rupees."

"What was that?" I said, a little taken aback by his brazenness.

"Baksheesh, Mr Peter, for bringing your escape. Five hundred rupees it is."

I fumbled a few notes from my pocket and found a five hundred rupee note and handed it to him. He took the money with a peculiar sleight of hand, like a conjuring trick that palms and conceals bank notes with a skill that any experienced street conman would envy. The money vanished as he pointed to the door through which I was free to exit.

I strode through the door just to hear Sid's parting words.

"I'll be seeing you again sometimes, Mr Peter."

I turned left and looked back to see Sid standing in the doorway smiling. It was obvious he didn't live there, but he must have known who did. I joined the traffic of people in the noisy alley and worked my way back to the main street. My worries waned and receded as I walked past the more affluent shops, but my thoughts wound and spiralled along the busy streets as I walked back to the hotel. I passed a slum opposite the hotel. The contrast between the adjacent hotel and the rough equal plots of slum land was stark. The hotel foyer was large and air conditioned filled with expensive and exclusive shops, with displays of jewels, silks and craft works for tourists. To the left was the slum, a sprawling couple of acres of wretched poverty with hundreds of tiny huts, housing thousands of the city's poorest people. Next to the hotel the neon lights and beautiful fountains. In the slums there was no electricity, no running water, no toilets and no certainty that the whole mass of human existence would not be swept away any day to make way for yet another shopping mall or hotel.

I turned my gaze from the expensive cars that had pulled up outside the hotel and began to walk into the slum. There was an open latrine near the entrance, concealed by some tall weeds swaying in the breezy heat. There were simple screens made from reed mats. The smell was appalling and so overpowering that I began to wretch as I could almost feel the stench settle on my skin and permeate into my soul. Gagging and swallowing back the impulse to vomit I hurried on. The air was hot and steamy in the close-set ally ways, but what little breeze there was dispersed the awful stink from the latrine. Further into the slum the smells of spices and cooking, incense and even flowers predominated. The huts I passed were pitiful structures made from scraps of plastic and cardboard. Roofs held up by thin bamboo poles and lengths of wood. More reed mats became excuses for walls and plastic sheets for roofs. All were erected on bare earth.

As I continued to walk along the narrow wood and plastic lanes of the slums, children started to gather and follow me. Sometimes a child would touch my skin quickly and whilst others would just stare blankly and perhaps unbelieving. Some though laughed and their eyes were wide with excitement and surprise. A group of boys played cricket and never gave me a glance, whilst other people could be seen standing in their doorways staring at me with such gravity and frowning intensity, that I felt sure they would perhaps attack me at any moment. They didn't of course. They were just staring at my fear. They were perhaps trying to understand what demons might be lurking in my head, causing me to dread my foray into their sanctuary of slum life. My fear had reached breaking point and I suddenly needed to get out of the slum. I turned and as the sweat soaked my shirt, I hurried back to the safety and pleasantness of the beautiful fountains and limousines dropping off rich clients outside the hotel.

I suddenly felt pathetic and ashamed, dishonourable and disgusted, all at the same time.

The cool dry air in the hotel foyer was blissfully welcoming as I slowly walked across the highly polished marble floor, but feeling the hot sweat, turn cold and chill my back.

"Mr Ianson," a voice from the front desk called. I turned to see a young receptionist waving an envelope at me. He ran over apologising for shouting, but he had this urgent letter for me. He had been asked to hand it to me personally. I didn't recognise the handwriting. Taking it and thanking him I hurried on and into the waiting lift to get back to my room.

I ripped open the envelope. It was a handwritten letter from Dr Singh, which surprised me as all previous correspondence here in India, had been computer generated and printed. It was asking me to meet his wife for lunch today. Neelu would pick me up at eleven thirty and take me to a restaurant close by. It was already ten thirty and I needed to shower and change after my early morning foray.

Initially, as I showered, I didn't think too much about it, but as I dressed, pulling on fresh chinos and a salmon coloured linen shirt, I wondered why I was to meet her alone, albeit with Neelu, but not with the doctor and without the children present. But then I assumed the children would still be away at school and no doubt Dr Singh had patients to see perhaps.

The foyer was remarkably busy as I waited for Neelu to arrive. It was eleven thirty exactly when the doors of the hotel swished open and the beautiful and elegant silhouette that was Neelu, parted the throng of busy guests and was stepping gracefully towards him in a pale fuchsia pink and gold sari. As she reached me, I could see inside her beautiful dark eyes and I knew she was an amazing woman.

She held out her hand.

"Hello," I sighed, copying her gesture. She gently shook my hand. It was cool and soft.

"Shall we go and find a taxi, Mr Ianson?" she purred at me with a huge smile and a fixed gaze. I returned her baleful stare with the fixity of a lamb about to be slaughtered.

"You see, Mr Ianson," she half whispered my name, never taking her eyes off me as we turned to leave, "we have to take a short taxi ride as, although the restaurant is only around the corner, it is so incredible hot today that it would be more comfortable, don't you think?"

I agreed and she responded by lifting her matching pink silk scarf to slip over her head as we stepped out of the hotel. I let out a soft moan and my eyes closed as the sun hit my face. A waiting taxi whisked us down the drive and into the grindingly slow, horn honking traffic, where we spent the next thirty minutes struggling through Mumbai's relentless congestion, even though the restaurant was easily in walking distance.

Chapter 7

Lunch was at a small, secluded restaurant in the old part of Mumbai. I could see the "Queen's Necklace" from the first-floor dining room. We spent most of the time preparing the plans for the painting, determining where I would be able to purchase supplies of paints and canvases.

At first things seemed to progress quite nicely, but then I found myself looking at Neelu in a way that troubled me. She was obviously very bright and able. Professionally qualified no doubt as well, but she seemed distant and perhaps a little uneasy as our discussions progressed. The food was minimal and seemingly not important. Dishes came and went, and we all had little here and there. I caught a remark that she made to Dr Singh's wife, who had introduced herself as, Mahima.

I don't know why I resented the remark. Perhaps it was the tone, not the words.

"I think you will be able to manage a few hours sitting for Mr Ianson. It won't be too difficult with the children," she had said with a smile that seemed a little forced.

"Don't you think so, Mr Ianson?"

When I didn't reply, she fumbled with her serviette for a moment, looking across at the view of the sea. Although we had had a light lunch and some water. Neelu ordered three glasses of white wine. When they came, she held up her glass and looked over it at me, and said, "A toast to the painting of the Taj Mahal."

Again, I was surprised by her words, but I raised my glass as did Mahima and said, rather solemnly, "To the portrait of Dr Singh's family, at the Taj Mahal."

Neelu's eyes met mine as we all sipped our wine together, then I looked away, embarrassed without knowing why.

Mahima was unaware and put her glass down and asked me if I was married. When I told her I wasn't, she smiled and gesturing to Neelu said, "Well, perhaps you might find a bride in India while you are here, Mr Ianson," she looked at us both in turn.

Neelu glared at Mahima. I caught the look and for the third time, over the past hour, I found myself troubled again.

With a sudden flurry regarding the payment of the bill, Neelu had decided that our meeting was over and suggested, rather gruffly that we should call a taxi, to leave.

I wasn't in the mood to be sharing a car with her right now and so suggested that I would walk back to the hotel as it was only a few minutes away and anyway, I said I needed to walk off my lunch. Before either Neelu or Mahima could reply, I had folded and dropped my serviette onto the table and headed for the door. As I hit the street, the heat hit me, full on, as did the thousands of people outside. Where they were all going or what they could possibly be doing, I had no idea. How these hundreds of extra souls squeezed themselves into these already overcrowded streets, I had no idea. With subtractions for the space taken up by cows and goats, shops, storage areas, streets, lanes and latrines, that allowed about a square meter for each man, woman and child around me. The crowds caused me some tension as everyone seemed to be shopping for something, but I could never figure out what it was, except for those with small parcels of eggs or milk, tea, rice, cigarettes or vegetables. Some carried cans of kerosene and some children's clothes or rolls of cloth. Everyone seemed to pay with large wads of notes, so the place was certainly thriving.

Suddenly I found myself with plenty of room around me as if the sea of people had suddenly parted as I walked into their space. A child screamed, not out of fear, I found out, but with scared excitement in her voice. There in front of me was a cobra. Body and head raised as if ready to strike, with its hood fully extended. I was sweating already from the heat but the sight of the cobra with its black eyes and flickering tongue caused a sudden river to run down my back. The snake charmer man, seeing me stop, smiled and with a stick prodded the cobra back into the wicker basket, which was on the pavement, dropped the lid over it and secured it with a bamboo slip-catch and placed a large stone on the top. The children ran forward laughing and dancing around the basket. Just as I was about to walk round the basket a mischievous monkey scampered over the top of the snake man's shoulders dropped onto the lid and removed the stone with one hand and flicked the catch open with the other. He jumped off quickly as another monkey, arriving seemingly from nowhere, opened the lid. Both monkeys from a safe vantage point of the snake man's shoulders, shrieked and flailed their arms about as if in mock panic.

"Saap alla! Saap alla! Saap snakes are coming, snakes! "The children screamed with delight again and ran behind their mother's sari skirts and father's legs. Everyone laughed but all I could see, through the haze of sweat on my brow, were the nut-brown faces of all the shoppers. They were laughing at me as I hurried on like a scared rabbit, trying to escape from a pack of baying hounds. They were only having fun, but it seemed at my expense.

Among their many other skills, the monkeys had also been trained to be excellent thieves. Like so many of the streets in Mumbai, the street I was on was a thief's heaven, so the monkeys were in pilferers paradise. Each day, the embarrassed owners and snake charmers were forced to lay out a cloth, where all the items the monkeys had stolen were displayed, and if possible reclaimed by the rightful owners. Tourists of course were usually unaware of this practice and they were also obviously more fruitful targets for the thieves. The monkeys seemed to show a marked preference for glass beads and bangles, brass anklets and bracelets and display them on their own hairy arms, as if showing off their skills. I had noticed a rather expensive gold chain wrapped round the arm of one little fellow though. I doubted whether that would be on the cloth the following morning waiting for the aggrieved tourist or rich Indian to return. I continued down the street feeling a little calmer, when I saw two monkeys stalking me, their eyes huge with simian guilt and mischief. One of them had a string of red beads round its neck. They walked on their hind legs, in tandem, squeaking and holding onto each other with both their tiny hands.

They looked so sweet. That was before they struck. Bouncing off a bench as I passed it, they landed on my back and tried to rip off my watch. I was so shocked I fell sideways onto the bench smashing my elbow and letting out such a cry of pain that the pair of them jumped off me just as quickly. I glared at them and swore. All they did was bare their teeth as if grinning at me, did a somersault, in turn and then scamper up the side of a crumbling building chattering angrily as if I had cheated them out of their deserved prize.

The rest of my journey back to the hotel, apart from crossing roads through streams of horn blaring traffic, taking a left turn by the tall date palm instead of right and being bombarded by a multitude of street vendors, calling out from flamboyant and brightly coloured bowers like birds of paradise singing for mates, was uneventful.

Back in my room, I had time to reflect on both my brief meeting with the doctor's wife and Neelu's behaviour.

I was due to fly up to Delhi the following day and then travel to Agra and onto the Taj Mahal to start work. Drawing and sketching with maybe some photographs taken across the day to determine the variations in light, would be my initial tasks. The subject matter had obviously already been decided, as had the angle. The backdrop was to be the famous view that has been photographed a billion times, that of the mausoleum, looking across the ponds and pathways to the front of the world-famous great marble monument. Having never seen it before, apart from in books or on posters, I was extremely excited and so looking forward to being there at last.

Chapter 8

The following morning Neelu arrived to pick me up. She was wearing a very elegant cream sari, hemmed with gold thread and she smelt faintly of peaches ripening in a green house. We talked briefly about nothing except the pending journey to Delhi. Dr Singh wasn't with her and so I asked her whether he was intending to join us.

"No, but I will be travelling with you to Delhi and Agra and then leave you to get on with your important work," she said.

Neelu put her hands together and looked down for a moment. Then said quietly: "He is rather busy at the moment, in Aurangabad."

"What's he doing over there?" I said, watching her. Her smiling, easy look had gone and now her lips were compressed, and she had turned pale. I suddenly realised she was on the verge of getting agitated. In a panic I tried to make a joke: "Well, perhaps I can get a contract to paint the family out there and we can join him there instead?"

The joke was not appreciated and all I got was an extremely startled stare. After that, she didn't seem to want to say any more about it. It was odd. A few minutes ago, Neelu and I had been, in one sense, perfectly content, chatting away. I had spent time with her over the past few days and although it had all been very professional, my admiration for her had been unbounded and yet it seemed I obviously didn't know her at all and certainly should not of asked her about Dr Singh.

I checked my watch and saw it was nearly nine o'clock. I picked up my suitcase and we hurried off to the waiting car outside.

We drove to the airport in silence. I watched the world outside. An old rickshaw stopped besides us. The old man sat on the cycle in the front in his yellow and white checked shirt and no teeth.

Sitting in the back of the white and green two wheeled cart was a woman and her son.

The letters ANS stencilled to the side and the numbers 0123, which I found strangely bemusing. The red frame for a hood was folded behind the seat but there was no fabric attached. It was tied up with a piece of old string. The boy was naked apart from a stained pair of grey looking shorts and his stomach was rather extended. He was gnawing on a cob of corn with relish. His eyes shone and he caught my gaze and smiled. His mother sat quietly beside him in a red top and scarf covering an ankle length red and green striped skirt. Her hair scraped into a bun and gold hoops hung from her pierced ears. She also caught my gaze and scowled as our car pulled away.

We drove on past a park with its colonial railings and huge trees. Most of the traffic lights didn't work and those that did were ignored by everyone, including our driver. The pavement kerb stones were generally painted blue, black and yellow, although most were obscured by mounds of rubbish and dirt. As we struggled on through the traffic, a motorcycle drew alongside. It had five people straddling it. A young father had his four sons with him. No helmets of course, but each wore a new shirt and trousers. The shirt sleeves were crisp and sharply ironed. Dad had his hand on the handlebar grips whilst his eldest son's hands held onto the space in between. Behind the father the other three sat rigidly, each holding on to the one in front, the smallest squashed between his father and the next youngest brother. All five, hair blowing in the wind watched me as we slowly drove past them. Their beautiful dark eyes never leaving my face.

We reached the airport late, as predicted, but as the flight was delayed, it didn't matter.

The flight was uneventful.

We jumped into a yellow and green tuk tuk and then driven at high speed across the city to the railway station where we were to catch our train to Agra. We passed a sign that said, "Chai Time" and blue umbrellas advertising

Pepsi, and even an old stand supposedly selling Camera Film. Kodak Gold 200. 36 EXP FILM. Its faded yellow and black colours looked sad and outdated. The only building I remembered seeing was the Parliament House, the Sansad Bhavan which contains the Lok Sabha and the Rajya Sabha. Built in 1927 by two British architects, Edwin Lutyens and Herbert Baker, so Neelu informed me. It was the only conversation we had as we hurtled on towards the station.

We were taking the afternoon train and travelling first-class which meant we would be served some sort of a meal. The platform was heaving with hundreds of travellers. We had been told to stand at the top end of the platform as the first-class carriage would be just behind the diesel engine. The train arrived and it appeared that first-class was, at the rear of the train. Trying to move through the crowd with a suitcase the size of an elephant, was to say the least, challenging. Neelu seemed to skip her way through quite easily, often glancing over her shoulder to give me another hurry-up look.

"I thought we were at the front of the train," I wailed, getting farther behind.

We sat down in our seats like civilised people once I had managed to stow my suitcase and wipe the perspiration from my brow. She looked at me, reproach and disappointment brimming in her large soft-brown eyes. She pulled two tickets from her bag and handed one to me.

"That is your ticket," she said, looking away. There was a long silence before she spoke again.

"Anybody can make a mistake. If you had preferred to make this journey by yourself, then you should have let me know. You don't need a Mumbai guide to buy a ticket in comfortable, empty carriage. But you do need a very excellent Mumbai woman, like me, like Dr Singh's personal secretary, to get you into this carriage at Delhi station and get good seats, isn't it? This is my job."

Our seats were awfully close together and the table dirty and warped. I reflected awhile and felt a little guilty at being upset as I looked around the crowded and dimly lit carriage. I was just about to comment on the fact that the carriage wasn't empty or comfortable as the train suddenly lurched forward and slowly started to grind its way on its journey.

The man opposite me shifted his feet, accidently brushing his foot against mine and then apologised with great gestures for the unintended offence.

On what was my first journey out of a city and into India, I found such sudden politeness amazing after the violent scramble to board the train. It seemed so hypocritical for them to show such deferential concern over brushing my foot when, minutes before, they were almost pushing one another out of the bloody windows.

The scrambled fight and courteous deference. The amount of force required to board the train was necessary. It was part of Indian culture and philosophy but the consideration after boarding was necessary to ensure that the cramped journey, even in first class, was a pleasant as possible.

We trundled on through the sprawling slums of the city. I watched people openly defecate in the fields by the tracks, cows roam with total freedom across the rails and beggars huddled at every crossing and station. All driven by the concatenate complexity of the bureaucracies that rule India, taught by the British in the past. The contrast from the gorgeous, unashamed escapism that is the Bollywood movie, to the accommodation of hundreds of thousands living below the poverty line in the slums. This is a country already too crowded with sorrows and needs.

The carriage was filled with farmers, travelling salesmen, itinerant workers and returning sons and fathers being agreeable despite the cramped conditions and relentlessly increasing heat. Every available centimetre of seating space was occupied. A whole family sat close together. Perhaps they were on some pilgrimage to Agra and the Taj Mahal as well. Yet there wasn't a single display of grumpiness or bad temper.

It wasn't long before we were served with a meal. White starched tablecloths were spread in front of us. The waiter wore white gloves that had seen better days and perhaps hadn't been washed for many a serving. Polished silver cutlery was laid on the cloths alongside a cracked gold rimmed plate and a cup and saucer. The table was at a jaunty angle and I wondered whether the cup and saucer were going to slide off at any moment. Fresh Indian tea was served. Milky and sweet. The waiter spoke to me, drifting between English and Hindi until we both finally understood what I was going to be served. Every one of my fellow passengers, except Neelu, looked at me. Some smiled and some scowled. An elderly gentleman muttered a curse that made one of the other passengers splutter into laughter and one young man commiserated with me patting my shoulder. I watched and listened, literally rubbing shoulders with a well-dressed salesman on one side and Neelu on the other. It seemed a little too close for her, I think.

My first excursion by train from the city did please me though. Everyone seemed to use the famous Indian head-wiggle. I had seen it everywhere in Mumbai. It had taught me that the wiggling of the head from side to side was the equivalent of a forward nod of the head meaning – *yes, I would like that.* What I learned, on the train, was that a universal message attached to the gesture, when it was used as a greeting, made it uniquely useful. Everyone that entered the carriage and the waiter when serving me, gave a little wiggle of the head. I watched it happen at every station and every time Neelu and I were served. When my eyes met the waiter's, I gave a little wiggle of my head and a smile. The result was astounding. The waiter beamed a smile at me so huge that it even made Neelu smile too. I knew he wasn't indicating – yes, I agree with you because nothing had been said, but it was just a signal to me that he was amiable: *I'm a peaceful man and don't mean you any harm.*

It was the first truly Indian expression I had learned, on that journey of crowded hearts.

We left the railway at Agra along with many other travellers. It was bustling and busy and people were rushing everywhere. I constantly wondered where everyone was going to in Indian. Everybody always seemed to be going somewhere, but I still never understood where.

Cases, glass, wood and textiles, were all being unloaded as we alighted. As we struggled through the throng, a range of other goods from pottery to hand woven tatami mats were arriving for dispatch to the city. I smelt the fresh mixtures of newly harvested spices, vegetables and flowers as we crossed a vast open patch of rough ground that served as a car park for the taxis and long-distance coaches. Me with my bulky luggage and Neelu with her small carry-on. I couldn't read the Hindi texts on the buses or signs, so allowed Neelu to lead me forward.

We stopped by a gleaming black car. The driver and Neelu spoke and we got in. The driver packed our luggage into the boot, while we settled into the clean airconditioned vehicle. The silence was cutting. Neelu hadn't spoken much to me on the train journey and even less so now.

The sun was setting by the time we arrived at the hotel. Large, white and colonial.

I was too tired to really take in the surroundings and anyway my mind was suddenly engaged in the immense significance of the work that I was about to undertake. This commission was worth not hundreds, but thousands of pounds to me and I was also becoming a little concerned about my relationship with Neelu.

Back in Mumbai, Dr Singh was sitting brooding in the back of his Range Rover. Vijay sat behind the wheel glancing in the mirror at his boss. They sat outside the villa as the sky grew darker. The front of the villa was lit from below by a small bank of flood lights, the pillars either side of the door rose like stalwart sentinels. The pillars were flanked by a shadowy row of columns.

They sat in silence, both concealing the deceit and hate. Vijay for his boss, Dr Singh for his wife.

Vijay wasn't looking forward to his task, but he yearned to gain his freedom and escape from the doctor so much that he knew he had to do it.

"You have to clear your mind for the task in hand," Dr Singh said quietly leaning forward to whisper into Vijay's ear.

The muscles in Vijay's broad back tightened as he listened to the plan once again. The sound of Dr Singh's voice haunting his soul.

"Release your hatred, Vijay," continued the doctor. "Remember that your freedom depends on it."

Looking up at the two pillars, Vijay dragged his mind back to horror of the request that he was now listening to. He knew the stench of death, the cries of the dying and the final sobs of a forgotten soul. A shiver ran down his spine as he remembered when he had left home when he was ten.

His father enraged by his inability to feed all his family, beat his mother regularly, blaming her for having so many children. When Vijay tried to defend her, he too was savagely beaten. One night his father had gone too far, and his mother never got up. Vijay as a small boy had stood over his lifeless mother and felt unbearable guilt that somehow it was his fault. Soon after, Vijay fled home but found the streets of Mumbai equally unfriendly. He slept under an old oil skin in a shop basement, eating stolen rice and vegetables. His only friend was a skinny goat that helped keep him warm when he was around. Over time he became like an untouchable until one day Dr Singh found him unconscious under a flyover and took him home. He thought he had been saved until he woke to find himself in shackles. He was ridiculed and often marched round the garden naked and hungry. Over the years he was allowed into the house and trained to cook and to serve the good doctor when he still a young registrar, but he always thought of himself as a weightless ghost. Just existing, being there, but not really being a person and he longed to for his freedom. He knew that he probably owed his life to the doctor but nevertheless, he resented him and his family just the same.

Upstairs in the villa, Mahima had gone to bed early. She hadn't been sleeping well of late and her and her husband had been arguing more than usual. She and Dr Singh slept in separate rooms most of the time, these days.

Although it was late, she had heard her husband's car draw up outside. Although the front of the house was always lit up, her bedroom was at the rear and overlooking the sea, where there was no light except from a pale moon. She suddenly felt a cold sweat breaking across her brow. Mahima turned over and tried to get back to sleep, but her attention was still drawn to the arrival of the car. She hadn't heard the front door open or the sound of her husband or Vijay talking as they normally did when they arrived home late.

Mahima suddenly felt very alone.

Climbing out of bed and without turning on the light, she tiptoed over to the door. It took only a second to realise that something was wrong as a light went on in the hall below and she could hear muffled whispering. Mahima's ears strained to hear what they were saying. She slid back the gold chain that dangled from the bolt and opened the door. A shaft of light from below struck her pale face.

To Mahima's utter amazement, the two of them were huddled together. The broad, sculpted head of Vijay was bowed as her husband handed him a long knife. Mahima felt a shiver run up her spine as if a ghost had walked through her.

"When the time comes, you will know what to do," Dr Singh said to Vijay with his hand on the servant's shoulder.

A tightness gripped her throat as she realised something terrible was being planned.

"Use it well," he continued, "and you will find it easy."

Mahima closed her door and slipped back into bed. What were they planning she wondered as her blood ran cold?

The following morning, skirting the edges of consciousness, Vijay stirred as dawn was breaking. His bed was soft like a cloud and the air around him smelled of the sea. Suddenly, realising where he was, a silent scream of anguish startled him from his slumber. His body leapt out of bed, staggered towards the window where the early sun was glowing pink. He saw the glint of the blade in the warming light. The knife that Dr Singh had given him the night before lay on the chair by the window.

He remembered that last words from the night before.

"Thank you, my friend. Soon all this will be over," Dr Singh had assured him.

Today was the day of reckoning. Vijay's thoughts were with the awful task he had to perform. He wasn't eager to progress with the preparation, he wished he could change the promise he had made. But he could not. The doctor had seen to that.

"It is for your freedom," the doctor had explained. "I know it will be difficult, but if you fail the results will be disastrous for you."

Vijay knew he was right. The doctor was an exceptionally clever and careful man. He would have ensured that his plan would work perfectly and had proven himself a man well worth obeying, even if Vijay hated him for the way he had been treated in the past, but after all, he had obtained the knife and organised and made the necessary arrangements surrounding his wife's whereabouts across the day. These had been the things that had convinced him that they were truly capable of delivering the murderous plot without being discovered.

"Vijay," the doctor had told him, "I have made all the arrangements. "For my plan to succeed, you must follow my instructions to the letter. You must call me as soon as it is done. You will not speak to anyone else. I will communicate with you only on your mobile phone only."

"You, my trusted servant, deserve all that is coming to you."

"Yes, master sir. Then I understand," Vijay had replied and the doctor smiled.

"Excellent, then our desires are in accord."

Vijay felt a renewed confidence that he would not fail. Freedom and faith were powerful motivators.

Chapter 5

Mahima had woken early and roused her two boys, calling them for breakfast as the sun streamed in through the library windows. She gazed out across the Indian Ocean watching the small fishing boats, and the sun glint off the crests of breaking waves.

She turned as she heard the thunder of her son's feet thumping down the stairs to join her. They were laughing as they enjoyed their rough and tumble play together.

The boys spent most of the time away at school but sometimes came home for weekends and holidays. Vijay had picked them up from boarding school the night before. It was the weekend, so they were relaxed and looking forward to playing cricket together out on the lawn after breakfast.

Their mother was sitting on the veranda when the boys finally stopped giggling and joined her. Vijay watched them from a distance on the other side of the garden. The sun was strong, and the temperature was steadily rising. It was going to be another hot, dry day, he thought as he ran the back of his hand across his forehead and felt a bead of sweat run down his temple.

Mahima sat with a boy on either side of her as they ate dhal, homemade flatbread, yoghurt and a couple of mangoes each. They never stopped eating and chatting. A cricket bat was propped against the back of the eldest's chair and a well-used ball rolled under his feet.

Rohit was nine years old and his brother Rakesh, three years older. They were both mad keen on cricket and glad to be home albeit just for the weekend. Their father had told them they were to meet an artist and he was going to paint them. They disliked their school with its uniformed rigour, always having to be dressed and in the refectory at ten to eight for breakfast. The prefects waking them at seven, a cold shower after a sprint round the playing field. This always seemed like a form of punishment to the boys as the system was open to all kinds of abuse. Prefects would settle scores with the younger boys they disliked by sending them round the field twice which meant they would inevitably be late for breakfast resulting in real punishment. Rakesh was nearly always late for breakfast.

Being at home meant no Prefects, no early run and cold shower and, therefore, breakfast on time, at least for Rakesh and he was in a happy mood and ready to thrash his brother at cricket. Rohit too was glad to be at home as he looked up to his brother and adored his mother. Having finished breakfast, they both ran onto the lawn to play. It was a fantasy world of India where they could smell the sea air and not the stench of the city sewers or slums, this India without poverty and sickness, this India in the morning sun to play with leather and willow, this India circumscribed by a white crease and laws and bats and wickets.

Rakesh caught Vijay staring at them from across the garden and his adolescent dream vanished, dispersed like smoke in the clogged city streets with their traffic jams, murders, and disgusting masses of poor and starving people.

"Come on, Rakesh," Rohit shouted as he drove the last wicket into place with a large, heavy pebble they had taken from the beach for that exact purpose.

"I'm batting first," he said.

Rakesh's mind clicked back into fantasy mode and he picked up the scuffed red leather ball.

"Play!" he shouted as he brought down his arm hurling the ball at his brother. His ball was of full length, but Rohit swept his bat elegantly forward to block the ball and smiled.

Rakesh bowled a second, but the ball had already gone past Rohit who looked round in total disbelief to see his middle wicket lying on the ground. He marched to where his brother now stood and thrust the bat into his hands shaking his head as if he had been guilty of some appalling crime.

Mahima watched the boys from the veranda of the library and smiled. Vijay, deep in thought, watched all of them, and did not smile.

It was hot in my room over-night. The central fan hummed but failed to cool me at it swirled the hot air pointlessly around the room. I had seen the glimmer of dawn through the shutters and decided to get up. It was only four in the morning, but I thought it would give me the chance to see the dawn. The hotel was not far from the Taj Mahal and famously had a viewing tower facing east where you could see the sun rise from behind the beautiful monument, silhouetting it initially as it rose.

I took a refreshingly cold shower, before slipping on my shorts, sandals, and a white linen shirt. I took my camera and room key and set off to find the tower. Reception was quiet and the night porter a little surprised to see me but kindly directed me towards the other end of the hotel, whilst rubbing the sleep from his eyes at the same time.

The tower was like a tall, white minaret with a central staircase that spiralled upwards to a circular veranda at the summit. I climbed the stairs, reaching the top in no time and gasped when I saw the hazy view. The light was a strange deep crimson red and orange. Four grey spires sat in a deep grey green surround. The smog hung over the Taj and Agra, diffusing the rays of light as the sun slowly rose, shimmering angrily red determined to light another new day.

I stood open mouthed and stared, wide eyed at the sheer beauty of a rising scarlet arch of sky. Somewhere, music played on a radio and over it was a fine sweet soprano and boasting tenor of a duet from an Indian movie. Birds began the morning chorus and below me in the grounds of the hotel, the staff talked, nourishing one another with their smiles and conversation. The love song continued as did the rising of the sun changing the landscape as it did, reassuring us that a new morning had arrived and we had survived and the world unfolded into another day and I felt complete and my heart began to swell and my heart beat quickened as the sun shone brighter behind the glory that is the Taj Mahal.

Two hours later, having had breakfast, Neelu had taken us as far as possible towards the Taj Mahal entrance. We left the car and started to walk. There were suddenly hundreds of people all travelling along the same road towards the great marble monument. A hand cart carrying a dead body that was wrapped in white linen and tied at the feet and at the head, decked with orange marigolds hurried past us. Several mourners were pushing it quickly, wailing as they went, heads bowed, not wanting to be seen perhaps, but certainly wanting to get past with their terrible cargo. As the cart passed by the smell was appallingly overpowering. It was like a physical element permeating the air. I glanced at Neelu who had her head scarf wrapped tightly around her face. She didn't look at me. The air was hot now and the smell of incense and spices grew stronger and fitful gusts of wind whipped up the dust on the road.

At last we reached the first entrance and the high outer walls that lead to the gardens beyond. The density of people grew rapidly and the queue to the first arch already long was growing longer as we reached it. Soldiers manned the gates and the obligatory x-ray scanners that everyone had to go through. It seemed to take an age to reach the first check point. Neelu had the tickets and thrust them into the hands of a tall captain on arrival.

We all shuffled along in a line and through the x-ray machine, that wasn't even plugged in. Bags and back packs were searched. I had a camera and a sketch pad and pencils along with a small set of watercolours and a canister of water in mine. The tall slim soldier with his pencil thin moustache wobbled his head as he searched my backpack asked me where I was from and what I was doing here. I was on the verge of being rude and stating the obvious, but declined as Neelu, standing behind me, explained quickly and succinctly. The soldier waved us on quickly. The long pathways edged with lawns and the water rills all thrusting directly to the main structure gave the mausoleum its exacting importance and grandeur.

Standing at the main inner gate staring at the four minarets across the length of the rill looking at the monument's reflection in the water and the terracotta brickwork along its sides, made me gasp. The lawns with their zigzag patterns and cropped Cyprus looking trees, were magnificent. Hundreds of people ambling along both pathways leading to and from the gorgeous white domed building. This was the view I wanted to paint. I sat down on the step by the water. There were fountains running along the middle of the rill, but sadly they weren't working. I sketched a while and took some photographs. Neelu was nowhere to be seen, not that I had missed her. So engrossed was I with the magnificence that was the Taj Mahal, that I couldn't take my eyes from it. I walked on to another square pool and sat on the incredibly famous bench that many a president and princess had sat on before me. As I approached still closer, the body of people grew again. I joined yet another queue, this time to get a ticket to a deposit box in which to place my shoes before being allowed to walk on the hollowed marble.

My first step onto the beautiful white marble steps, made my heart leap. The cool, smooth surface where millions before me had walked, shone. Polished by their feet sliding gently across the huge solid slabs, gently veined in pale hues of pinks, browns and greens. I walked under the high main arch where the light, suddenly changed the colour of the marble. The intricate detail of a mass of carvings made me smile and opened my eyes wide. Inside it was cool and suddenly the marble walls looked dark green and mysterious. The amazing lattice work was stunning. I found myself drifting through the internal space of the cool interior before reaching the other side and finding myself gazing now at the river. Wide and dirty and slow moving, with the occasional boat battling the current. The blue grey marble slabs under my feet felt like silk as I ran my fingers around dark green leaf patterns on the walls and creamy white flower motifs in central panels. I had no idea what they meant, nor the history and meaning behind any of them. I felt ignorant, stupid and unworthy but I was totally in awe of this amazing and wonderful place.

Hours later, having sat and sketched and painted, Neelu had come to find me. The sun was dropping and as it did so, changed colour and with it the colour of the monument. The Taj was suddenly bathed in a wonderful orange pink glow and the deepening shadows in its many facets and arches turned it into a truly majestic sight. We half walked, half ran back up the pathway and around to the river just as the sun, now deepening into wine red seemed to set the main building and each minaret on fire with its shimmering light. The bright blue sky deepened in hue and then turned orange; and the few clouds that there were became ochre smoke trails. I looked at the reflection of the sky in the polished marble floor and the dark silhouette that was Neelu, standing in front of me. It was time to leave.

chapter 10

I checked my watch and saw it was seven o'clock. We were back at the hotel and I was tired, and the sun had burnt a nice stripe across my forehead. Neelu and I had driven back, almost in silence. It was odd. It was as if we had been total strangers and were just sharing a cab together to go about our personal business. I had spent time with her over the past week or so, quite a lot of time, but it had all been rather professional. My admiration for her ability was unbounded, but I was completely ignorant of her personal circumstances. I hadn't asked her a single question about herself or indeed her apparent closeness to Dr Singh.

It had been a long day and I was too tired to go through my sketches or photographs with her, not that she had seemed particularly interested anyway.

I made my excuses about needing to work on the sketches, stating that I was going to have room service and making my apologies, escaped up the stairs and along the veranda to my room. It had been a magnificent day and I just lay back and smiled, once I had put some soothing after sun cream on my sore sunburnt forehead.

It was time.

Vijay felt ready as he made his way along the corridor from the wine cellar, next to the kitchen. The sun was setting over the sea and Mahima and the boys were talking about the day, waiting for dinner. The evening breeze rustled their loose-fitting robes as they enjoyed the moment. Dr Singh had phoned saying he would be home late as he had to see an old patient and not worry about leaving him any dinner. He would pick up some street food on the way home.

Vijay knew the task before him would take more finesse than force and so he left the long knife, Dr Singh had given him, in his room under his pillow, but did take his sharp pruning pen knife. It was easier to conceal but in his hands, just as deadly. The house and grounds were quiet and deserted at this hour. The gardeners had gone home. The only visible souls were a couple of fishermen out in the shallows as the tide came in. He flexed the muscles in his arms and shoulders and making a fist with each hand, prepared his body and mind. For many years, Vijay had remained loyal and silent. He had sacrificed a lot. Considering the poverty from which he had come, he was looking forward to his rewards. He was eager now to prove himself to the doctor, the one that had assured him his actions would set him free.

Pausing in the shadow of the doorway to the dining room, he took a deep breath. It was not until this moment that he truly realised what he was about to do and what awaited him inside the dining room. He raised one of his clenched fists and knocked on the door. A voice came from within, summoning him to enter.

Although the shutters to my room were closed, I had left the windows open and the warm evening breeze moved them back and forth enough to make the hinges creak just a little. I had hungrily ploughed my way through a chicken madras, aloo gobi and a garlic nan and was washing it down with a bottle of cold Kingfisher, when there was a knock on my door. Thinking it was probably room service come to collect my dishes, I jumped off the bed.

"Coming," I shouted, picking up the tray of crockery.

I turned the knob and swung open the door to find Neelu standing outside, dressed in a beautiful but tight translucent pale cream sari. The light from the veranda beyond shone through it, outlining her perfect body straining underneath it.

As my jaw dropped, so nearly did the tray, out of my now trembling hands.

For what seemed several seconds, I stared in wonder at her and felt as if the floor was beginning to spin beneath my feet. In my wildest dreams I could not fathom why Neelu would want to visit me in my room.

"Hello, Peter," there was a pause. "Well, are you going to invite me in, or am I to stand in your doorway all night?" Neelu said, her eyes urgent and sparkling.

I had closed my mouth but opened it again although nothing came out.

Neelu's eyes widened and as she smiled as she gently pushed passed me and closed the door behind her. She went and sat on the bed curling her legs under her. I glimpsed at her thighs beneath the material of her sari and the round firmness of her breasts. She cradled her hands in her lap and her long black hair was loosely tied behind her head. She stared at me with an expression of calculated appraisal, one eye almost closed. It reminded me of a marksman about to take aim at his target on a firing range.

"So, did you enjoy your room service?"

I sat on a straight-backed chair and folded my legs and arms, trying to look relaxed.

"I did indeed," I said rather shrilly.

She laughed gently. It was a pleasant sound. Quiet but rich and sensual. She took the bottle of Kingfisher from where I had left it on the desk and took a swig. I was surprised, especially as it exposed one round breast with the movement.

"I'm not sure why you have come to my room, Neelu," I said nervously as she took another swig.

"If you want to see what I've been working on, I can show you my sketchbook and photos."

"I'll make you a deal, Peter. I'll look at your sketches if you agree to take all your clothes off here, in front of me."

"Assuming you can manage that and anything else that comes up," she whispered, smiling again. "Goodness it's hot in here," she continued spilling the loose tie of her hair until the long black curls fell over one shoulder. With her hand poised there, on top of her head, the sari's loose folds opened again exposing her breast once more.

I thought she looked so beautiful, relaxed and with an expression that was gentle and compassionate. Her cheeks were slightly flushed and her molten eyes chocolate brown. She was a woman with the face of a girl, unmarked by the rigours of living in Mumbai. From the few things I knew about her and her role working for Dr Singh and that her life had in fact been harder than most, none of that showed in her face.

Neelu pulled aside the sari showing her nakedness, touching at her breast clumsily.

"Are they nice? Do you like them?" she said, but it sounded wrong somehow.

"They're ... very nice," I muttered.

"Nice? They're absolutely beautiful is what they are. They're perfect! You want to touch them, don't you? Or maybe start with my thigh. Here!"

She snatched at my wrists with surprising speed and pulled my hand onto her thigh by her hip. The flesh was warm and supple under the thin material.

"I... I think you should go, Neelu," I said, withdrawing my fingers from her thigh and my hand from her weakening grip and stood up backing away from the bed.

My heart was beating faster as I watched her rise from the bed, covering up her body at the same time. She continued to slide towards me as I reached the door to open it.

Mahima heard loud knocking on her door that startled her as she wasn't expecting it. Usually the servants would knock lightly and then enter. She opened it and she stood facing the size that was Vijay. The dining room was spacious and welcoming even though it was slightly eccentric in its décor. It was built to enable the diners to gain the maximum view of the sea and its footprint was a miniature version of the Grand Gallery in the Louvre, in Paris, with its beautiful parquet flooring and a fire place that housed an enormous black grate that looked like something out of an English medieval castle. It was dimly lit as if it were a cavern.

Vijay squinted into the semi darkness beyond Mahima. He was looking for the boys.

"Vijay," she said, surprised at seeing him. She stepped back, a little concerned.

Vijay was not surprised by this. He was accustomed to Mahima being uncomfortable in his presence.

"What is it that you want? I wasn't expecting you nor did I call for you, Vijay."

"No, I know that you did not call for me, madam," Vijay responded. "I had my own calling and I have now come."

Mahima shook her head. She was a small woman with gentle eyes but at this moment they were wide open with surprise. Vijay had never come without being called and had never spoken this way either.

You have no idea, Vijay thought.

Her small stature, which Vijay could incapacitate easily, allowed him to follow her into the room, where the boys were busy in conversation.

"I am sorry to disturb you just at this moment before your dining," Vijay said, stumbling over his words.

"Not at all, if you have something that you need to discuss," Mahima replied, turning back to face him.

"Actually, madam, my reasons are not for discussion."

She gave a nervous laugh: "I am sure then that you will tell me what it is that you require."

Vijay felt his eyes focus on the boys. He stopped walking as he stood only inches away from the boys and then turned his massive body towards the small woman, and he could sense her fear as she gazed up into his deep black eyes.

"If it does not seem rude, please sit down next to the boys," he said and placed a firm hand on her shoulder, forcing her to sit, facing the window.

Sitting there in the darkening room as the sunset, Mahima peered silently through the large bay window and out to the sea beyond the garden walls. The sudden dread in her heart made it hard for to sit still. She remained seated but watched Vijay move around her from the corner of her eye.

Soon I will be a free man.

Searching in his pocket, Vijay found the folded pen knife and flicked open the sharp blade. He usually used it to cut the roses in the garden, but it would serve a far more deadly purpose this evening. Vijay stood in front of her and held up the glimmering blade. His dark eyes flashed fear, but he smiled and moved closer as Mahima recoiled in terror.

"Be still," Vijay whispered, raising the blade. The boys had stopped talking and sat frozen, staring at the back of Vijay standing over their mother, not realising what he held in his hand.

As the knife descended, Mahima closed her eyes and clenched her teeth.

A slash of pain tore through her chest. She cried out, unable to believe she was about to die here in her own dining room in front of her darling boys, unable to defend herself through fear not knowing what was intended for her sons.

Mahima felt the scorching pain and terrible warmth spreading across her chest and she looked down to see the blood flowing freely soaking her sari. She felt her body sag as the fire spread and her eyes began to close. The two blurred images that were her sons, were the last thing she saw before the blackness closed her eyes for ever.

Although the air in Agra had cooled that evening, the temperature and humidity in most of the hotel was still high. As the evening throbbed and the crimson sky gave way to darkness, the hotel filled with returning tourists, all had been visiting the Taj Mahal and now the restaurant was full and noisy.

Neelu stood in silence for what felt like for ever, by the door, waiting for something to happen.

"So, what do you want to do, Peter?" Neelu whispered to me.

"You are very beautiful," I said.

Neelu smiled. "I am beautiful and very capable of pleasing you, if you want."

I looked at her and shook my head.

"You look like an Indian Mona Lisa, but we have to remain professional," I said, trying to sound both sophisticated and in control. Neelu laughed and I felt embarrassed at the ridiculousness of my remark.

"Mona Lisa?" she replied knowing that the conversation was not going any further.

"I'm going back to my room," Neelu declared, her voice hollow and flat.

"I don't think I am particularly welcome here tonight."

I felt guilty about turning away a generous and perhaps genuine offer to satisfy my most obvious desire for her. She grasped the handle of the door and looked back at me as I nodded in agreement that she should leave.

Although I hesitated as she opened the door, I said, "You had better go. Now."

Neelu gave me an almost grateful smile and it was then that I realised that her intentions had perhaps not been genuine, and it was even perhaps, part of a greater plan designed to please me and ensure I completed my commission. As the door closed and I found myself alone in my room again, the shutters creaked open with the breeze and I heard the joyful chatter and cacophony of noises that was the restaurant. I slumped overly frustrated, onto the bed and picking up the bottle of lager, finished it off in one gulp.

"Stupid bugger," was all I could say before closing my eyes to dream.

Chapter 11

It was well into the night by the time Vijay had moved Mahima's body and secured the boys in the kitchen pantry, next to the wine cellar. He had tied them together round their ankles and wrists to the shelves of vegetables and cans. Although he had been instructed to dispose of the two boys as well, he hadn't been able to muster enough courage to do so yet.

Dr Singh wasn't going to be back that night, as previously agreed, but Vijay knew he only had until very early morning, before people started to rise, to deal somehow with getting rid of the boys.

Vijay was not a bad man, not really. He had realised that he could not personally kill the boys, but panic and fear was beginning to cloud his mind as a red mist was slowly colouring then darkening his thoughts.

Perhaps he could hide them somewhere or take them and leave them to fend for themselves amongst the poor and the untouchables. At least he wouldn't have killed them, even if someone else probably would. However, Dr Singh would probably want proof that he *had* killed them as well, or else he would never gain his freedom.

He had spent several painful minutes pacing up and down the hallway, sweating more profusely as the time passed.

Suddenly he decided what he would do and grabbing Mahima's bag, hunted for the keys to her car. He rushed to the pantry and grabbed both boys, who were still sobbing with the pain of their mother's execution and the thought and horror of their own probable murder.

Vijay bundled them down the rear stairs from the kitchen and dragged the boys to the car that was parked in front of the garages. He opened the boot lid electronically as he reached it and threw them carelessly into the empty small space and slammed the lid shut in frustration and fear. He could hear them crying now and rubbed his eyes and the sides of his temples as a dull pain crept across his damp brow.

"Shut up, shut up," he whispered hoarsely in Hindi.

Vijay opened the garage doors and searched round until he found a petrol can. It was almost full, judging by the weight.

He was beginning to lose control of his physical and emotional senses as he yanked open the car door, throwing in the can of petrol and slumping into the driver's seat. Turning the key and starting the engine at least drowned out the plaintive cries of the children in the boot.

Vijay slammed the car into gear and put his foot hard on the accelerator and sped off down the driveway and through the gates onto the road towards Mumbai's suburbs.

He had to find a solution and time was running out.

He had been driving on the motorway and had just driven over a couple of acres of slums, nestled under a flyover. He came off at the next junction and back to a track underneath the flyover, parking the car just by one of the concrete flyover supports, but away from the slums and near the outfall pipes. He opened the window, but the putrid smell from the drains forced him to close it again. He quickly grabbed the can of petrol and emptied it across the seats of the car, tossing the can in amongst the rubbish and debris in the stream of filth, down from the pipes. He looked across the black shadows of the huts in the slum. All was quiet and humid except for the constant hum of the traffic on the flyover above. Vijay needed to get away from the car before it caught fire and so he had placed a thin silk scarf he had found in the car, on the floor of the driver's side and lit it with a single match. Closing the door quietly he ran as fast as he could towards the slum's outer fencing, leaving the boys in the boot and the scarf to slowly burn.

He was a few hundred metres away when suddenly a gorgeous plume of orange flames erupting skywards. A dull explosion followed and suddenly faces appeared at the doors of the huts and some people started to run towards the direction of the flames that rose into the night sky like dancing yellow spears. Vijay stopped and looked round, bewildered and scared as he considered his terrible deed. He watched the spiral of smoke and the wall of flames. The red and yellow flames fanned by the sea breeze started to advance through the dry grasses, towards the outer huts of the slum as the fire headed towards Vijay's position, at a slow but dangerous walking pace. The slum was a huge pile of tinder dry kindling that a strengthening sea breeze fanning the flames, would easily burn through its fuel of wood and human lives.

Stunned and afraid, Vijay was in a state of panic and turning away from the fire, ran on through the slums to escape, on along the narrow twisting lanes, pushing women and old people out of his way. He thundered on, bumping along the lanes, still in the opposite direction of the fire. Families came out of their hovels carrying their possessions of clothes, cooking pots, stoves, bits of tarpaulin and sticks. The smell of smoke and burning drifted in the wind. It was acrid and unnerving. Vijay turned a blind corner and then another until finally he found himself on the main road where he could flag down a passing vehicle.

Dr Singh was sitting in a small restaurant on the west side of Mumbai with a fellow medical colleague. A perfect alibi of course. He had a cup of tea by his side and Indian music was plying on a radio somewhere behind them. It was his second cup of chai having eaten a meal of roti bread, rice and bhaji. The curried vegetables had been deliciously spiced, and Dr Singh was cleaning his plate with the last bit of roti, when a news flash came over the radio about an explosion and fire on the coast road, south of the city, close to where the doctor lived.

The news startled him, but there was little information, the presenter said.

"Goodness gracious, Satwinder," said his colleague, not noticing Dr Singh's sudden movement. "No doubt another exploding kerosene stove in the slums over there. Every one of those several thousand huts has a stove. This time of night they are all pumped up and under pressure. It only takes one and then all the rest explode once the flames reach them. They should demolish those damn places," he said, sitting back in his chair and shaking his head.

"The last monsoon rains stopped weeks ago, so there is a lot of dry timber around there, so no doubt there won't be many people who will survive."

"No, I think not. Crying shame though," Dr Singh replied slowly, but his mind was elsewhere as he quietly spoke the words.

Vijay had managed to flag down a passing truck that gave him a ride back along the motorway to Mumbai. He found himself on the sea wall on Marine Drive. The broad footpath beside the sea wall was bare and clean. A few drunk tourists were wandering aimlessly along, laughing and talking loudly. The wide road separated him from the curving crescent of affluence. The fine homes and expensive apartments of the now rich Indians. They used to belong to the British, but not anymore. Now there were first class restaurants and hotels as well, and they all looked out beyond the "Queen's Necklace", to the black and heaving sea.

There were only a few cars on Marine Drive at this time of night and there were few lights shining from the opulent rooms of homes and hotels. A cool wind carried the clean, salt air. It was quiet now, which was unusual for this city even at night. It wasn't always safe walking alone on the streets at night, but Vijay was big and strong and unlikely to be troubled and anyway it wasn't the city that he feared. He felt safe on the street . Strange and trouble as his life was the city enfolded it and him, within the millions of others.

He had allowed his life to be swept up in the broiling manic struggle and allowed himself to be bound to Dr Singh and *his* sins.

He tried not to think of what he had done, not to think of the boys and Mahima. He could feel her behind him as he spoke her name, in shame.

Standing on the sea wall, he felt the cool breeze wash across the skin of his lined face like water poured from a large matka. There was no sound other than his own breathing and the crash of the water on the rocks beneath the wall. The waves splashed up to him, pulling him towards them.

Let go. Get it over with. You don't deserve to live. Just fall in and die. The world would be better off without you. Child killer, Murderer…

The voice came from deep inside him – the shame that smothered his self-esteem as a once hard working, upstanding and proud Indian, was overpowering.

The sea surged over the rocks below Vijay. One step and it would be all over. He could feel the fall, the crash, as his body hit the rocks, the cold sliding death of drowning. It would be so easy.

A hand suddenly touched his knee. He was startled and looked down to see a tiny boy. The touch was gentle but firm. The little boy's hand now gripped his trouser leg as the other hand slowly opened along with his big sad empty eyes. With the palm of his tiny hand open and pleading, he seemed to be reading Vijay's thoughts and begged him with a gesture of pinched fingers up to his open mouth, that he needed food.

Vijay took a 10-rupee note from his pocket and handed it to the boy. The boy smiled easily and grabbed the money, took away his other hand to run it through his thick, dirty slicked back hair and then disappeared into the night as quickly as he had arrived.

Vijay suddenly stood up straight, as if re-awakened from a terrible dream.

He gestured to a passing tuk tuk that drew up beside him, and Vijay jumped in and off they trundled in the direction of the villa, a few miles up the coast. He managed to run the last few hundred meters or so along the dirt roads to the gates without being seen. His next task would at least be more straightforward. His thoughts were now focused on deepening the trench he had started digging much earlier, behind the garden shed, into a grave in which to place Mahima's body before dawn.

Later that evening, Dr Singh had checked into a local hotel. He was in his room when his mobile rang. It was Neelu on her phone, but he told her to call him back on the hotel phone and ask to speak to a Mr Sidhu and hung up. Dr Singh had booked his room using a false name as he didn't want to use his real one, to avoid him being traced, should there be an issue in the future.

He pulled up a chair and sat down. He was nervous and concerned about the news flash. It had disturbed him as he didn't know whether it was anything to do with his family, or Vijay, or whether it was something else and totally unrelated. His mind was eased when the phone rang at the side of the bed. He picked it up and the lady on the switchboard informed him, in a smooth voice, that a young lady wished to talk to him.

"It's Neelu here. Is that you, darling?" she said.

He said hello and put his hand over the mouthpiece. "Oh! my angel. It is so good to hear your sweet voice," he whispered, sitting up straighter in his chair and loosening his shirt collar.

"So Neelu. How is the project going with Mr Ianson? Did you manage to *look after him* this evening?" he enquired.

Neelu said, "We are on track, Satwinder, don't worry."

"A little more detail would be good, my sweetness."

"I'll have to talk that through with you tomorrow. I don't really want to discuss these things tonight on the phone."

"Specific details are what I want, Neelu," said the doctor cheerfully, but with a nervous menace in his voice.

"He wasn't interested in me helping him relax or *looking after him*, as you put it, after our rather long visit to the Taj today," she said a little sharply.

"I want you to give me a full briefing as soon as you can tomorrow then. I don't want any dramatic developments that we can't control. Talk to me tomorrow as I want to know everything that was said. It would be better if you could get back here as soon as possible. Can you get back tomorrow? Nothing about this conversation must be discussed, Neelu. Okay? Goodnight," Dr Singh said, raising his voice. He had suddenly become quite agitated at Neelu's unwillingness to give him the information he wanted about her time, and especially her evening with Peter Ianson.

After the conversation with Satwinder, Neelu's mood changed. He had appeared rather jealous after all and she had put the phone down glowing with pleasure. Having said that she knew it would be better if she could persuade Peter Ianson to get back on a train and plane the following day.

It was early morning when I woke with a start. I had closed my eyes thinking about Neelu's rather glorious figure, but after the busy and exciting day, both the food and beer had sent me off to sleep quite easily.

I struggled to get up, as the memory of Neelu the previous night was difficult to get out of my mind. I wanted to go through my sketches before breakfast. The smell of Neelu's aromatic perfume had long since disappeared, which helped clear my mind and focus my thoughts. There was a note under my door. Neelu wanted to meet for breakfast at eight. I had just enough time to shave, shower and dress.

When I arrived down in the restaurant there was a smell of delicious spices and fruits coming from the kitchens. People were busy scurrying around and waiters hurried past with trays. Neelu was seated at a table by the window, overlooking the rather green looking swimming pool. Her thick, long black hair was shining like running water over black granite. She wore a long-sleeved Indian salwar top that reached over her thighs to her knees and below were a loose pair of trousers in the same crimson red silk fabric. She looked radiant.

I said hello and asked her how she was. She told me she had slept well, and would I like her to pour me some fresh mango juice.

This was unlike her.

As I had noted before, Neelu always seemed to be in a rush, immersed in her own needs and even quite curt. Here she was, smiling sweetly and appearing very relaxed, serving me juice from a crystal jug.

I drank some juice from my glass, watching her over the rim.

"This is really good," I said after a mouthful. Neelu laughed a little and said something about how delicious freshly squeezed fruit was. I noticed a twinkle in her eye as she said it.

She sipped her juice too and asked, "Do you have any idea how long we need to be here before we can return to Mumbai?"

"Well, that's a difficult question," I said, putting my glass down. "I told you that I need to ensure I have enough material in order to paint the Taj as a backdrop on the canvas first. I am not sure we need to stay any longer than perhaps another day."

"It's just that Dr Singh would like to see what you have done so far, and as soon as possible. He is extremely excited about your progress and I need to call him today to update him and tell him when to expect us to return," Neelu said without a smile.

I said it seemed a bit hard to be able to be totally sure, but that we could probably finish today.

Neelu frowned at me and said: "Why do you need another day? What you have done already seems particularly good and I would have thought more than enough. With the photographs you took, you should be able to start work back at the villa tomorrow."

It was happening again. Neelu was behaving like one of India's pre-colonial Rajas. For her, attack was not just the best form of defence, but the only form of defence.

I didn't want to argue with her. On the contrary I wanted to enjoy my time with her. Despite my intention to keep the conversation as convivial as possible, I did find myself getting a little annoyed and even irrationally irritated.

I remember saying that I didn't think she really understood how important it was for an artist, such as I, to ensure that I had truly captured the spirit and magnificence of the monument.

Although she calmed down a little, she explained that it was necessary to move to the next phase of the project to show Dr Singh that things were indeed moving on well.

The previous evening's events weren't ever mentioned. It was as if nothing had ever happened, and in my mind, I wished they hadn't either.

It was as if I was being tested or teased or purposefully lead astray, or all these things. It had confused me. She had confused me, but now it had suddenly started to worry me.

Something was going on. It was just that I didn't know what it was, and whether I should or shouldn't be concerned about it.

chapter 15

In the shadows of the concrete pillars under the fly over where one of Mumbai's many slums spread like a pandemic, a youngish man sat huddled, wrapped in a woollen cloak which was his only protection from the evening chill. He lived in the slum but had needed to get away from the noise and hubbub of the place for a while. Climbing through the broken fencing he had found a concrete slab to sit on. He had eaten a meagre meal of rice and lentils. The stench of putrid faecal water from the slum mixed with the motorway run off spilling from the outfall pipe would be enough to keep even the most audacious thieves away from the area.

He was resting his back against the cool concrete, the cloak over his head when he saw the bright glow of a car's headlights bouncing up and down over the rough terrain and heading his way. He drew his knees up to his chest, making himself almost invisible to the oncoming car.

He watched the car suddenly stop amidst a cloud of dust. The front driver's door swung open and a large man climbed awkwardly out of the front seat, having emptied a large can of liquid inside the car. As the man in the cloak watched, he saw a faint yellow flame suddenly appear on the front seat. Soon after the big man threw the empty can into the stream of sewage and started running to the fence where he struggled to get his large frame through the gap. He tore his shirt but then ran on towards the slum huts. Almost immediately the cloaked stranger heard the cries of two children coming from the car as the flames in the front grew a little brighter.

Without thinking of any danger, he threw off his cloak and ran to the car. The banging and shouting from the boot set his heart racing. Two children were obviously trapped inside the boot. Their cries for help growing loader as the man banged on the boot lid. Panicking a little, he found a large stone and smashed at the lock several times. Just as the flames grew higher and black acrid smoke billowed out of the front door, the boot lid sprang open and two pairs of very scared eyes, wide with fear, blinked out from the darkness of the space.

The young man pulled them out by their arms, telling them to run into the shelter of the outfall pipe just beyond the pillars. They set off and he followed, wading quickly through the sewage and debris before climbing up inside the pipe. As they did so, they saw the sky outside suddenly turned bright yellow as a sheet of flames lit up the underside of the flyover. Seconds later an explosion followed, sounding like a shotgun blast. It thundered and rebounded off the underside of the motorway flyover. The boys screamed and they all sat frozen and motionless like three rabbits caught in the headlamps of the very car that they had just escaped from and had suddenly burst into flames.

"Who are you?" asked Rakesh, staring wide eyed with both trepidation and relief.

"Maza nao Sidharth," replied the young man as he peeled back the cloak from over his head.

"But you can be calling me Sid," he said and smiled, and his big ears twitched, along with his pencil moustache. The boys noticed his pointed chin and big brown eyes and they smiled back at Sid, their saviour.

"Thank you... Sid. You just saved our lives," said Rakesh, and a tear ran down his cheek.

"I am Rakesh, and this is my younger brother, Rohit. He's only nine but I'm twelve," he said, sitting up as straight as he could puffing out his chest.

"Very pleasing to be meeting with you," Sidharth replied and he smiled again. "But we must be getting you out of here before we are all being burning to a frazzlement."

I was waiting for Neelu under the external canopy of the hotel, hiding from the strength and heat of the morning sun. I watched a water cart stop on the other side of the road. Two young Indian men walking behind carrying big pots of water on their heads, went into the house opposite. The old man in the stairwell had to move to let them pass. On the wagon was a great big plastic container with metal straps around it to hold it place. It didn't look particularly hygienic. The wheels were iron rimmed. Another guy jumped up onto the back with a bucket and started dipping it into the huge plastic cube on the cart and filling the big carry-pots with water.

As I waited, I watched the men make several trips. When Neelu arrived, I asked her what they were doing. She told me that was the water for the old man's shower. That the shower came from a tank on the roof and these men filled the tank from the pots.

"Yes, you are very lucky, Mr Ianson, that you have such a nice life, nice hotel and come from a world of plenty," Neelu said.

I wasn't sure that I needed a lecture on western affluence, as that what it was sounding like, but I acknowledged the point she was making.

"At least these people have an honest job which enables them to support a family with their wages."

The men then got ready to run onto the next house, pushing their water wagon. I knew what she really meant and what she wanted me to see. They were strong, proud and healthy. They weren't begging or stealing. They were working hard to earn a living and they were proud of it. Most poor people in India are proud. They are a proud nation. When they ran off, joining the traffic, with their well-developed muscles, I noticed Neelu give them a sly look of admiration.

Did she consider my work to be less worthy, I wondered? Un worthy of the huge fee that I was being paid for the painting of the good doctor's family in front of the mighty Taj Mahal. Not worth spending any more time in Agra "photographing" it, "sketching " it, trying to capture the colours and tones, texture and light that made it glow so magnificently.

"I've packed my suitcase and gear up, ready to go back, Neelu," I said as I had pre-empted her desire and determination to get back to Mumbai as requested by the doctor.

There was a hint of surprise as she turned and said she had better go and do the same then and with that she almost ran back into the hotel through its brass handled revolving door, leaving me standing with just the doorman for company in the now sweltering heat.

Dr Singh had slept badly and had woken early. He left the hotel without breakfast and headed out of the city towards his villa, before the usual traffic jams built up into gridlock.

Vijay looked up, sweat pouring from his forehead, to see a black Range Rover powering up the drive, a thick cloud of dust billowing from its wheels. He carried on with his digging until the car pulled up and stopped. The doctor opened the door, and almost falling out, shouted over to him.

"Vijay. Is it done?"

With a troubled mind, Vijay rose again and turned to face him.

"It is. All of it. As you commanded," he said. "Your wife… Your lady wife is here and the boys, they are..." he stopped and couldn't finish his sentence.

"Was that you last night?" the doctor enquired. "The blast under the motorway. Was that the boys?"

Dr Singh looked pale and very drawn as he struggled to look at the body wrapped in white linen, lying next to the trench that Vijay had now finished digging. The body that he assumed to be that of his now deceased wife. He looked up at Vijay who nodded his bowed head but said nothing in reply.

"Get that body buried. Now. It's already light. Now, damn you, man!" The doctor almost screamed as his expression tightened suddenly. His eyes were riveted to the white-clad corpse.

"Mahima," he choked, a fearful bewilderment sweeping across his face. "It is done."

Dr Singh slowly closed his eyes: "Finally, I am free."

Vijay paused and shot him a glance.

"Finally, we are both free, I believe, master!" He said, faltering a little.

chapter 13

The drive back to the station from the hotel with Neelu sitting quietly next to me, her perfume filling the car despite the air conditioning, was again, a silent one. We hadn't travelled far when we drove through a corpse of tall trees. The sun was high, and many people were sheltering under the canopy for shade. The dappled light playing across their faces. Some old men were huddled round a seat while a family of young women and children, filled shiny aluminium pots with water from a roadside pump. The driver had to slow the car down, almost to a standstill to avoid the crowd of people.

"You see poverty, but although it is everywhere especially in the countryside, people still seem happy," I said quietly to Neelu, not really wanting or needing a reply. I didn't get one anyway.

I was about to say something else when I saw, walking through the wood an irresistibly beautiful young woman. She was walking away from the crowd at the pump and balancing a tall aluminium jug of water on her head. The dappled sunlight glinted off the jug and moved across her shoulders as she walked, very upright and elegant. She was wearing a deep emerald green sari embroidered with gold thread. Ornate gold earrings swayed from her ears that matched her necklace that was clearly visible around her slender neck and hanging down to her breasts. Her black hair was free under her scarf but burnished with copper tints from the sun. The green of warm shallow water in a dreamed lagoon blazed proudly in her eyes. She was almost too beautiful; as a blush of summer sun streamed through the trees and caught her face as she walked on slowly, step by step to keep the jug balanced. As poor as she was, she had dressed in her finest sari to fetch the water. I noticed the gentleness in her face, as one hand helped steady the weight on her head as she caught my gaze. An ironic half smile turned up the corners of her mouth. Within a moment we had passed her and were driving on along the road. I could feel my heart beating a little faster, wishing I had had my camera to catch that moment of pride and beauty. It was a fleeting image that would stay with me all my life.

Neelu wanted to stop at a roadside stall to purchase some fruit. It gave me a chance to stretch my legs although it meant getting out of the cool air-conditioned car and into the scorching heat of the over-head sun.

I wandered behind the stall to some huts and saw the poverty, yet again. A part of me shrivelled in shame. Someone once told me that "fear and guilt are the dark angels that haunt rich men." I don't know if it's true, but I did see the despair and humiliation that haunt the poor.

To one side a gin still had been set up next to a large sugar cane field. Four young men stood around an old steam driven engine and a battered copper still. The floor was littered with dried up, brown sugar cane leaves. One of the young boys fed the crusher with cane and another stocked the clay clad fire pit, its sides black with soot as thick smoke poured from the wide, low chimney. They both wore bandanas, and despite the heat, short sleeved striped woollen jumpers over dirty buttonless shirts. A third young man scowled at me as he stood on top of the drystone wall that surrounded the steam engine. I noticed the boss, with his purple turban and thick gold chain, prominently dangling from around his neck. He slouched against the wheels of a hand cart stacked with the next lot of cane to be crushed. Behind them was a series of reed covered, open shacks.

I turned back to the huts by the stall.

"Come in, come in. This is for chapatis, yes?" Two men had invited me into their hut and offered me a wooden stool to sit on as they picked up a plastic bag.

I looked around the small hut, their gaze followed mine. It was a shabby threadbare hovel. It was mean and cramped with a cracked bare earth floor that had lumpy undulations. The reed matting of the roof sagged and had even given way in a few places. A single-burner kerosene stove and a few containers of spices sat on some bricks. Some water was stored in an earthenware matka. I saw the cracks in the wooden supports and the stains of mildew. The door was held together with wire and string. Large holes punctured a couple of walls exposing not only the bustle outside but movement in another room. I peeped through one of the holes. The two men suddenly stood up dropping their plastic bags. I looked back at them as one lit a cigarette and blew smoke out through the side of his mouth. As I looked back again through the hole, I saw two small boys, probably no older than eleven or twelve, tied by their ankles with a dirty rope to a central wooden pillar. They were sitting making chapatis. Both had a pile on either side of them, piled up on cracked plates.

A rush of irrational anguish seized me. I was suddenly unbelievably angry at the fact I had seen the boys and the unlovely truth that they were, for all intended purposes, slaves.

"What are they doing through there with those small boys?" I suddenly shouted at the two men. One had picked up a thick stick while the other continued to smoke his cigarette watching me through half closed eyes. He suddenly raised his left eyebrow in a high arch, challenging me to repeat my question and meet him face to face. He was threatening as well as judging me. He looked at me, seeing into my soul, seeing what I felt.

"Don't you be telling me what I should and shouldn't do, British," he snarled. "You don't rule India anymore," he continued. "We were so many slaves to you British, so don't be coming in here and telling me," his voice was shrill, and he was about to speak again and took a step towards me.

"It's fine," a voice at the door said. It was Neelu. "Come with me, Mr Ianson, quickly," she said firmly. As I turned towards her and the door, I heard her swearing at them in Hindi.

She stormed ahead of me to the car.

"Get in," she insisted, slamming the door.

She sat on the other side of me, staring intently. I stared back but neither of us spoke.

I had been struck by the poor boys' expressive little faces, hair that was night-sky black and dark bronze eyes. Each wore a grave expression of despair and fear.

I had physically done nothing. I had said little to help, and even perhaps had made it worse for them.

We continued our journey to the station in solemn silence. All the while though my guilt and upset grew.

The journey back took up the rest of the day. The train was overcrowded and heat and smell unbearable. The airport wasn't much better. I slept a little on the plane and I was dropped off at the hotel late in the evening. Neelu had said her goodbyes quickly and sped off in the car, leaving me outside the hotel. The doorman wobbled his head and smiled as he opened the door. The cool clean air in the foyer, was refreshing as was a cold beer at the bar. I went to bed feeling miserable and still riddled with guilt.

The following morning, I felt shattered from the day before. It had been an emotional trip and I had felt bilious all night.

Despite that, I was up at six, went for breakfast and was ready and waiting by the reception desk when a young smartly dressed Indian said good morning. I turned to see who was addressing me. It was the driver and he saw that I was a little surprised.

"Where is Neelu, err, Miss Prabaktar?" I enquired, sounding as surprised as I looked.

"Madam will be meeting with you at Dr Singh's villa, which is where I am taking you now sir," he said politely with clasped hands. His brass bangle on his wrist jangling against his shiny watch bracelet before he ushered me towards the doors. He had looked at me in a not very friendly way and asked me if I had had a good night's sleep as we walked to the car. He had obviously noticed the bags under my eyes and pale complexion.

The streets were already hot, smelly and busy and the traffic slow. The constant horns blowing, and the general street noises were making the journey more unpleasant. Traffic lights turned red and green and back to red many times, but nothing stopped the traffic's endless noisy crawl.

We had stopped by some park gates. A dead dog lay on the side of the road next to our car. We were outside one of the park entrances. I looked at a row of women sitting on a low wall with the park railings behind them. One young woman saw that I was white, and as she caught me looking at her, immediately covered her head and mouth with her shawl. Sitting next to her was an old woman dressed in black and two children, one with a straw hat on and lottery ticket stuck in the hat band, played behind her. She was propped up by another elderly lady in pink holding a baby wrapped in a pale blue length of cloth. Four other women in red and blue saris, sat alongside the gate entrance, bangles at their ankles and beads in their fingers. One old woman wore a pair of black socks but no sandals. All of them just stared at me as I did them, until our car moved on another few feet.

A brightly painted red hand cart, wheels wedged with rocks, came into view. Three Muslim men sat on canvas covered iron chairs. Two looked like they were brothers and the third possibly their father. He was dressed in pure white with his cap sitting on his head at a jaunty angle. The two young men had the same moustaches, same white shirts, sleeves rolled up to the same place and identical blue grey trousers and sandals. They saw me looking at them and smiled. One held up a poster of a man in a white gown. I think he was a local politician. They all raised their thumbs, so I raised mine as a sign of agreement not knowing who he was or what he represented. It didn't really matter to me.

Half an hour later we were just about leaving the city boundaries when we stopped again, next to a watering hole. By it was a waist high steel pump with a young father cranking the handle up and down as his children watched and played gleefully in the spurting water. Their oxen drank greedily from an aluminium bucket that the owner had placed under the tumbling water. The father held the chain that was fastened tightly around the animal's neck. The children waved to me. Their mother had been squatting by the runoff, washing the few cloths that she had brought. Her purple sari and scarf covered her head and face, but I watched her hands scrubbing vigorously with a bristle brush at the pile of garments. Soap suds running down her arms to her bright cadmium yellow tunic. She turned as she wondered who her children were waving at. Then I saw her face and her high cheekbones, tight with malnutrition. Her dark brown sunken eyes and her furrowed brow. She was probably only thirty but looked twice that.

The car moved on once more and I saw that we were slowly following a horse drawn covered wagon. In the back were about twenty school children. They all wore purple jackets or jumpers and underneath, white shirts and their purple and gold striped school ties. They were all boys about eight or nine years old, all with neat haircuts and round smiling, healthy faces. Their satchels and school bags were strapped to the tail gate and swung back and forth as the blue, two wheeled cart meandered on down the road to their school. As we passed the school cart, I noticed two were playing chess and didn't look up while the rest saw me and waved, laughing and showing their rows of beautiful white teeth. They were happy to show me their big smiles and cheeky, well fed faces.

Finally, we reached the motorway where the traffic eased and we made reasonable progress, reaching Dr Singh's villa midmorning.

We drove through the gates and up the dusty drive, but no one seemed to be around in the gardens. I was expecting to see the boys maybe, out playing, or at least some life around the place, but all was quiet. As I got out of the car the driver handed me my sketch book and paints, before getting my luggage. I had my camera in my bag as I wanted to show Dr Singh what I had been doing up in Agra and having hopefully gained his approval, would be able to start on the painting and get the outline of the Taj Mahal on canvas, before setting to work sketching ideas with his wife and children.

All my canvases, oil paints and brushes had been brought and stored at the villa, ready for me to start work, so I was eager now to get going with the real job in hand and especially meet the boys and Mahima.

The front door opened and from the dark interior, the bulk that was Vijay appeared. His eyes were black and hooded and his forehead large and wrinkled. He bowed his head and beckoned me to come in.

Dr Singh, having greeted me with a big smile, rushed me through the hall, and talked nervously as he marched me through to the lounge.

"I am assured by Neelu that you have many technical things to discuss, but they would probably bore me to death if you went into all the artistic details, but the upshot is that you think that a great painting can be made, yes?" he said, without taking a breath before continuing.

"I am sure that, as a lover of great art, I will be most impressed and thrilled. Neelu rang me up and I said bring him here as soon as possible and we can start this great work that he is going to do for me."

Dr Singh appeared to be talking just for the sake of it, but there was no way I could even get one word in to stop him.

"I will be giving you anything that you want to make this thing happen," he continued, as he paced nervously around the room. His eyes kept on darting back to me as if he had something to hide.

We finally got to discussing the painting some ten minutes later when tea arrived. Neelu had brought in three cups and a large silver jug of milky sweet tea on a silver platter and placed it on a side table. I had to go through all the trivial data about the sketches and possible positions and views. Vijay joined us for a few moments and was issued with a few instructions before he disappeared again.

"I am very pleased with your proposal and the drawings of our beautiful monument," Dr Singh finally said.

I replied that it was just luck that I had managed to capture the beauty in such a short time.

"It is not luck, Mr Ianson, it is God's wish. He has given you a gift and passed on that gift to me through the painting that you will now produce. You are the right man at the right time, but already I know what I need to know about the painting," Dr Singh said as he turned to pour another cup, smiling at Neelu as he gazed deep into her eyes.

"Now it is time for you to start your great work," he said, turning to face me.

"Fantastic!" I said, standing up to meet the man's gaze.

"When do I meet the boys and Mahima, so that we can start to get some sketches of them?" I asked excitedly.

chapter 14

Sid had taken Rakesh and Rohit through the slum to a friend who owned a tuk tuk, who drove them to a drop off point along a wide, tree lined, and relatively empty avenue that followed a curve of the bay, by the stone arch of the "Gateway of India". The street at the front of the monument was crammed with all kinds of pedestrians and cars. Many people came in the evening to see the arch and enjoy the expensive restaurants. The usual noise of car horns and general commerce sounded like hail stones on a tin roof.

There were hundreds of people there, traders and tourists. Groups, large and small, standing talking and laughing. Shops, restaurants and hotels filled the street on one side with the sea on the other. Each place had a suitably dressed doorman, either standing, or sitting on folded stools. There were Africans, Arabs, Europeans and Indians, all together, enjoying the evening. Languages changed with every step and music played from every restaurant and shop. The smells of different spices and cooking spilled into the boiling night air.

Sid took the boys by their hands and ran over to follow a bullock wagon that was weaving its way slowly through the heavy evening traffic. They stopped by a cart selling watermelons and sacks of rice. Sid stole a large piece before the owner had noticed and handed it to Rakesh. They trotted on past racks of clothes for sale and a stall selling cigarettes. An old man was selling ice. Sid again stole a chunk handing the melting shard to Rohit, as they ran on. He sucked on it gleefully and giggled as the cold water ran down his front as well as down his thirsty throat. Sid had noticed a man counting his thick wade of bank notes and as a passing juggler distracted him for a second, Sid had deftly dipped his hand in the man's back pocket and acquired several bank notes for himself. They stumbled around some acrobats performing for the tourists, mesmerised by the snake charmers, musicians, astrologers and palmists who were all trying to sell their wares along with the pimps and the pushers. The whole street was filthy with rubbish and rotting food. As the three moved on they were nearly hit by a pale full of vegetable peelings thrown from a window above, without warning. Large amounts of garbage were heaped in piles on the pavements or the roadsides and they were alive and moving as the fat rats feasted among them.

Sid stole a sideways glance at the boys' faces as they skipped along.

"How is it that you are both feeling?"

"Tired," Rakesh replied, "and a little scared."

They had just passed a group of beggars who were sitting in a doorway playing cards and eating a meagre meal of fish and rice. The boys were unnerved by the sheer density of the area, the carnival of greed and need. The pain of the "untouchables" banished from even the slums had made Sid's heart miss a beat.

He smiled at the two boys though, as they passed the group. He smiled easily and no matter how dangerous or scary the streets seemed to be, he was happy.

He was happy to have saved the brothers. He himself was a fugitive but he always seemed to remain one step ahead of all those that may want to catch him. He was free. Every day, he was on the run. That was his life. Every free minute that he had was a joy and he was always willing to share that joy, that short story of his life.

Kneeling outside by the door, Vijay had been listening to the conversation in the lounge. He was pretending to clean the floor should anyone suddenly find him there. Turning his head to the right, he gazed out towards the garden and to the shallow grave where he had buried Mahima's body. He looked towards his victim's resting place and a chill ran up his spine. He didn't trust Dr Singh, but what could he do now but wait and hope.

Slowly, Vijay let his eyes trace the outline of the ground where the body lay. He stood up and walked out towards the plot. As he made his way towards the strip of newly dug earth, he surveyed it from left to right. The sweat on his brow grew as he realised how obvious the grave was, like a slash wound across a beautiful face. The strip cleaved the garden bed in two. Maybe the location was wrong. Maybe he would have to move the body again to another less obvious place or even remove it from the garden altogether. He noticed a sundial with its brass top a few feet further down the path by the rose garden. He looked at the perfect but worn north-south axis. It was an old English looking sundial of sorts, a vestige of the British that had once ruled his India. The sun's rays, hit the shining brass and the shadow formed indicated the passage of time, time that perhaps he didn't have. He then noticed that stone slabs supporting it were loose and could be easily removed. He strode over to the sundial, glanced behind him to make sure nobody was looking and shouldered the dial a few inches. It moved easily. For a moment, he thought he heard a door open in the house. He turned and gazed at the house for several seconds. Nothing.

Standing with his strong legs slightly apart, he faced the sundial again and heaved it to one side.

Tonight, he thought, if all goes to plan, he will move the body, dig up the area under the sundial, re bury the body there and replace the sundial before the morning. Dr Singh would never know. It would be Vijay's secret and possibly one he could use in the future against the doctor, should his promise not be fulfilled.

The silence in the room was deafening as we looked from one to another. Neelu was staring at Dr Singh and he in turn was trying to look anywhere but at either her or I.

"My wife was here," The doctor said, dropping suddenly into an armchair, just a few feet away from Neelu. She turned quickly on her heels and glided across to another chair by the window.

At first I said nothing, but my senses were tingling. There was something strange about my host's reaction. Why wasn't Mahima here, and where indeed were the children? Surely they knew I was returning to the villa to see them and to start sketching them in various poses.

"But I am afraid she had to leave suddenly," he continued. "I know she will have probably left a message, but I just haven't found where it is yet," he said, quickly getting up and striding over to where the tea was. He poured a cup for himself and stood facing away from the window and he had his back to me.

"Surely she wouldn't have left without a reason," I whispered, stepping closer to Dr Singh. "I suggest we had better find the message that you think she has left then, and as soon as possible," I said, a little more forcefully than I had intended.

I was both confused and frustrated. I didn't really know what to do or think. The whole situation and his explanation just didn't ring true and yet why should I disbelieve him. What did it matter to me if she had suddenly decided to go off for the day? I had plenty to get on with regarding the painting. I had the whole back drop, the Taj Mahal to paint before superimposing his wife and boys as a group on the top of it.

"There's nothing in here that I have found!" Dr Singh said through gritted teeth as he walked over to Neelu.

At that moment I saw a glimmer of fear in his face as he reached down and grabbed Neelu's wrist and slowly raised her up.

They both froze for a second.

"We had better search the house to see if we can find a message," he spoke harshly, looking straight at me but obviously aimed his request at Neelu.

"I suggest that you start to draw and develop a few things on that canvas of yours, Mr Ianson. I will get Vijay to take you to your studio room that I have had him prepare, so you can begin work on the masterpiece that I know you are dying to create for me," Dr Singh enthused as he helped Neelu to the door at great speed.

Out in the corridor, Dr Singh stared in astonishment at Neelu's pained expression. The silence between them seemed to hover in space, casting a jagged shadow across her frightened face.

"The message," he whispered. "You must write the message to prove that she has gone on a trip or something. I need time and to think of how to placate Ianson!"

"The deed has been done. Mahima and the boys are dead, but I need that man to do this painting without asking any more questions about where they are," he continued. "Do you understand?"

Neelu looked at him in confusion: "You understand how difficult this is going to be, darling?" she said a little icily.

"It will be flawless; the plan, it will be flawless," Dr Singh said, nodding as his thoughts churned. "I just need a little time to sort out the fundamentals of the next step."

Neelu looked baffled at the idea of writing a message that was supposedly written by Mahima. What on earth was she going to write and how was she going to ensure that her handwriting was different enough from her own usual style, to avoid any future scrutiny.

Neelu remained silent, staring at the doctor.

"Mr Ianson needs to believe that they have taken a sudden vacation or something and that they won't be returning for some considerable time. I will have to find some photographs of them and tell him that he will have to use those," he said thoughtfully. "Maybe, we have to say that her sister has been taken ill very suddenly and she had to leave immediately to see her, and with the boys as they would require looking after."

Neelu's expression remained uncertain.

"It doesn't really sound too feasible and hardly flawless. She doesn't have a sister," she said.

Dr Singh understood her meaning. Should the message be less or more prescriptive? Should it be mysterious? Should there be a question that would throw doubt, and Mr Ianson off the scent or not, or should the message remain simple and without detail?

His mind was still grappling with the awfully bold clarity of what had happened. But the message needed to be written and produced, and soon.

So dark the evil of man, he thought. So dark indeed.

He was troubled at the thought of the brutal violent end that his wife had no doubt suffered, but the method had been inspired as much as it had no doubt been horrific.

She had died because of his infatuation for another younger woman. His thoughts were that his wife was rightfully punished for her lack of unquestioning care and attention to him.

An absolute sin by any standard.

It was that that gave birth to the idea that she should have perhaps even been burned at the stake for her lacking. This woman, once celebrated as an essential half of his life, had now been banished from the temple of his world. The once hallowed act of sexual union between man and woman had been recast by him as a shameful, but inevitable act with another. His new woman was the only woman that he wanted even though he feared his own sexual urges as the work of the devil, collaborating with his favourite accomplice – Neelu.

I was left standing alone in the lounge looking out at the sea, when suddenly someone knocked on the door and opened it straight away, rather unexpectedly. It was Vijay, who stood by the open door and gazed at the floor, not wanting to look at me. He shuffled his feet a little, clasping his hands in front of his stomach. The grip of his hands turning his knuckles quite pale.

"Sir, I have been asked to show you to the room that is to be your studio," he said quietly, his head bowed. "Your equipment, easel and paints are on the table, Mr Ianson, and there are two large canvases prepared and ready for you, I have been informed."

It was the first time we had been alone. I have to say I didn't think it was going to be the easiest of moments, but I did want to try and find out a little more about where Mahima and the boys might have gone to. He didn't look like a man who would tell many jokes, but I did expect him to tell me the truth as he understood it. He struck me as being a bit of a pedant, but I didn't want to give him a hard time, although I did want to let him know who was in charge. After a while I realised that he wasn't too bad and that he was, despite his huge build and obvious strength, possibly quite a gentle man. It was just his manner perhaps, mixed with quite a lot of apprehension at finding himself alone with me in Dr Singh's lounge.

I asked him if he knew the whereabouts of the doctor's wife and children.

He blinked and looked at me in surprise, then said, "I don't know anything, no, I know nothing about where they are, sir."

I asked him if that was his opinion, or whether he had been told to say that.

He paused and thought for a moment and then said that as far as he could remember, Madam often just went away on trips, sometimes for weeks: "I don't really know the answer. I think there may be many places that she could go."

"Try and remember some of them for me," I suggested, sitting on the arm of the chair, spreading my legs and folding my arms.

"She may have gone to visit friends in Pune or her guru. It isn't always about seeing friends, but about her faith," he said, wobbling his head.

"You've lost me there, Vijay," I told him.

"I mean," said Vijay, sweat beginning to form on his brow as his hands gripped harder, "that where madam wants to go sometimes is to demonstrate to god that she is a good person and that miracles can happen. Maybe her guru will help her come back quickly."

There was a silence. I didn't go for the religious stuff and guru miracles, and anyway he wasn't making any sense.

I shook my head. "No, Vijay, I have not understood one word that you have said. It doesn't make any sense, but I am thinking that I need to talk with Dr Singh again. Can you arrange it, sometime soon?"

"I might be able to arrange that," said Vijay. "He will be available later. I will try and speak to him and let you know, Mr Ianson, sir."

I stood up and asked him mildly, to show me the studio. As he turned towards the door I said, "Thanks for talking to me Vijay." He walked on and didn't look back but opened the door for me and led the way, up two flights of stairs to a room at the top of the villa that was to be my studio.

The room was large with a single wide window facing north, which was good. Northern light is always good for painting. The room had a tall ceiling and with the help of a humming ceiling fan, kept it cool. I closed the door and looked over at all my painting accessories and a canvas, already perched up on the easel.

There was a bed in the far corner and a table with two chairs. It was obvious that this was to be my living, sleeping, as well as painting quarters.

I felt detached and miserable. It was raining in my heart. Vijay's bizarre and trite words rattled around my head and would not leave me. I felt hollow inside remembering Dr Singh's announcement that his wife and children had suddenly gone away. And while I should have been thinking about the composition of the painting, especially now that I didn't have half the subject matter available and concerning myself with the usual problems and complexities that should have engaged every moment of my time, I was thinking about why they would have left so suddenly and without even telling Vijay or her husband.

I unpacked my luggage and started flicking though the sketches I had made in Agra. Each time I looked at the large white empty canvas, my heart sank.

Picking up a 5HB pencil, I attempted to draw some images on the canvas. They became extended lines and scribbles with no depth or perspective. Angrily, I threw the pencil onto the table and flopped onto the bed. The mattress was hard and smelt musty and I felt confused and a little frightened.

It was early evening by the time I had completed a basic outline in thinned burnt sienna oil paint. My outlines always seemed to start this way. I had just placed my thin bristle brush back into the white spirit, when there was a knock on the door. Taking off my smock and wiping my hands on a spirit-soaked rag, I opened the door. Dr Singh was standing soldier like, holding a piece of paper in his right hand. His smile was thin, and his eyes half closed. Neelu was standing further back in the shadow of the corridor. He glanced over my shoulder at the canvas.

"I am so glad that you have started your masterpiece, Mr Ianson," he said, wobbling his head and staring straight into my face. "I have some good news. I told you that Mahima would have left a note," he said, waving a single sheet of crinkled paper under my nose. "It was in my bedroom all along; silly of me to have missed it initially."

"Shall I read it out to you?" he said, raising his nose in the air as if he were extremely proud of himself that he had been correct all along.

"Well I am sure it is a perfectly acceptable explanation, Dr Singh," I said, not wanting to appear that I had ever doubted him in the first place. "I certainly don't need to know the intricate details of your family's comings and goings, nor her reasons for having to leave. I am sure..."

I was about to finish me sentence but was interrupted, as Dr Singh thrust the paper into my rather oil paint covered fingers insisting that I read it for myself.

He stood in front of me, perfectly still with his hands clasped behind his back. I glanced at the rather long note, written in English with a black biro, which seemed strange. The style seemed somewhat haphazard, with some letters sloping backwards in one sentence and forwards in the next.

I didn't want to read it and handed it back almost as quickly as the doctor had given it to me.

He stared at me and smiled that narrow disapproving smile that I had seen before with Neelu.

I felt as if I was being forced to accept something that seemed quite understandable, and yet something didn't seem right. Why *was* I being shown this note that seemed more like a letter than a short explanation anyway. It didn't seem to have been written quickly. Quite the opposite and why had she written it in English. I would have thought a personal note to her husband would have been written in Hindi.

They both remained standing in the doorway as if waiting for me to say something perhaps.

"Good, right then, that's settled. Good. So, we will see you at dinner, Mr Ianson. No doubt after all your hard work you will be very much hungry."

With that they both turned and left me standing somewhat bemused, in my studio come bedroom, staring at the ceiling fan and listening to its incessant hum.

Outside in the garden, Vijay carried his garden shovel over his shoulder and walked round the shed to where he had buried Mahima's body. He eyed the sundial as he passed where he was going to rebury the body. He trudged on a little further and sat by the sea wall. From his position he could see Dr Singh, Neelu and Mr Ianson having dinner in the dining room. The air was warm, and he could smell and hear the sea. The crashing of the waves he hoped, would drown out the sound of shovelling, that he was going to be making as he dug beneath the sundial. He could not afford to make any considerable noise. Iron striking the stone could be heard from the house on a still night no doubt.

Would the household hear him? They should be asleep by midnight when he would start the digging. It was a chance that Vijay was not wanting to take, but he had no choice.

Over the next few hours, he sat alone in the dark with his cloak wrapped around him. The lights finally went out around eleven o'clock and so he waited another hour to be safe before removing his woollen cloak and standing naked, except for his loin cloth and boots, picked up his spade and headed to the sundial. Then he aimed his spade at the base and drove the blade under the dial. It moved enough for him to manoeuvre it out of the way and allow him to dig. He created a sort of compartment as he pulled aside the slabs and steps that surrounded the plinth.

Quickly, pulling the remaining pieces away and digging deeper Vijay gazed at the deep ditch he had created. His blood pounded in his head as he stood and looked into the void.

He needed to move quietly and quickly now, retrieving Mahima's body from the shallow grave , placing it here and replacing the slabs and sundial.

An hour later, Vijay was stunned with his own devilish plan completed. The new secret location that only he knew about. *Clever Vijay,* he thought, barely able to contain his excitement. Looking up at the house, he gazed across the windows just to make sure that no one had seen him and couldn't help but smile.

Up in the top floor studio by the window, I was standing shaking. Moments ago, I had witnessed a large man pulling a cloak over his shoulders, and I was overcome with a horrified bewilderment. The man was clutching a spade in one hand and a white cloth in the other, as he walked along the pathway from the sundial, back towards the garden shed and the garages.

In breathless silence, I left the window not understanding any of what I had just witnessed.

Only moments before I had been woken by the sound of stone grating on stone. It had come from the garden in waves, as the sound of the rolling sea took over every now and then.

I was drawn to the window where I could easily see across the expansive gardens and that's when I noticed a semi naked figure pushing the sundial into place. I had no idea what he was doing, but nevertheless I felt suddenly afraid.

Back in the garden, Vijay had walked silently back to the garden shed and leaving the spade outside, entered his small abode. His whole body was sweating now as he found his bed in the dark and lay down. He ran his fingers across his wet brow.

Now it has been done.

He spoke the words as tears ran down his cheeks. Confused, he said the words again, sensing that his terrible deeds and the wrong he had done, would at some stage be discovered. He sadly realised that it wasn't really, *done,* and he would soon have to pay the consequences, despite the doctor's continued promise of freedom.

Chapter 15

"So, Mr Ianson is not really your friend…" Dr Singh said to Neelu, finally finding themselves alone. I had gone up to my studio room having finished a rather delicious glass of 25-year-old Talisker whisky and left my hosts to themselves. I was tired and feeling a little uneasy, so had hoped that I would be able to sleep well after such a simple, but pleasant meal, a couple of beers and finally the scotch whiskey.

"I warned you that Peter Ianson wasn't a man to try and bribe, not a man to want sexual favours thrust upon him. You might be able to do everything else with him, but not that. He obviously finds you extremely attractive, but then most men do, my darling. But you didn't listen to me, did you?"

"You still need to keep him interested in you so that you can watch his every move. The second part of our plan has yet to be put in place," Dr Singh said, leaning forward and taking Neelu's hands.

"Mr Ianson did exactly as I knew he would do. In his own mind, he considered a trade of his affection for me, but realised that it would be futile. He would never try anything like that again with me," Neelu whispered, knowing that what she was telling the doctor wasn't entirely the truth.

"Is he afraid of you?" Dr Singh asked, smiling as he continued holding onto her hands.

"Yes, perhaps he is a little bit, but he is also in awe of me too. That's one of the reasons I despise him. I can never respect a man who didn't have the strength to *look after* a woman, unlike you my darling Satwinder. And now I must get to bed."

Neelu stood up and the doctor rose with her and gazed lovingly into her dark brown eyes.

"Tomorrow," he said, "when I go to the surgery, try to help Mr Ianson relax into his painting. Tell him that, in India, he has to surrender before he can win." Then he laughed out loud. Neelu smiled back at him sweetly.

"You have always got some wise advice, haven't you?" she said, laughing gently too.

"That's not wise, Neelu. I think wisdom is very over-rated. Wisdom is just cleverness, with all the guts kicked out of it, but I am certainly very clever having just kicked the guts out of my god damn family, haven't I? I would rather be clever than wise, any day. If I *were* giving wise advice – which I am not – I would say don't have another glass of that fine whiskey, don't spend all your money on trivia and trinkets and don't fall in love with a pretty Indian secretary. *Tha*t would be wise," he said, still holding Neelu's hands and laughing again. "Okay, let's go to bed. Come and see me in my room when you think Mr Ianson is asleep. I'm looking forward to it. I really want you tonight."

She kissed his cheek and turned away. He couldn't obey the impulse to pull her into his arms and kiss her full, delicious lips. She twisted sideways and he watched her swaying hips, walk out of the room. She moved into the warm half-light of the hall where she stopped at the bottom of the stairs. Dr Singh's watching eyes made her shadow come to life, as if his heart had painted her from darkness with the light and colours of his love. She turned with one leg raised as a stilettoed foot rested on the first step, to see that he was watching her, before she slowly and quietly climbed the staircase to her room.

Sid woke early, just as the first rays of sunlight hit the tattered sheet of blue plastic that he had found the night before, in a place he knew well enough. The two brothers were still asleep, wrapped up in each other's arms welded into Sid's slim but warm back. He folded back the plastic that barely covered them but at least it had hidden them a little and provided some protection from the rats and general misery that was Mumbai at night. Sid had taken the boys to a red-light district he knew in the north party of the city, near the posh hotels where there were always white, rich foreigners looking for young Indian girls. He had a friend, a beautiful girl but a prostitute. Sid had pleaded with her to let them stay the night in a disused room at the back of a rundown hotel.

She had returned late and had taken the small rusting bed on the other side of the room to sleep on.

Sid got up and walked across the room and drew back the woollen blanket draped across her.

"You are so fat but in the most important and most serious of places," he whispered, not really wanting to wake her. "Men can be grabbing big handfuls of you with so much glee and enjoyment."

Bhupinder turned over and rubbed the sleep from her eyes. She was not at all impressed with his description of her.

Although she was a little rotund perhaps, she didn't need Sid to remind her, but she knew he was only really teasing her.

"Don't talk to me like that, baba. Only first you get bumping and jumping and give me money, then your silly mood will so quickly change, *futt-a futt*!"

"Maybe you are very much right, Bhupi, but I think I will pass, all the same, yes," he said, wanting to change the subject of having to pay Bhupinder for sex.

"I will pay you 100 rupees for the room though, even if it is not much better than my slum hut."

"I am needing to have some place for these boys to sleep. They were nearly burnt to frazzlement in a car last night, but I am the rescuing man here. A hero you might say even," Sid said, smiling and beating his chest with a clenched fist to show how strong and proud he was.

Bhupinder pulled the door of the small hotel room shut and locked it. Something she had forgotten to do the night before. The hotel was more than a hundred years old and built to serve a different more splendid age. The room, albeit small having been divided up many times, had a high ceiling which featured part of a fine detailed cornice and a ceiling rosette, from which a single bare wire and a dim bulb hung. The furniture was a single shoddy bed and a shabby carpet with holes in. The paint was peeling, and the walls bruised with dirt.

Bhupinder, dressed in her usual red and yellow sari, looked tired and pale. On the bed a dhoti and white cap lay. Her last client, a farmer from Aurangabad had left suddenly!

She fixed her gaze on the two brothers and they stared balefully back at her. She was a pretty woman, though wide faced with a bulbous nose and lips so thin and curled that the boys thought her mouth resembled a clam that they had poked with a stick. She wore make up on her face that was geisha thick but when she smiled finally, they smiled back as her scowling expression disappeared.

"You see, boys?" Sid muttered, never taking his eyes off her. "You see what I told you?" he continued and wobbled his head. "She is a very lovingly lady."

The three of them had slept on the floor. Bhupinder had been in and out of the room all night, as she was obviously busy elsewhere. Sid told the boys that they would have to leave soon but he would find somewhere to eat.

"This place that I am going to be taking you is such a very fine place that very often you can be sitting down even while you are eating," he enthused and smiled his big smile.

As good as his word, Sid took the boys to a hovel, about twenty minutes' walk past a busy bus stop by a park. With a plate of dhal, rice and a roti, they forced themselves into a corner, crushed and dusty, with several others all eating on a narrow stone bench. The others were workers, farmers and a routine assortment of law breakers who Sid knew. They all wore sullen and sad expressions and said very little as they ate. It was a grim and pleasureless experience for the boys, who had been used to much more refined dining, but they were more than grateful for the meal. Then suddenly, a Hindi love song jingled from an old radio by the cooker and one of the shabby waiters started to sing along. Although off key, he drew cheers and passionate approval from the morning diners, that made the boys smile and Sid laugh out loud.

It was another day in Mumbai city and already the hot sun and deafening endless street noise had set the scene for Sid and his new young acquaintances.

The boys were scared and bewildered by all that had happened and yet if Sid was with them, they were not only grateful but felt somehow, safe.

I woke quite early having had a rather disturbed night's sleep. The light from the window was pale blue as it just crept between the slats of the shutters. I turned over to feel yet another uncomfortable spring that easily found my spine. The mattress wasn't the most luxurious one I had every slept on. Sitting up, the image of last night's figure in the garden suddenly entered my head again.

Who was that? What were they doing at that time of night? A cold shiver ran up my spine as I dragged my tired body out of bed and headed to the wash basin, trying not to think about what I had witnessed.

I was halfway through shaving when a knock came on the door and a meek female voice said in broken English that breakfast would be ready in the dining room.

It was Dr Singh's cook.

She had also kindly left me a cup of sweet Indian tea that I only found on opening the door to leave. It was cold but I drank it anyway.

I ate breakfast alone, which pleased me as I really wanted to get on with the painting now and needed no further interruptions and excuses from anyone.

I would paint the Taj Mahal backdrop and take things from there.

Back in my studio room, I folded back the shutters that hung tentatively at the single north facing window and turned to assess my task. The outline that I had already prepared the day before, drew me in. The need to immerse myself in the use of colour and paint, was suddenly the most important thing in the world for me to do.

Standing in front of the canvas I lost my worries. I was just a simple painter, at one with my oils, my whole being concentrated on my next step and my next stroke of the brush. I watched my own bold marks play across the canvas and see the paint glisten, without apparent effort, and great forms begin to appear as my movements became easier. I painted with economy and skill, so much so that I somehow surprised myself to see the form of the monument appear. I became lost in time, forgetting everything except for the immediate moment of placing oil on canvas, paint over paint, blending and mixing as I went.

It was in the end, quite a peaceful time spent.

I was tired; shattered from the previous day's outings, exhausted by the worry about what had been happening, but as I painted, a sense of deep calm flowed through me, a feeling that perhaps everything would be alright; the doctor would have his painting, Mahima and the boys would show up to be added to the picture and everything would be fine and I would be happy again.

Then I heard a voice from down in the garden. It made me look up.

Putting down my brushes and wiping my hands, I walked unhurriedly to the window and looked down. Coming along the path from behind the garages towards the house, was Vijay. His top half naked. On his head was a scarf to keep the sun off. I heard his feet scrunching on the gravel path as he hurried along, and I realised that Dr Singh had called him to the house.

There was a sudden recollection that the body I was looking at now was the same shape and bulk of that which I had glimpsed the night before, almost in the same place.

So, was it Vijay that had been digging by the sundial so late?

The two men met on the path. I couldn't hear much of what was being said as the sound of the sea and breeze drowned out their conversation.

I did hear Dr Singh when he raised his voice.

"But that's not what we had agreed before," he shouted up close to Vijay's face.

"It doesn't matter if everyone thinks they were taken there on purpose. Any other way is too risky now," he paused and rubbed his forehead with his hand. Then he added, "The important point is you should say that you only heard it on the streets or in the bars, that you are absolutely sure that you were here all that evening if you are ever asked."

"There must be more you can tell me. You will be in a hell of a lot of trouble if someone finds out," Dr Singh said finally, before turning away.

I saw Vijay grab the doctor's jacket sleeve and stare down at him. He said something to him, but I couldn't hear as the wind blew the words away. I did however see Dr Singh's look as he tore away Vijay's hand and marched back to the house. There seemed to be a lot of anguish on both their faces.

As the boys finished their meagre breakfast, three farmers dressed in lungis and singlets approached them brazenly. One of them carried a wire basket containing hot chai. A second grasped a plate, and on it several sweet ladoo.

"Will you drink tea, boys?" one of the men asked politely in Hindi. "Will you have a sweet?"

Sid smiled and wagged his head. The men advanced quickly, handing a glass of chai to Sid and the brothers. They squatted on the ground by the stone seat and smiled at the two boys. Sid drank the chai but insisted that the boys left theirs. The men remained with them and watched the boys' faces intently.

"The universe is getting more complex every single of days and this is because that is its nature to be doing so," Sid said to the boys in English, trusting that the men couldn't understand him, but still they stayed and watched.

"The tendency towards complexity has moved most very much the universe from simplicity to the complex world that we are most living in now," he continued, trying to separate the boys from the men.

The boys were amazed that Sid even knew so many big words but had no idea what he was talking about. As they were so surprised, they just sat and smiled at him, mesmerised, as were the three farmers.

Suddenly Rohit realised that this wasn't normal and nudging his brother said.

"I think I know where you are going with this."

Sid laughed and the farmers laughed with him.

Sid then turned his full attention to the two boys, with one eyebrow raised, as if he were going to make some major announcement. It was an expression that the boys had seen before and knew that it meant something was about to happen. Sid's fearlessness had taken the boys by surprise before. He was impudent but street wise, beyond words. Whatever the cause for his endless smile and now arched eyebrow, whatever was going to happen would happen soon.

"It is now that we must leave you," he said to the farmers, glancing at them sitting at his feet. He exchanged a broad smile with them and suddenly jumped up, catching the plate of sweets and glasses of hot chai, spilling everything over the farmers. With hot chai spraying the farmer's laps and sweets flying everywhere, Sid grabbed the hands of both boys and dragging and stumbling over the three men, ran straight out into the searing heat of the street to escape.

It had been a close call, as the farmer's intentions had no doubt been to kidnap the boys and sell them or worse. They ran through the side streets as fast as they could. Sid kept looking round, but the farmers hadn't followed them.

It was about eleven o'clock and hot and finally when they were all out of breath they finally found time to stop. They had passed a number of small shops as the street wound through two right turns until eventually, they arrived at a small courtyard. The oval space, although open to the sky, was shaded by the inhabitants' cloths, all drying on balconies or lengths of wire. It was paved with large square Maharashtrian stone and surrounded by brick arches that gave it a colonial effect. An elderly gentleman sat in a cane emperor chair, reading a book.

Salaam aleikum," he smiled. *Peace be with you.*

Sid smiled back and raised an eyebrow again and nodded but said nothing.

The man was sitting next to a fountain. It was a circle of marble with a single huge stone centre piece. Water seemed to spout from the very core of the stone. At its peak, the small fountain curved into a lily-shaped plume before splashing gently back onto the smooth marble.

"Hello very much," said Sid, his eyes huge at the sight of the water.

The old man returned to his book and without looking at the boys asked them if they wanted a drink. Their eyes flickered a tiny, hopeful smile in response. Sid looked back at the gentleman reading his book, who returned the look, staring straight into his soul.

"Please, go ahead. The water is good."

The boys weren't sure, but Sid tugged at their wrists with both hands, pulling them closer to him. The boys shook their heads and told him they weren't thirsty. He could see the fear in their eyes. He planted his feet and tugged harder at their wrists. Rohit told him in Hindi that he wasn't that thirsty. Sid was adamant but let go of them and they all scampered up to the fountain to drink. Frustrated and wavering, the brothers hesitated initially, but seeing Sid, his hands and feet wet, they too stepped up, and leaning over as far as they could, cupped the water as it cascaded down.

"The water's good," the old man said, after a while. "Have you noticed that the water's good here? I mean really good. You'd expect it to be slime, I mean Mumbai and all. People are so scared of the water, but it's really much better than the chemical-tasting camel piss that comes out of most watering holes."

"It is very hot, no?" continued the elderly gentleman, closing but holding his book firmly in his hands.

"God, I hate this time of year. It's usually always worst just before the monsoon, but it shouldn't be like it now. It makes people crazy. Doesn't this weather make you boys crazy? This was my seventieth monsoon, I think. You start to count in monsoons when you get to my age. Seventy goddamn monsoons. How about you?"

Rohit suddenly spoke up, not afraid anymore: "This was my sixth here in Mumbai. I was looking forward to it. I love the rain, even if it does turn the garden into a swamp."

"Ah! So, you must be a rich little boy, to have a garden," the old man said, gazing at Rohit.

Rohit's eyes lowered as he looked down at the water so the old man couldn't read his expression. The man's eyes glittered in a radiant, almost inviting smile, but his mouth was twisted in a disdainful sneer.

"You are both very nice young boys. How did you get hooked up with this fellow?" he said, turning a hooded gaze towards Sid.

"Do you like children?" he said slowly.

"I don't. They are being very innocent. Except that they are not. They are very much worldly boys. You are being very much creepy, sir, that is making me sick to my stomach."

The old man seemed to be immune to the words that stumbled out of Sid's mouth.

Sid turned back to the fountain and cupping his hands together, took another scoop of water and drank it in a long, slow swallow. He wiped his lips with the back of his hand. The set of his jaw - angry and dislikeable - relaxed into an expression that was surprisingly gentle, as he turned back to face the old man. There was a lengthening silence.

He stared at him blankly.

Suddenly, using the old man's grip on the book as leverage, Sid smashed his head onto the point of the old man's chin as he tried to pull away. Alarm surged through the courtyard. A dozen pair of eyes suddenly appeared through windows. He dropped his book and screamed. Thrashing wildly, he tried to get out of his cane chair as Sid picked up the book and ran across the courtyard to a steel gate. The boys followed him, with their hands reaching out for his back. Grasping the bars, he shook the gate and screeched for help. It was suddenly opened by a young woman and the three of them scrambled through the gate. Rohit's T-shirt stretched behind him and for a second he was stuck there, his legs running but his little body quite still. Then the T-shirt gave way, and he was left with a chunk of it left on the gate latch as he escaped through the opening. They turned a corner and cowered behind some refuse bins; their backs pressed against the wall. They heard the gate slammed shut, but nobody had followed them, so they moved on quickly until arriving at a busy street, squeezed their way through the busy throng of shoppers and to freedom, once more.

I needed a break from painting, and I was also very curious about what I had seen and heard in the garden the night before. Wandering down the stairs to the hall, I bumped into Neelu. She looked as if she had just come out of the shower as her hair was wrapped in a towel and she had no makeup on.

"God," she said, "I must look a mess. Thank goodness it's only you, Peter. I'm sorry to have let you see me like this. I was just washing my hair."

"You look absolutely fine to me," I said, obviously surprised.

She looked at me and gave a sad smile.

"That's very sweet of you," suddenly, she leaned forward and kissed me briefly and coolly on the cheek. She then continued, saying over her shoulder, "Give me five minutes and I will join you in the lounge."

I went through to the lounge and as I sat there waiting I could still feel the touch of her lips on my cheek.

Almost twenty minutes later she arrived back, and I explained that I just needed to get out, perhaps for a walk or a little shopping locally.

She drove us to the nearest village and down to the river where we walked along a path on the west bank. After a while, we sat on the ground under the shade of a Sandal tree and listened to a mina bird singing in the branches above us. I had my back propped against it as we listened.

I had thought there would be a constraint from the night in Agra and that both she and I would feel embarrassed by the fact that I had rejected her advances. As we sat there, I had a feeling of contentment I hadn't known for a long time. The sky was a dark blue and black kites screeched and wheeled far above us. There was little vegetation apart from a few dry bushes and tuffs of grass that were fading from green to brown awaiting any possible rain, to turn their colour back. The river was not particularly wide, and it was dissected by the dried-up banks of shingle, as the tide was out.

I said to Neelu, "Lovely spot, this, and so close to the sea." I rolled onto my side to have a look further up the river.

Neelu smiled at me: "You look like a little boy who's been let out to play for the first time," she said. Then her smile faded. We were looking at each other and there must have been an expression on my face that gave away the fact that I did find her extremely attractive.

"Peter, I don't think..." she started to say in an uncertain tone, but I had caught sight of a movement behind her. Someone was coming.

Neelu turned round and we both saw a young woman walking towards us. She was very dark skinned and thin and dressed in a brightly coloured sari of jade green and fuchsia pink and she wore her deep crimson head scarf in a way that hid her face from the burning brightness of the sun. She looked very striking as the breeze forced her sari tight across her slim frame. On her head she carried a pitcher and in her hand she carried two tin cups. As we watched her approach, I saw that she had come from a hut along the riverbank where several goats were tethered, chewing the green shoots from the top of some bushes.

As the young woman approached she gave a shy smile and said hello in Hindi. She took the pitcher from off the top of her head, knelt on the ground next to where we were sitting and poured water from it into the two tin cups. Then she reached into her sari and drew out two chapatis, wrapped up in a cloth and handed one to each of us and gestured to us to eat and drink. The chapati was delicious and the water refreshingly cool. We smiled and Neelu thanked her. She sat with us for a while and I marvelled at her simple act of kindness. She had seen two people walking in the heat and she had put aside whatever she had been doing and came to give her service. Because it was her custom and her upbringing, her action was as natural to her as the water that she had poured for us. Once we had declined the offer of a second cup, she rose and clasped her hands together, murmured her farewell and turned and went back to her hut further up the river.

I never saw her whole face, just her smile and her slender hennaed hands.

The young woman's act of kindness had given me a chance to change both the situation I had found myself in with Neelu and also somehow, had reminded me of the unkind words being spoken, some of which I had overheard, between Dr Singh and Vijay.

"Can I ask you a question?" I said, looking into Neelu's half-closed eyes.

"Of course, Peter. What is it?" she said with a rather forced smile, no doubt hoping that I wasn't going to ask her about the night in Agra.

"I was wondering whether there were any problems with Dr Singh and his family," I said slowly. Neelu didn't look away, but I noticed a slight sudden twitch of her left cheek.

"I am not a political man nor a nosey one, Neelu, just someone who wants to produce a joyous painting for a generous client and show him that I can fulfil his every wish."

"With your skills and our amazing monument, Dr Singh will no doubt have an amazing picture soon enough," said Neelu, "and then you can expect that handsome fee for all your hard work."

"I think you meant an amazing portrait of the family *and* the monument," I replied, a little surprised that including the family in my intended picture had been left out of her description.

"I don't think Dr Singh quite understands the urgency of my needing to meet with and to paint his wife and children as soon as possible. Perhaps they will reveal themselves to me one day soon, do you think?"

The two of us sat together in silence. Neelu didn't look at me for several moments and I wondered if she was ever going to respond to my question at all.

She surprised me by turning her eyes upon me and saying, "You are far too inquisitive, Peter."

I didn't know what to say. I flushed and was thankful we were under the shade of the tree so that the change in my colour was probably not obvious.

I saw Neelu look at me intently.

"Oh... am I? I certainly didn't mean to pry, but it is going to be a little awkward if I have to try and paint a decent portrait from Dr Singh's photo collection," I continued. "Is there an illness in the family or something?" I was getting more exasperated.

"No, it's nothing like that," she said between gritted teeth.

"Then don't tell me, for it's none of my concern. But I will regret to see the outcome. I would rather perhaps come back when the family has returned so that I can put my whole heart and mind into the project. You need to understand, that painting a live person is far better than..." I stopped as Neelu had suddenly burst into tears.

I was horrified. I hadn't realised the conversation was getting a little deep or that my approach was that aggressive. Neelu made a gesture with her hand as she turned away to hide her tears.

She took a little time to pull herself together but as soon as she had done so, she got up and suggested that we should return to the villa, as no doubt I needed to continue with the painting.

Both the return walk and the drive back were carried out in total silence that left me both upset and deeply concerned, and yet I had no idea why.

Chapter 16

I spent the afternoon back in my studio room continuing, as best I could, to focus on the painting once more. I kept thinking back to the walk by the river with Neelu and her sudden breakdown when I had asked her about Mahima and the boys. Something wasn't right, something had happened, between us going to Agra and our return to Mumbai.

I should never have allowed myself to get involved. As soon as I saw Dr Singh and Vijay arguing and seeing Vijay, in the middle of the night in the garden and now Neelu's behaviour, I should have thought then that things weren't quite right. I should have packed my bags and left. Perhaps I should still do that now, I thought. Stop the project, put down my brushes and tell Dr Singh to drop it. After all, what did it amount to at the moment?

A half-finished painting of the Taj Mahal and no portrait of a single member of the family included in it.

I blamed myself, all the way.

I should have insisted that I at least sketched the family when I first saw them at the villa, and then gone to Agra.

What would it matter if I hadn't completed the painting? A lost commission ? Is that all?

I suppose Dr Singh might have refused to pay for my return flight or worse, insist I repay what he had already spent.

Those were all the questions I should have been asking myself if I had been focused on job properly.

But I hadn't, and now here I sat, chewing the end of my brush and worrying. I thought about the changeable behaviour in the doctor and Neelu. What relationship did they have? What did she mean when she had said, *"No, it's nothing like that"*?

Why would anyone want a portrait painting when those needed, weren't available?

What had Vijay been actually doing in the garden and where on earth were Mahima and the boys, really?

It was all rubbish.

I needed to get back to the painting. Thumbing through some of the sketches and colour tones I came across several photographs of Mahima and the boys. They had been given to me by Dr Singh for me to use in the absence of his family. I found myself studying them with an intensity that I hadn't applied before. They had been taken fairly recently, looking at the age of the Rohit and Rakesh.

I think Mahima had said they were nine and twelve, respectively. In the photographs they appeared to be about that age, but with not having children of my own I found it a little difficult to determine their actual ages.

The boys were smiling in all but one photograph. It was a photograph which included their mother and father, and nobody was smiling in that picture. The ones where both boys were sitting side by side made me smile, as they both looked happy and relaxed together.

Suddenly, amongst the pile, I came across a coloured image of Mahima, by herself. She was standing very upright in a gold embroidered silk sari. Her makeup was immaculate, and her jewellery pronounced and obviously expensive. She looked very elegant and yet, as I looked at her head and got close enough to the photograph to see more of her face, her eyes seemed sad and empty.

A slight shiver ran down my spine that made be jump back in surprise. I put the photographs back in the folder that Dr Singh had presented them to me days before and stashed it underneath my sketch book.

Sitting there gazing out of my solitary window, listening to the hum of the fan and feeling the warm air circulate around me, I suddenly felt afraid, isolated and very vulnerable.

It was getting a little cooler and the sun was sinking a little further when I sat back to admire the day's work. The painting of the monument was almost complete, and I was pleased with the pale blue colours of the sky and water and brilliant golden creamy whiteness of the Taj itself using Naples Yellow and clean mixing white. The long lengths of lawn leading to the monument that edged the pathways, I had used both Phthalo Green, the yellow shade, along with Sap Green and created a deeper look to the pathways by adding in Burnt Sienna and Venetian Red and Alizarin Crimson to plenty of Zinc White. The water reflected the colour of the sky, whilst the trees between the water and the pathways, a deeper Sap Green with Ochre.

I was still in two minds whether I should add some of the hundreds of visitors that were a constant part of the scene or leave them all out. Perhaps I would decide tomorrow. I wasn't particularly happy with the reflection of the Taj in the water. It had shimmered beautifully all day and was a slightly deeper cream, but I hadn't quite managed to capture its true reflective beauty yet. As part of the lower third of the canvas, I had left three "shapes" at the bottom of the picture. The shapes sat like outlines of three Russian dolls with the mother doll in the centre and two smaller dolls on either side. The left hand one being slightly larger and taller than the right, representing Rakesh and Rohit.

I'll finish it tomorrow I thought and with that I bathed and changed, and went downstairs, as I had been invited to join Dr Singh and Neelu for dinner.

I don't think anybody spoke a great deal for most of the evening. Dinner was a formal, silent affair. Vijay waited on us, treading soft-footed behind our chairs and serving us with a most delicious murgha biryani accompanied by some Reserve wines from Pune. For me, it might have been dried rice on my plate and vinegar in my glass. I pushed the food around and sipped at my wine without tasting it. Dr Singh didn't have much to say, after one or two unsuccessful attempts to draw him on the subject of the painting.

I saw Neelu glance at him several times and then at me once or twice and realised my expression must be giving something away about how uncomfortable I was feeling. I have never been very good at hiding my feelings.

For a while there was no sound except the clink of cutlery on plates and occasional slurping of wine. The doctor was keeping social conversation to an absolute minimum as there were obviously things that he didn't wish to discuss. The progress of the painting seemed an obvious one. There were things to be discussed or there were not. There were the day's events to be exchanged or there were not. Neelu was beginning to feel the discomfort and had tried, unsuccessfully, to lighten the mood.

In the end I couldn't stand it. I could see that they both were unwilling to engage with me despite one or two conversational gambits, directed at me by Neelu that had gone nowhere.

Finally, I said, "Dr Singh, as you know, I have almost completed the painting. That is to say, the Taj Mahal background and now I need to add the images of your family.

The doctor smiled and said, "I am sorry that my wife and children are not here. It must be very difficult to add something that isn't available in the flesh, so to speak. Something you want to add so much and never do it."

"Well I am sure I will be able to produce something that will perhaps suffice but I won't be able to capture the true elegance and beauty of your wife nor the vibrancy of life that the boys have."

Dr Singh's smile disappeared, and his stare was dark and menacing.

Neelu had bowed her head and avoided my gaze.

"What I really mean is," I said, "that an actual physical sitting is and would be far more favourable to create a truly wholesome portrait."

"Of course, it would be, but as I have no idea when my wife and family will return, you are now required to do the best you can with the photographs I have supplied. It took me a great deal of time and care to choose the ones that I find most appealing and I will assume that you are competent enough to be able to easily add them into the painting, making them as life like as possible."

I noticed that he stumbled a little with the last few words, which made me feel concerned once more.

Dinner was over and so Vijay, looking sombre and discreet and moving noiselessly in front of me, showed me back to my studio room.

"Tomorrow morning, sir, breakfast will be at eight."

"But I don't particularly want breakfast at eight, thank you, Vijay," I said, a little annoyed. "What I really want is to ask you a couple of questions, if that's possible?" I continued, trying to see into the depth of his hooded eyes. He didn't answer me, but instead turned quickly on his heels and saying goodnight, marched quickly along the landing to the stairs.

I stomped upstairs to my room and threw myself onto the bed and staring at the ceiling, felt a profound sense of frustration and fear, steal over me. It was as if I was drowning in a deep dark pool of freezing water. I was away from home, away from England, and I had had the wholly unexpected feeling of dying, alone, isolated and in terror.

My thoughts were totally irrational and ridiculous, I realised, but nevertheless, I tried to sleep having securely locked and bolted my door.

Rohit suddenly collapsed by the roadside and burst out crying. Rakesh was trying desperately to console him as tears left rivulets in the dried mud and dust that caked his young cheeks, when Sid finally stopped and turned to see them both sitting in the gutter. He could see the look of sheer exhaustion and despair on their faces. As noon approached the heavy heat in the streets was taking its toll on the young boys. The city sounds, colour and commotion were at their height.

"I want to go home, Rakesh," Rohit was sitting in a pile of rubbish and pleaded with his brother.

"Why did Vijay put us in the boot of mama's car?" he sobbed.

"Why does he hate us so much? We did nothing wrong except break the window in the green house, but that was last week."

"It was your bowling that made me do that, Rohit," Rakesh murmured.

"Vijay must hate us more than... I've never been treated like this in my life. Not even by Mr Hamid, when he caught me and Rajan smoking a cigarette at school did anything like what Vijay did," Rakesh said, as he too started to sob, and the tears welled up in his big brown eyes.

"He must have been so angry with us, that it sent him crazy maybe, if you know what I mean."

"The thing with the fire in the car. He could have killed us if he hadn't changed his mind and let us out," Rakesh went on staring at his brother in disbelief.

"What is it that you are saying and thinking there?" Sid suddenly exploded running round them, his hands flailing the air.

"I was the very one person that was getting you out of that car boot. Not the big fellow that I was seeing running off towards the slums," he said, quite upset and staring from one boy to the other with his left eyebrow raised.

"That's right! Me. I came to be rescuing you from that burning car inferno," he said, as the boys looked wide-eyed back at him.

"So, Vijay was going to kill us? Let us be burnt alive in the boot of mama's car?" Rakesh said, totally beside himself.

"But why? Why? What had we done that would make him want to do that?"

Rohit was now almost hysterical with disbelief and exhaustion. He and Rakesh sat sobbing and hugged each other.

"Come on. We have to be getting out of this. I don't know what is going on. I don't know why the big man did this. If you hadn't been the naughtiest of boys then things are bad. If he was going to kill you then things are much worse. I will give you what is being my money and you must just … go."

"And go where?" Rakesh said through his tears that poured endlessly down his little face.

"Anywhere."

"Are you coming with us?"

"No. I don't know. I am having unfinished business here in Mumbai. But you should go."

Rakesh's mouth was twisted in pain and his reddened eyes and tear streaked cheeks suddenly struck Siddharth's heart and he had to turn away and bite his lip, remembering his own harsh past.

He pulled out the rupees from his pocket that he had stolen earlier and offered them to the boys.

"You can't do this. You can't leave us here. Please, Sid," Rakesh insisted, wiping the flood from his eyes.

"We don't want your money. We just want to go home, and we want to go back now."

Sid's head dropped to his chest and he knew he couldn't leave them or send them off by themselves. He knew he would have to take them home, or at least close enough so they could find the rest of their way.

"Okay, this can be working," Sid wobbled his head and smiled as he put the rupees back in his pocket and held out his hands to each of the brothers.

"I can be feeling it in my bones that we can make these things all possible. I don't have any education like you boys, and I am not as smarting as you either. I am not trained to do anything. But this... this I can do and this we will do today and so I am doing something good."

"You *are* good. You'll do good wherever you go and whoever you are with," Rakesh said quietly, politely and feeling much calmer.

Sid stood with his hands on his hips and smiled his usual wonderful wide and welcoming smile.

Rohit ran up to him and hugged him round his slim waist.

"Thank you, Sid," he said and smiled up at his new hero.

The three of them linked arms and march off in the direction of the slum by the World Trade Centre. A couple of hours had passed before they entered the compound of the slum, the boys remembering the last time they had found themselves in those bleak and tormented acres, where Sid had rescued them. They walked past a chai shop and the owner came out to greet them trying to persuade them to buy a cup. He was wearing a yellow shirt and dark blue pants with a dark blue silk scarf tied at his throat; he was clinking the metal cups together. They walked on as a little boy clung onto Sid's sleeve and people greeted them from every side, calling out invitations to share chai, food, or a smoke.

They walked on a few more seconds when a friend of Sid's called out that there was a surprise in Sid's hut.

"Well?" he asked, after a while. They spoke in Hindi

"Well, what?"

"Well, who is it? Who's in my hut?"

"Oh!" he laughed. "Sorry, Siddharth, I thought you liked surprises."

"Well it's not a surprise now, is it? As you have just told me someone is in my hut."

"No, no!" he insisted. "You don't know her name yet, so still you get the surprise. And that is a good thing. If I don't tell you there is somebody, then you go to your hut, and you get the shocks. And that is a bad thing. A shocks is like a surprise when you are not ready."

"Thank you!" Sid replied, his sarcasm evaporating as it was uttered.

They arrived at his hut to find Bhupinder sitting in the shade of the crooked doorway on a stool and fanning herself with an old Vogue magazine.

"My goodness it's Bhupi," Rakesh informed Sid, grinning happily.

"Yes, so it is being," he said to the boys and smiled at Bhupinder.

She rose, clasped her hands and bowed.

"This is a good surprise. It's good to see you."

"And good to see you, dear Siddharth," Bhupi replied and smiled at the two boys that were now gazing lovingly up at her, despite the distressing heat. "But I must admit, you all look a little *worse for wear*, as the British would say."

"It's been an interesting journey," said Sid, stripping off his shirt and pouring a third of a bucket of clean water from his clay matka, and talking to her in Hindi.

"But why are you here? What had brought you all this way over here to see me," he continued as he washed his face, arms and chest.

"Shouldn't you be working?"

Neighbours smiled as they passed by, looking at him, Bhupinder and the boys. There is no art to washing in the slum.

You didn't waste water or use an excess of it.

He gave the matka to the two boys and they did the same.

"Would you like me to make chai?" he asked Bhupi as he slipped on a clean white shirt, standing in the doorway of his hut; he gave the boys two of his smallest T-shirts, both of which swamped them.

"No, I came to tell you what I have heard," she said, fanning herself again.

They all sat down on in his rickety hut. He had a table made from an old bedroom dresser, a patchwork plastic roof and a bench made from planks resting precariously on two piles of bricks. All the materials had been looted from the building site behind the slum.

Sid appraised the table with a suspicious squint, then slapped at it with a filthy rag, tucking the cloth inside his clean shirt.

He grinned at Bhupi, shaking his head of dark curls and raising the palms of his hands.

"Okay, then be telling me what it is that you have been hearing," his broad smile filled his face.

"We are being very fatigued, it is true," he said, managing a shrug of amazing self-pity.

"You must be understanding how difficult it has been to get us all back here, as I am a simple man. The simpler the man, the more effort it is requiring."

"I have all the latest news for you about the fire and the car that you rescued the boys from."

The two boys suddenly drew closer to her, and staring wide eyed, waited for her to tell them all, the news.

"You do know the difference between news and gossip, don't you? News tells you *what* people did. Gossip tells you how much they *enjoyed* it," Sid said, wagging his finger.

"Right, where to start? Oh yes, I heard on the radio that there had been a car found on fire underneath a flyover and initially it was thought to have been an accident, but as there were no bodies or people hurt and no obvious sign it had careered off the road, that it probably wasn't the case."

Bhupinder stopped and smiled at the boys before continuing.

"Well? Go on then," Sid coaxed her.

"It seems that the car was totally burnt out and so they couldn't hardly identify the make let alone the registration details."

"The car was our mother's," Rakesh said after a brief silence. He looked over at his brother who had started to cry again.

Even Bhupinder's soothing arms couldn't console him as he sobbed uncontrollably into her chest.

The boys didn't see the look of shock on Bhupinder's face. She stared, wide eyed at Siddharth, who just waggled his head and sighed.

"I will help you get back home to your mother and family," Bhupinder spoke quietly to the two little boys who were now cradled in her arms. She looked up again into Sid's face for his approval and he waggled his head once more, in agreement.

"Thank you, Bhupi," Rohit said as the tears still ran down his face and dripped off his chin onto Bhupinder's lap.

The simple truth about India and all the different peoples of India is that their hearts always guide them more wisely than their heads. There is nowhere else in the world where that is quite so true.

Sid was running on his instinct as always and therefore always pushed his luck. The boys had already given their hearts to him and now would have to trust his luck as well.

chapter 17

It was already ten o'clock the following morning when, having started work on the canvas straight after breakfast, Neelu knocked on my door and entered my studio room. We exchanged greetings, but rather brusquely.

Finally, she said, "Peter, as you know, Dr Singh is a passionate client. That is to say, he is extremely interested to see how the painting is coming on, if he ever gets any free time."

I smiled at her and said, "I'm sorry he hasn't the time. It must be very sad to love something so much and never have sufficient time to be part of it let alone see it."

"Well, the doctor is a very busy man. I'm sure you understand, but, when you get the painting finished, he'd really love the chance to come and see it, just as soon as he is able."

"The doctor will be most welcome, if he ever finds some free time, as you said," I announced with a hint of sarcasm that was, of course, instantly picked up by Neelu.

"What I really mean is," she continued, "that perhaps an *official invitation* could come from you some time nearer the completion of the painting. When I say that, I mean when it includes Mahima and the boys, it would be looked on most favourably by Dr Singh."

"Of course, Dr Singh is most welcome to see the painting then, or at any time that he is *available*. He has only to say, and I will receive him in my modest little studio up here and he can join me with his passion for art for as much time as his busy life will permit him to stay. You too, are most welcome, Neelu. Would you like to have a closer look at my work now?"

Neelu was getting more annoyed as she knew I was being antagonistic on purpose.

"I don't know anything about art; never had the desire or inclination to learn about it. I'd like to come with Dr Singh though, when it's complete, that is."

"Then I would be greatly honoured, but it might take some time to paint the family in and do them justice as I have only a few photographs from which to work," I said, turning to look her in the eye.

"I don't suppose you or the good doctor have heard when his wife and family will be returning?"

"I have no idea how long they will be staying away, but I am sure Dr Singh will let you know as soon as he has any such information, but that should not prevent you from starting to include them in the picture, should it?" she said, sounding a little nervous.

She came closer to have a look over my shoulder at the canvas.

"I notice that you have already allowed spaces for them to be added. Does this suggest that you will be starting on painting them in, as of today?"

"That, I will have to consider," I said, replacing my brush in the jar of murky coloured white spirit, and folding my arms, leaning back in the chair.

Neelu's half-closed eyes and thin-lipped expression told me everything as she turned and swishing her sari, and left the room hurriedly.

The door slammed shut, leaving me alone with my anger and frustration once more.

Neelu had reached the hallway and was on the way to call Dr Singh on his mobile about the conversation she had just had with Peter Ianson when the home phone rang. Picking it up, she was surprised to hear an unfamiliar male voice on the line: "Good day, Madame."

"I have a message for Dr Singh. Is he there?" the voice demanded, sounding rather aggressive.

"I am his personal secretary," Neelu said, a little suspiciously." Who is this on the line, please?"

"It is Mumbai Central Police calling and I want to speak with Dr Singh as a matter of urgency," the voice shouted down the phone.

"Yes, sir. Dr Singh is down-town in his surgery, but I can reach him if needs be and give him a message," she said, suddenly feeling very uncomfortable.

"No, I want to speak with him personally, so I will need the number for his surgery."

Neelu's heart was beating so hard she was afraid that the policeman on the other end of the phone could hear it too. She gave him the number and he rang off.

Immediately she called the doctor's mobile number, hoping to get through to him before the police did.

Luckily, he had his mobile phone on and answered straight away.

"Satwinder, Neelu here. You are about to get a phone call from the police. I don't know what it's about as they wouldn't tell me, but it sounded rather urgent."

"Yes, okay, thank you, Neelu. I am very glad you called. They haven't tried to phone me yet," he didn't sound at all concerned about the call. "Did the policeman leave his name?"

"No, he didn't, and I forgot to ask. Aren't you worried?"

"Never mind, I will wait for his call, and no I am not at all worried. I have done nothing wrong and have a perfect alibi as you know. Where is Peter Ianson?" he enquired.

"I have just left him in the studio. He is not at all happy about painting in Mahima and the children without them being here."

"Don't worry about him, Neelu darling, I might have to put a little pressure on him to help him complete the damn picture a little sooner than I had anticipated."

Dr Singh quickly severed the connection, without saying goodbye to Neelu who was left holding her phone to her ear.

As Neelu put her phone away, she wondered what the police had discovered so soon that they wanted to discuss it with the doctor, and her heart continued to beat even faster as she bit her lower lip. At that moment Vijay came in from the garden and glowered at her. He hadn't heard all the conversation, but he had heard some and had also recognised the look of fear in her eyes and so wondered who she had been talking to.

Neelu didn't want to engage in any sort of conversation and anyway she needed to get down to the surgery. She marched straight past Vijay, telling him where she was going and that she and Dr Singh would be back after lunch but before dinner.

A few minutes later, in Dr Singh's surgery, the line began to ring.

He picked it up and a young Indian male voice spoke to him.

"Hello, is that Dr Singh? This is the Mumbai Central Police. Hold the line."

Dr Singh was uncertain if he should reveal who he was and felt himself hesitate.

"Yes, this is he."

"One moment." There was a click on the line.

After a long wait, another man came on, his tone gruff and concerned. "Doctor, I am glad I finally reached you. You and I have much to discuss."

Bhupinder stayed with Sid and the boys that night. She usually worked but had decided to stay and help Sid prepare some sort of meal. The following morning, she called a taxi driver friend of hers, a young man who often took her to meet some of her clients.

When Mumbai worked and was throbbing, she would often busy herself with chores, needs and small pleasures. But at night, when the sleeping slum dreamed, Bhupi was busy in the black caves of the steamy world of sex. Her friend would pick her up most nights, while the city slept. Bhupi worked and forced herself not to think of the wall of danger that surrounded her, but just the money she would earn in order to survive. At midnight, every night the police would be out in force, looking for young women like her. Half an hour before twelve, police jeeps would gather in the main streets of the central city, to begin the hunt for the prostitutes and their clients as well as the beggars and junkies. Most would try and hide or were already in seedy hotels. The rest were chased from the footpaths and pavements. Steel shutter would come down over shop windows and white calico cloths thrown over tables in all the markets and bazaars. Quiet and emptiness would descend. In the whirl and crush of people during Mumbai's daylight hours, it was difficult to imaging those deserted silences when it became soundless, beautiful and threatening.

At night, Mumbai became a haunted and desperate house and Bhupi knew it well.

For those few hours after midnight, police would patrol the streets looking for the likes of her as well as criminals, suspects and homeless unemployed men. More than half the people of Mumbai are homeless and many of them live, eat and sleep on the streets. You have to earn *some* money to even afford live in the slums. Bhupi was for ever tripping over stretched out sleepers with only a thin blanket and a cotton sheet to keep out the damp of night, or coming across families who had escaped from some drought, flood or famine, to sleep on the stone paths and in doorways, huddled together in bundled survival necessity.

It is technically illegal to sleep on the streets in Mumbai and the police enforce the law, but they are also pragmatic about it as they are about enforcing the laws against prostitution on the *Street of The Thousand Whores.*

Some women of the night, like Bhupinder, if they are clever and are clean and respectful, can usually talk their way out of an arrest, usually with the promise of free sex in the future, or more commonly, if they can pay baksheesh.

Her friend had a fare in his cab when she called but said he would be with her within thirty minutes. This, as they all knew, meant at least an hour, if not longer if the traffic was bad and it always was. Bhupi often paid for her cab rides in kind and this ride was going to be no different.

Sid knew this and yet there was little he could do. The boys had no idea either way.

When her friend finally arrived, it was already hot and dry. The slum was humming and the smell from the open latrines overpowering. He phoned her from outside the slum, as no car would ever survive once inside. It would be brought to a halt and stripped of every useful part whilst the driver was still trying open his door to escape. Bhupi got the boys ready as Sid wrapped some boiled rice and lentils in a cloth to take with them. They hurried through the throng of people in the narrow lanes to the main road. A black and yellow cab was waiting. The driver waved when he recognised Bhupi and they all hurried over to climb in. Bhupi sat in the back with the boys and Sid sat up front to ride shotgun.

Sid hadn't underestimated the difficult and potentially dangerous task that had been set. He knew things could go wrong and so he had tucked a knife in a leather scabbard into the waistband of his trousers under his shirt. It had a long, heavy, sharp blade. He knew that with a good knife he could handle the man he had seen setting fire to the car the night he freed the boys. Sid sat in the front of the cab, silent and still. He was preparing himself for a fight.

A little movie, a preview of what might come, played itself in his mind. He would have to keep the boys and Bhupi safe and maybe attack the people at the villa. His right hand might have to force a path through any resistance. He wasn't afraid. He knew that if there was to be a fight, he would slash and punch and stab without thinking.

Bhupinder's friend was a well-heeled cabbie. The cab bluffed its way through the tangle of traffic, and they picked up speed on the wider streets near a steep overpass, the one on the other side of the slum, under which Sid had rescued the boys.

He recognised it, the others didn't. Sid opened the window to get a better look and a blessing of fresh wind that cooled them. His thick wavy hair that had been lank and wet with sweat was dry in seconds. Bhupi, sitting in the back fidgeted and complained about the rush of air spoiling her hair. Her friend, the driver sniffed loudly and adjusted his mirror to get a view of the back seat more clearly.

"Bollywood music anyone?" he shouted, smiling.

"Very best film in India right now," he said, tapping his fingers on the wheel and straining to see the boys' faces. "You like to hear?"

He punched a CD into his dashboard player and threw the volume to maximum. Seconds later, a jolly Indian song thumped out of the speakers behind the back seat with numbing plangency. Bhupi whooped with joy and the boys laughed as she sang along to the music. They all sang the chorus together and drove past a thousand years of street, from barefoot peasant boys on bullock carts to businessmen buying laptops.

Within sight of the villa, the driver pulled over beside an open chai shop. He pointed to it, with a jerk of his thumb and told Bhupi that he would have to drop them there but would wait if she wanted him to. Sid knew enough about cab drivers in Mumbai, to know that an offer to wait was a decent gesture of concern for her, and not just hunger for tips or something else. He liked her. She'd seen it before, that quirky and lustful infatuation. Bhupinder was young and attractive, sure, but most of men's reaction was inspired by the way she used to deal with them. Bhupi paid the fare and promised a big tip next time she saw him and told him not to wait. Both she and Sid knew that he would, just in case!

The villa was walled, but the gates were open, and they could see a large low building, double fronted with a long drive to the main entrance.

They all got out of the cab and started the walk towards the gates. Rakesh and Rohit suddenly became quite reticent and scared. Rohit slipped his hand into Bhupinder's as they slowly continued up the dusty road towards the villa. The boys were home and yet they somehow, didn't want to be. Sid felt for his knife under his shirt and turned to look at Bhupi. He saw her hand gripping Rohit's and instinctively he put his arm around Rakesh's tiny shoulders and looked down at the boy's slumped head.

"It will be very much alright; I am promising you," he quietly said to Rakesh and ruffled his hair with his free hand, having first made sure his knife was securely in place.

Chapter 18

I had been struggling with a sketch of the two boys all afternoon. Getting the height of them to sit easily on either side of Mahima was proving harder than I had anticipated. There wasn't one photograph of all three together and so I had been trying to draw the two of them from one photo alongside that of another of their mother.

The studio was hot, even with the window open the benefits of the sea breeze and the fan ceaselessly revolving like a manic carrousel on drugs. I was ready to call it a day as I had a headache starting to gnaw at my temples from looking at too many images of a mother and her children. I knew no one was in the house as I had heard Neelu leave hours before and Vijay was nowhere to be seen either.

My poor attempts on paper, my inadequate sketches of the boys, full of over drawing and rubbing out had annoyed me. I hadn't managed to capture the grace and beauty of Mahima's personality either. When the doctor had spoken about her I didn't detect any love for her, nor had he mentioned any of the obvious beauty that I was seeing in the photographs. His words kept echoing in my head and remained in my memory and yet my dreams had portrayed a different woman.

Now though my thoughts had become somewhat darker, there was somethings I was trying to forget as if they hadn't happened. I had to find out where she and the boys were. Maybe I had to go to wherever they had travelled to! Had they gone to see a family friend or on a short holiday somewhere?

My head was beginning to ache more, and I needed to find some pain killers and go look at the deep blues and turquoises of the sea.

When I left the studio room to skip down the stairs, through the landing window I saw a black and yellow cab out on the dirt road beyond the villa gates and walking up the long drive, a couple with two young boys. The cab had stopped by the chai shop and the driver was leaning against the door.

The boys looked familiar, but I didn't recognise the man and woman. I hadn't heard the cab arrive but then it was quite far away, but seeing the group walking up the drive had given me a start. My natural instinct was to ignore them as it wasn't really my concern, but before I had chance to continue down the stairs, I suddenly recognised the two boys.

They saw me standing at the window and the whole group stopped. That gave me a chance to have a really good look at them, and my heart rate quickened to way above normal. It suddenly became obvious to me that they were Rakesh and Rohit, but who were they with. The woman was young and attractive and there was something about her companion that seemed familiar. He was tall and thin faced with largish ears, a pencil thin moustache and thick black wavy hair. His complexion was dark, and his eyebrows were arched over a pair of deep brown eyes. I sort of recognised him as they drew closer but couldn't remember where I had seen him. None of them were smiling, but the young man waved a greeting as they moved forwards again.

I ran down the rest of the stairs and threw open the front door just as the entourage arrived at the foot of the stone steps leading up to the covered entrance.

"Who are you? What are your names?" I asked the boys. I think my voice must have been trembling. They had startled me, arriving so suddenly and seemingly, from nowhere.

They didn't tell me their names. They looked frightened and so recoiled at my questions, hiding behind the young woman's sari that billowed in the sea breeze. The young man stood on the first step to address me. He simply said that the boys originated from this villa and that they had something to tell me. Then he said, and his words jolted my memory.

"It is being a lot better for me if you are not knowing who we are, but these boys are Mr Doctor's himself."

My jaw dropped and I couldn't say a word.

"Are you trusting me in what I am saying?" he said after a pause, realising that I hadn't responded.

"They are both being very well and healthy and there has been no harming coming to them."

I was suddenly very alarmed, as I recognised the young man as the one who had saved me from the angry crowd in the back streets of Mumbai city.

"You!" I said and smiled. "You're the young man who saved me in Mumbai and now you've saved them?" I said in total disbelief.

I was overwhelmed by the need to know how this had happened and what on earth was going on; I wanted him to tell me everything.

He suddenly smiled, having recognised me too. The others looked totally bemused and the boys still hid away from me, behind the woman.

"Yes, sir, I am Sid the person that very much saved you from being much harassed in the alley. I am glad that you are remembering me now. And what is it that you are doing here?" Sid asked me.

"I am painting a commission for Dr Singh, of his wife and his two sons here, but never mind that, Sid, tell me what's going on," I replied impatiently.

I didn't really want to get into the reasons for my presence as much as I wanted to learn more about what had happened to the boys and indeed Mahima, if they had further information.

I knew he would not have harmed the boys and looking at the young woman I thought, neither would she have done so. I nodded at his recognition, still not sure I could trust myself to speak without a quaver in my voice and again the boys looked scared when I couldn't speak. It made me feel something I never expected to feel, a sense of total pleasure and relief, but there was also a sense of threat.

I invited them to come inside but Sid refused saying that it would be better to talk outside, perhaps in the garden.

I followed them into garden by the side of the garages and the garden shed, where they turned down a pathway leading to the sundial and the pergola.

We sat round a wooden table under the shade of the pergola and its climbing roses. It was cramped but as it was quiet, we could talk openly, without whispering.

Before I could ask them any questions, the boys asked for some water. I nodded and ran to ask the cook and in a very short time she came scurrying out to the table with a large jug of water and some tin cups.

A scream of delight followed when she saw the boys and having hugged and kissed both, apologised and ran off back in doors.

She didn't seem at all concerned about seeing two strangers, although she did pass a quizzical eye over Bhupi.

"Maybe we are not supposed to being here," Siddharth said, without any preliminaries. "I'd probably been in a lot of troubles if I was found here, so please take the boys and forget that we have ever been around, as soon as we are leaving."

I promised that I would. I looked at him, willing him to get on with it, and say whatever dreadful things were as yet unsaid. I knew we would not be sitting there if he was going to tell me anything good.

Then he told me how he had saved the boys from the boot of the burning car and seen a big man run away just before. He told me that the boys knew him as Vijay, the valet, driver and gardener to their father, here at the villa.

I was suddenly quite shocked at hearing what Vijay was being accused of and that all too familiar shiver ran back up my spine as, the memory of seeing him in the garden a few nights ago, flashed into my mind and made me feel quite ill. I took another gulp of water as I told him that everyone kept insisting that Mahima and her boys were away, and wouldn't divulge their whereabouts, for some unknown reason. I explained that I had been informed that they had left with their mother, but if the boys had been taken by Vijay, then where *was* Mahima?

"You have been given many of the lies."

"What do you mean?" I said.

He paused, then took a slow sip from his cup of water. He raised one eyebrow into an arch and looked at my cup. I knew he was telling me to have a drink before he spoke again. I drank a little water. It was cool and soothing but I barely tasted it.

"I mean that Mr Doctor's wife is somewhere she shouldn't be. She is gone away I am thinking maybe or maybe not. The bad news is the doctor is probably knowing where she is."

"Well of course he probably does," I said rather sharply, but there was a look in his eye that told me that perhaps something more sinister was scrolling through his mind.

I asked him what he really meant and where he thought she might be, but he just shook his head either not wanting to say or not really having any other ideas. The young woman continued to cradle the two boys, who had remained deathly silent throughout.

"What can we do?" I said.

I must have spoken very loudly because the cook suddenly appeared at the kitchen door, her head straining upwards to see what was going on.

She was staring at me. I tried to calm down.

"So, what can I do?" I repeated, quietly. "Why are you telling me? Surely you should be telling Dr Singh or the police if you suspect that Vijay tried to harm the boys?"

Sid leaned across the table and spoke with great intensity.

"Something terrible has been happening. Mr Doctor is very well known but to have his boys locked in the boot of a car and the car is belonging to the wife of the doctor and the car is burning on fire! These things are not all right.

"Someone needs to be blowing the whistle. You, sir, must be informing the police. You are a white man and although Mr Doctor is pretty well known and respected, so will you be," Sid said rather knowingly.

"You have to tell all police bosses. Get them to talk to Mr Doctor. Get them to be asking him the questions about Vijay and be dragging him out into the open space and be doing something about it," Sid was becoming more animated as he ranted.

"But what should I say?"

"Tell them what has been happening to the boys and all the details, except about me and Bhupi that is." He quickly lowered his voice and looked round at the young woman, who gave him a hard stare.

"I need to write all this down."

Sid gave me a moment to let me find a pencil and a scrap of paper I had with me, and then spelled it out for me.

"Be telling them Vijay was being seen running from the car after setting it alight."

"But that isn't enough proof that he kidnapped the boys, locked them in the boot and intended to burn them alive."

"How do you know he set it alight anyway? It could have been a terrible accident," I said rather unconvincingly.

Rakesh suddenly sat up straight and, moving away a little from Bhupinder, looked directly at me.

"I will tell them exactly what happened to my brother and me, that it was Vijay who put us in the boot of the car and only by luck did this kind and wonderful person save us from a probable terrible end," he said firmly, in perfect English and pointing across to Sid.

"It doesn't matter at this moment if policemen think it was or was not an accident. They must be knowing that Mr Vijay kidnapped the boys, putting them in the trunk part of Madam Singh's own car. Any other way and he will be getting off," Sid finished and wobbled his head, folding his young arms defiantly.

"The important point is that I should say I am acting on information received, that I am absolutely convinced that it is genuine, and the police urgently need to listen to the account of the boys here, and to place Vijay under arrest for kidnapping and suspected attempted murder," I said, quite pleased with my logic.

"But will they be doing it I wonder?" Sid was having doubts about the Mumbai Police Force.

"If I can get the police to come here and see the boys and listen to you and the boys as well, they will have to do something. Put it another way, Vijay is in a hell of a lot of trouble and if we don't do it then we have to get Dr Singh to do it, but with his wife missing too, who knows whether he would or not, or what the hell is going on," I said, feeling more doubtful than a moment earlier.

"Don't be involving me, mister sir. We will have to be going," said Sid, suddenly looking considerably more concerned about his potential involvement.

I stood up. "Don't go," I begged him, grasping at his arm. "There must be more details that you can tell me."

"Nothing any more sir," he said, staring wide-eyed at me. "For the sake of the boys, do whatever it is you can, and be doing it today. Tomorrow might be too late." And with that he stood up and, taking Bhupinder by the hand, they both left, scurrying back up the garden and away.

The boys and I watched them leave the garden and run back down towards the waiting taxi.

I was in such a state I could hardly string two words together, let alone talk to the boys and get them to give me as much information as they could.

I had been writing furiously during the whole time. I knew I needed to make an accurate record of everything that had just happened and had been said.

I couldn't believe that Sid had just left me with the boys, but I suspected that he might have been wanted by the police himself or perhaps they might have thought he was making the story up, and they would have blamed him and his young companion.

Dr Singh dropped the phone back into its cradle and put his head in his hands as he sat in his surgery. His pulse was thundering as he tried to work out what he was going to do next.

He called Neelu on her mobile phone. She answered straight away.

"I think they're dead!" he stammered into the phone. "Please, Neelu. I need you. They're all dead!"

He started to whine: "The police found Mahima's car. It was burnt out. I think the boys were in it but there were no bodies."

"How did they identify the car?" Neelu whispered loudly into her mobile, covering her mouth in case she might be overheard.

"They had identified it from the engine reference numbers, or something," Dr Singh whispered back in fear.

"Where are you?"

"Hang up the phone," Neelu said quietly. "I will be with you shortly and we can discuss all this then."

The doctor sat down heavily, suddenly terrified at what he had set in motion.

He didn't know if he was scared of the fact that the boys had been killed or whether, as there were no bodies, if they had escaped and were roaming the streets or had been taken away, or worse, were going to reappear at home.

Perhaps he had been played for a fool, by Vijay. Maybe he had the boys hidden away and would threaten the doctor, with exposing him later.

A sudden explosion of rage erupted behind the doctor's eyes. He had to talk to Vijay immediately to find out, as an overwhelming sense of foreboding, stabbed at his heart.

All three are dead.
My precious family lost for ever.
Or were they to reappear and destroy him after all?

Chapter 19

Vijay lay prone on the rattan mat spread along the bed in his small room, allowing his thoughts to gather heavily over him. The recent event on hearing the boys' voices in the garden had left him dizzy and weak. He had killed Mahima and dealt with her body, but he had no idea how the boys had escaped from the boot of the burning car, nor what would happen next.

Perhaps he still had a chance to get rid of them, or was it too late? Did the doctor know?

If not, he would soon find out when he returned.

I have failed the doctor.

Far worse, I have failed to gain my freedom.

Today was supposed to be his salvation. He had never wanted to harm anyone and had pleaded with Dr Singh, not to involve him from the start.

"It's impossible!" Vijay had cried out. "I cannot accept these demands!"

The doctor's words had terrified Vijay. He had prayed that he would change his mind, and even in those dark days, his trust in his gods never wavered. Yet here he was the soldier of evil. The battle was lost, and he had failed the tasks as well and now he would have to be sacrificed.

He lay there until the voices had fallen silent.

He had no idea where the boys had now gone to.

Had they left the villa or gone inside? He neither knew nor really wanted to know.

It seemed an age though before he then heard the unforgettable sound of the four-wheel drive and four litre engine of the doctor's car, thunder up the drive. Both doors slammed shut and the sound of two sets of feet on the gravel were heard getting closer to where he lay.

The door of Vijay's squalid quarters was thrown open and Dr Singh and Neelu stood in the threshold. Vijay scrabbled off the bed and fell to his knees before the doctor – the man who had promised him a new life - and he said, "I have failed. Do with me as I deserve."

"I told you that if you did as I commanded, and you were victorious, you would be rewarded with your freedom," the doctor told him. "But it seems you have indeed failed and spectacularly, putting all of us in a terrible position."

Vijay gazed at the bare floor and new that victory had eluded him. He had not been thorough and had panicked, leaving the boys alive in the boot before he ran. With his failure, all hope of freedom had vanished. Now much worse could befall him.

Overcoming enormous trepidation, Vijay crawled to his feet and clasped his hands.

"Doctor," he whispered, "all is lost."

Vijay truthfully told the man what he had done and how he had not performed the task of murdering the boys but had locked them in the boot of the car and lit the fire, before running off.

"Why am I not believing you, Vijay?" he said.

"There were no bodies in the boot of the car where you said you had put them. You didn't see them escape you say and yet you also say that you didn't hang around to see the car explode into flames. Unless someone let them out, how could they have escaped?"

He shouted into Vijay's ear: "What else do you know that you are not telling me?"

Vijay was sobbing and yet he suddenly realised that the doctor didn't know about the boys' return. He hadn't told him that he thought he had heard their voices and also that of Mr Ianson, talking with them and others.

"I think they are here, sir!" Vijay finally managed to say.

"They could be inside with Mr Ianson, unless they left again with the strangers."

Neelu turned to look at the villa from where she stood in the doorway, her jaw dropped, and her hands started to tremble. There was a look of horror on the doctor's face too, as he staggered and sat down suddenly and heavily on Vijay's meagre bed.

Although Neelu was obviously shaken. She had indeed been taken aback and was totally unprepared for Vijay's dramatic announcement, but she was already scheming and trying to figure out how best to deal with the situation.

"Satwinder, perhaps we could make the police think Peter Ianson isn't as innocent as he appears. Perhaps, we can find a way of implicating him?" she suggested to the crestfallen man.

Both she and the doctor didn't know what to do initially. They had been astounded and puzzled by the turn of events. Terrible burning images of the boys from that night in the city tumbled and turned in their minds. Their blood so thrilled with hope that they would be together and free, was suddenly spilled upon the rocks of their own abominable plan. Now their lives were thrown into the shadows of their terrible deed and they were no longer safe.

Dr Singh thought then of implicating Peter Ianson, and he promised Neelu that he would devise a plan. He struggled though, with developing a possible way out, as his mind was a red dense fog. Looking at Neelu he was surprised at her composure and her faint impersonal callousness.

Her unsmiling face intruded his thoughts so often, but now, at this moment, it seemed that she was inviting a challenge and even warning him not to turn away from their original plan and mess things up.

He wanted to take up the issue with her.

He meant to go there, and look for the real thoughts in her mind, but not yet and not now. Not until he had learned a little more as to how they could create Mr Ianson's potential involvement.

Neelu seemed to know so much more about events than perhaps she had been letting on.

The doctor's head remained extremely disturbed and to think beyond those initial reflections about his family, became fixed orbits around his own cold sphere and his solitude that he had created. His thoughts became more twisted around the unquenchable longing of what his hopeful freedom had cost him, as he thought about his family and his loss.

His day was now pierced by the spike of shame for what his freedom continued to cost him and the loved ones he might or might not ever see again.

Neelu was to have taken their place. She was to be the light in his darkness and yet now, he wondered as he gazed at her again, whether that was going to be true.

If his children were indeed still alive would he have to let them live and loose his future freedom or would he have to still see his original plan through in order to be with the new love of his life.

He had harboured several fantasies about his life with Neelu once he was rid of both his wife and the boys, but it was becoming apparently clear that he hadn't truly thought through the possibility that his plans might have been thwarted and the tasks he had given Vijay would end in failure. He was mystified as to why Vijay had not been able to accomplish what seemed such a viable and simple plan.

His primary focus now though, was to devise a new and alternative way out.

"Amazing, isn't it?" Neelu whispered.

Dr Singh glanced up. "I don't know. What the hell do you mean?"

Now there was a glint in Neelu's eye.

"Mr Ianson seems to be the only person that has seen the boys. We don't know who the other people are, that Vijay thinks he heard talking, or if they are connected in anyway or even if they know anything at all. They might have just found the boys and brought them back perhaps expecting a reward. Perhaps we can implicate Ianson with the boys' disappearance?"

Neelu could see the doctor's surprise.

"Peter Ianson and the boys' disappearance?" he muttered, looking again into her eyes.

"Yes. If we can blame him, then we could still pull this off. He was here alone and has no alibi. We could tell the police that he didn't want to, or was incapable of painting the family, as he wasn't that good an artist. He made such a fuss about not being able to paint them from the photographs, didn't he?"

Considering the latest events, Neelu knew the answer might have some interesting implications.

"He could have taken the boys, stolen the car and driven to the nearest slum and panicked, deciding to let the boys out before setting the car alight."

Dr Singh's eyes widened further.

Neelu explained that creating the story, admittedly would only be their conjecture, but what other explanation could there be, when questioned by the police.

A talented artist would not have had a problem and yet he hadn't been able to complete the portraits.

The highly logical suggestion, from a well-respected and highly competent medical doctor would not be questioned above that of a second-rate artist from England, who obviously just wanted to defraud them of money.

As the time passed, Neelu and Dr Singh worked on the solution to their dilemma and how they would explain their story to the police. Unfortunately, if the police suspected the story might not be true, they would need to ensure that Vijay would take all the blame anyway.

Whatever they decided to do, they obviously wanted, very badly to keep the real events secret, at all costs.

The doctor quickly explained that secrecy was of paramount importance, as Neelu furrowed her brow. Vijay, having such absolute ties to the truth, worried her much more than she had let on.

As the doctor finished his explanation, his expression seemed to tighten suddenly.

"Doctor? Are you okay?" Neelu asked him.

His eyes were riveted to a distant point.

"Peter Ianson," he choked, a fearful bewilderment sweeping across his face. "We must get to Ianson now."

They both rose and leaving Vijay, walked quickly across the garden and up the gravel path to the villa.

Chapter 20

The boys were exhausted and once inside the villa they cried a little, but it was obvious that they needed to rest and as nobody was around except the cook, I suggested they went to their rooms and got some sleep.

I was feeling extremely agitated though and even in the cool villa, I had broken into a cold sweat.

I had been granted a terrible insight into the probability of a deadly and horrible crime.

I needed to understand more and decided to take my concerns to the boys, despite having told them to go and get some sleep. I crept up the marble staircase and knocked on one of the bedroom doors, and Rakesh called to come in. I found them snuggled together on a single bed. They were already only half awake, but I had to talk to them. I told them that I wanted to help find out from them, everything that had happened and that I had an exciting idea which would get us back on the front foot to discuss with their father and maybe the police. Although Sid had told me probably everything, I wanted to get their side of the story before I worked up a plan of action. As we were just us three together, it was the best chance I would have to capture their attention.

We all sprawled across the bed. A couple of glasses of water sat on the low table. I offered them a drink, which they accepted but did not touch. I would have a glass of wine afterwards, I thought. I would need it. Rohit put his head on my lap, and I patted his shoulder to comfort him.

I hadn't given the boys any advanced warning of what I was going to say, obviously, but needed to get quickly to the point. I needed them to trust me and they knew hopefully, that if I had something to tell them, it would be worth listening to.

I made it clear that I was only here by invitation and they didn't have to tell me anything, but as they both smiled and nodded, it seemed my timing was just about right.

"Tell me generally what happened and then we can go into the detail once I understand what has been going on," I said, quietly trying not to sound like an interrogator.

They gave me an outline and I summarised what they had said, writing down each word quickly as best I could. I told them that we would put together their whole story, as their mother would want to know and then they eagerly provided information, so I knew my message was getting through.

When they had finished there was quite a long silence.

Rakesh picked up my pencil and looked at its point, then put it down again.

Rohit sat back and looked uneasy.

Then Rakesh said, "Mr Ianson, what will daddy say?"

"He might think we just made it up."

I stared at him. I couldn't believe that their father would doubt what they had just told me and that he wouldn't be anything but delighted at seeing them, healthy, unharmed and at home, and most certainly would never doubt what had happened.

His words threw me, although my own thoughts about the doctor had somewhat prepared me for such a possibility.

It was almost as if the last twenty minutes had counted for nothing at all.

I was about to say something in reply, that I might have regretted, when Rohit looked up and said kindly, "Mr Peter, mummy will be glad to see us though, won't she?"

For some reason, as Rohit spoke those few words, my eyes filled up with tears. I stood up and went to the door then wiped my eyes with the back of my hand while they couldn't see my face, before turning back round.

I felt so sorry for them.

I thought my task to paint them in front of the great Taj Mahal was going to be a wonderful opportunity and a great meaningful experience.

Why was it turning into such a nightmare?

I smiled gratefully at him. A tear ran down my cheek. Neither of them seemed to notice.

I left them on the bed then watched them wrap their arms around each other and fall asleep before quietly exiting the room with my notebook.

Downstairs, the late afternoon light glistened on the sea and bathed the lounge walls in a golden hue. I found a half bottle of white wine produced in Pune and poured myself a large glass and slumped into an armchair and watched the sun start to sink, along with my heart.

There, in that room, no sound apart from the gentle swish of the retreating tide beyond the garden walls, reached me through the quieting villa. The silence was sweeter, the peace more profound for the presence of the two sleeping boys in the room above. A balm of fantasy soothed me. There was a time, once, when I'd known such a life; when a woman was my own and we were both together asleep. Like they were.

The momentary fantasy of belonging, that little dream of love and warmth of another.

The truth was that I belonged nowhere and to no one.

The truth was that Rohit and Rakesh meant nothing to me and I meant nothing to them. I was always and everywhere alone. Worse than that I now felt hollow, empty, gouged out and scraped bare by coming out to

India in the first place, painting a picture that was seemingly never to be completed and now somehow embroiled in a foul and treacherous plot.

I picked up my notebook and opened it to find the pages I had just been writing on earlier. Scribing as much as I could, whilst listening intently to the boys, it was therefore filled with scribbled phrases and half complete sentences, in my appalling handwriting. I turned through the pages and read the words they had eagerly provided. It was fragments, culled from their story. There were lines and phrases and sometimes with a line added or changes as they remembered details or events. There were random streams of consciousness, passages that described what had happened to them on a certain day or a specific time. Sid and Bhupi were both mentioned frequently, yet they were never identified except for, he or she.

On one page, near the end, there was a single and disturbing reference to the name, Vijay.

It read:

Q. What was Vijay going to do?

A. Vijay was going to kill us.

My heart began to beat faster as I read those few words through several times. I didn't doubt that Vijay's intention was indeed to kill the boys, but somehow I knew that someone else had put him up to commit the gruesome murders.

Where was he at this present moment ?

Was he on the run and being hunted by the police?

Did they even know about the boys or the car being found?

Somebody else knew something about Vijay, and what he had tried to do. I wondered what it all meant and whether now, I too, was in danger as well as the boys.

And where was Mahima?

The boys loved her but was she too involved with their attempted murder? Had she escaped or run away or was she a possible victim too? Perhaps she was imprisoned somewhere in Mumbai.

I didn't know what frightened me more, the power that could crush me or my ability to avoid or endure it.

I raised the glass I held to take another sip, when suddenly and abruptly my silent peace was shattered.

I heard the front door slam shut and I turned round but before I had time to get out of the chair, Dr Singh and Neelu were standing together in the lounge doorway, staring at me.

Feeling a cool sea breeze suddenly come through the open patio doors of the lounge, I realised the two of them were now standing over me, with angry expressions.

"Stay where you are, Mr Ianson," the doctor said. "What do you know about the disappearance of my boys?" he continued, stopping me from rising up out of the chair.

"I don't understand."

"The boys are here. They came back this afternoon. They were brought back by two kind people, one of which had saved them from an unquestionable and horrific death, had he not reacted to quickly," I was beside myself with shock and surprise, as I looked up at both their wide-eyed angry faces.

I told them exactly what had happened, showing the notes I had taken, demanding that they go upstairs to see the boys, and see that I was telling the truth about their presence.

I couldn't understand why it wasn't the first thing that Dr Singh would have wanted to do anyway.

"I don't believe you, Mr Ianson. You'd better explain your involvement," he said coldly. "I don't think you have been honest with me."

"Are you suggesting…" I stammered, looking into his black eyes.

I was absolutely flabbergasted.

He was actually suggesting that I was responsible.

"I'm being framed," I said, trying to stay calm.

"I wouldn't dream of killing anyone. I had nothing to do with their disappearance either."

Dr Singh's tone didn't soften: "Mr Ianson, you were here alone with the boys and could have done this terrible thing. Why did you want to kill them and why are you still lying about it? You abused my trust. I'm astonished you wanted to steal my money and then kill my children. You came here asking to paint my family portrait so you could hide out in my home."

"I didn't kill anyone. This is madness. Why on earth do you..."

He stopped me from continuing.

"My boys were abducted and locked in the boot of my wife's car, and the police said it was set on fire and that you did it," Dr Singh looked further into my face with venom in his eyes, "and I believed you to be an honest, upright contributor to the arts."

"What? What are you talking about now?" I said, totally lost by the ridiculous ranting outburst of hateful nonsense.

Neelu did not move and the doctor stared at me for several seconds and scoffed derisively: "A desperate response and no doubt a ploy to distract me."

"I'm telling you the truth," I wailed. "It's time you went up and asked your own children to tell you their full story. I am sure you will believe what they have to say. Then you will hear the truth from their own mouths," I sounded desperate; despite the fact I had been falsely accused.

"I am sure you have already terrorised them into agreeing with your lies."

"If I had intended to... to remove your children, why would I come back, why would I bring *them* back?"

"Because you realised how dreadful your actions were, you realised you would never get away with it and your cowardly actions against innocent children, obviously got the better of you and your conscience."

He collapsed majestically into a chair opposite me with his head in his hands.

His acting didn't seem particularly convincing.

Neelu marched swiftly across the room to the doctor and put her hand on his shoulder.

"I'll handle this," Neelu pointed to the door.

"Let me take Ianson upstairs and we will get the boys."

After a moment of stunned silence, the doctor took his head out of his hands and then Neelu frog marched me out and up to where the boys were sleeping.

In the thick garden bushes outside the lounge, Vijay clutched a machete and gazed through the window. Only moments ago, he had circled the house and seen Dr Singh and Neelu enter through the front doors, then shortly after had heard the doctor talking very loudly to Peter Ianson.

Now, as he huddled in the shadows, Vijay peered through the glass, he was surprised at the way the doctor was remonstrating with him. Staying in the shadows, he inched closer to the glass, eager to hear more of what was being said. He decided he would give them five minutes. If they continued to harass the innocent Mr Ianson, Vijay would have to enter and persuade them with force.

Up in the bedroom, Neelu woke the boys who looked sleepy and bewildered.

"Boys," Neelu choked, eyeing me.

"Neelu?" Rohit replied dozily.

Neelu nodded, seeing the sleepy shock in their eyes.

"But why are you here? Where's daddy?"

"Daddy is downstairs waiting for you. He wants to ask you a few questions about what happened to you."

Neelu stepped back from them, shooting another glance at me.

I nodded at the boys who struggled to get off the bed, rubbing the sleep from their eyes.

"Didn't you tell daddy the story you wrote in your book?" Rakesh said, with a sudden look of fear on his little face, as he put his shoes on.

"So, you did make up a story and even wrote it down," Neelu hissed at me.

"I wrote down what the boys told me. All the things they had been through."

"We told him everything, even about Vijay and..." Rakesh said urgently.

"I suppose that's what *he* told you to say," Neelu interrupted, pointing back at me.

"No, it's all true. It all happened," he pleaded.

"Well, we shall see about that," Neelu grasped hold of each of the boys' arms and dragged them out of the room and down the stairs.

I followed rather sheepishly, still stunned by the bizarre turn of events, but now becoming more concerned about the accusation and what might be a rather nasty turn of events. Despite my innocence, I was not feeling at all comfortable or confident about my position.

Who would be believed?

The boys and I, or the doctor?

I still didn't know where Mahima was and now I was wondering where Vijay had disappeared to. I had assumed, he had been driving the doctor and Neelu, but he hadn't come inside the villa with them.

So where was he?

As we entered the lounge, the doctor was standing in front of the windows, with his hands on his hips. His silhouette against the crimson sky was quite foreboding.

The boys stood next to me and for several seconds, I stared at the doctor. My head was spinning a little and I felt that the floor was tilting beneath my feet.

"So, tell me boys, what has this man been putting into your little heads?" Dr Singh finally spoke, as he turned from looking out through the windows.

In my wildest dreams I could not fathom why he could say that.

"Now do you understand," he said, his eyes urgent, "why we ordered you to come down to speak with us, boys? This Peter Ianson person is the primary suspect," the doctor was pointing at me as he made the accusation of their abduction and attempted murder.

The only thing I understood at that moment was that he and Neelu looked so smug, as they accused me of being an abductor and attempted murderer, by name.

"What have you to say, boys?" He swayed on his heels and folded his arms as he looked from one boy to the other.

Rakesh, obviously frightened of his father and particularly under the circumstances, having to stand in front of him accused of lying, suddenly and bravely told him directly that it was not true.

"Why would Mr Ianson hurt us?" Rakesh demanded, his confusion not giving way to fear and tears.

"Yes," I suddenly piped up. "Why *would* I want to hurt the boys?"

"I have yet to uncover a real motive, but you have been alone with the boys. You have drafted some fictitious story of events. You couldn't paint them into the picture, but no doubt expect to be paid."

I opened my mouth in disbelief, but no words came.

"When we get the police here and they interrogate him, he will have to confess," Neelu said quietly to the boys, "so why don't you just tell us what really happened now and it will all go away."

"This is impossible," I stammered. "I have an alibi. I have been here all the time painting, or with you, Neelu. Ask the cook where I was today when the boys were brought back."

"Neelu already did. She reported that she saw you with the boys when they were brought back, yes, but that she had *not* seen you at any other time, before that. Unfortunately, the time frame of the abduction to their return, cannot be accounted for and you could have easily left here earlier, taking the boys," Dr Singh said slowly.

"This is insanity. You have no evidence!" I insisted, as a bead of sweat trickled down my temple, that didn't go unnoticed by Neelu.

Her eyes widened as if to say, *you're sweating because you are guilty as charged.*

"Mr Ianson, no evidence? Your story is written down in a notebook, I believe. You wrote it. Why would you do such a thing?" He paused. "I think there is enough evidence to take you into custody at the police station for questioning, straight away."

I suddenly sensed that things were getting out of hand and I would probably need a lawyer, except I didn't know of one and, as I was a white man in India, how fair would a trial be.

"I didn't do this."

Neelu sighed.

"This is not a British TV series about a backwards colonial continent, Mr Ianson. Here now in India you will be treated with respect and protected by the law. Unfortunately, in this case, there is also the media to consider. Dr Singh here, is a highly respected and well-loved figure in Mumbai and the abduction and attempted murder of his children, will be in the news very soon. Whether or not you are guilty, as you claim, you most certainly will be held by the Mumbai Central Police Department, until they can figure out what really happened.

I suddenly felt like a caged tiger, as I watched the doctor pick up the phone.

I knew that he was calling the police.

Chapter 21

That evening, hours after leaving the boys and Peter Ianson at the villa, Siddarth and Bhupinder lay back in the comfortable darkness, lit only by the soft yellow light of a kerosene lamp. He was tired but couldn't sleep. Outside the window of his hut in the slum, the alley that had writhed and toiled all day was silent, subdued by a night sultriness, moist with stars.

Astounding and disturbing images from the day tumbled and turned in his mind like leaves on a wave of wind, and his heart, beat hard with the hope that the boys were safe.

No one in the world that was Mumbai, knew where he and Bhupi were. No one in the doctor's household knew who he was.

With that thought, he smiled.

In that moment, in those shadows, he and Bhupi were almost safe.

Sid thought of the boys. He had promised Bhupi that he would return to see how they were doing, at some time in the future, when it was safer.

He thought of Bhupinder, again and again, surprised that her composed, smiling face intruded so often, surprised at how she had helped look after the boys and even more surprised how she had so willingly helped to take them back home. She lay next to him, her head resting on his shoulder having closed her eyes long before. He blew out the flickering flame of the lamp, then closed his eyes in the dark and breathed in the silence of the slum. He realised he had given his heart to the woman lying next to him, as well as to Mumbai and knowing none of it, he fell, before the smile faded from his lips, into a dreamless, gentle sleep.

The doctor placed the phone back in its cradle and informed me that the police were on their way. I understood the dreadful situation I was in but not the ease and speed at which I had been accused. My face was hard. My eyes were hard. And that hardness divided my feelings from theirs, as cleanly and inviolably as the space where I sat, separated from where they stood over me.

I thought about Mahima. I thought about the sadness that had glittered in her deep brown eyes when she talked to me in the restaurant.

Mahima was unhappy about something and desperately wanted her boys to be with her.

When we had lunch together with Neelu, I recalled the concern she showed and indeed a little fear of something. I saw it in those baleful eyes of hers.

She didn't tell me why she was unhappy, but I could see that she was. She hadn't mentioned what she was planning to do or where she was going to go. I didn't ask. I should have asked her, of course. It might have saved me all this trouble. In the long run it might have saved the boys from being kidnapped. But I hadn't been interested enough in Mahima, until now that is.

"One thing you still haven't told me, Dr Singh," I ventured, "is where exactly is your wife?"

"She's in Pune," the doctor said without hesitating, which I was very doubtful about as up until now he had never been at all clear or specific about her whereabouts.

"Where in Pune?"

"I don't know. One of the vineyards."

"There's a lot of vineyards in Pune, Doctor."

"I know, I know," he whined, flinching at my irritating tone.

"You said you knew where she was."

"I do. She's in Pune. I *know* she is in Pune. She wrote to me from a hotel there. I got her last letter only yesterday. She's somewhere in the northern hills."

"Why did she leave?"

"I don't know really," he said, looking more and more uncomfortable at my questioning.

"She must have said something to you. You're her husband."

Neelu laughed a little, but then stopped herself as the doctor gave her a frightening stare.

"She didn't say anything to me about leaving."

I became embolden as I suspected something wasn't right, especially when Neelu had laughed.

"If you want to know what I think, I am in the opinion that she left because of you. There must be more to her leaving. Was she afraid of something?"

Neelu laughed again and this time didn't care what the doctor thought.

"My wife wasn't afraid of anything."

The sudden use of the past tense made me stop talking. I turned, slowly, to stare at them both, searching in the faint light for some hint of a lie, some hidden meaning or allusion in the statement.

"What happened on the day before I was supposed to meet the family?" I asked him.

"She had left, and I thought she had taken the boys with her."

"Enough of this. You have no right to be questioning me. You are the one that will have to explain things when the police arrive."

"I know you are right, Doctor, but *you* will have to explain where your wife is and I for one will be delighted when she returns."

It wasn't long before I saw the faint blue light of a police car and its headlights bouncing up and down as it sped up the drive to the villa.

Neelu let them in. There were two burly police officers and a shabbily dressed inspector.

There was little in the way of formalities. The doctor shook his hand and spoke in Hindi to the inspector who in turn bowed his head before turning to me without any introduction.

"I will talk to the boys in a moment, but first you, sir, please describe the initial reasons for your involvement in being here at Dr Singh's villa?"

"Don't you know who I am and why I came?"

"You are Peter Ianson. Please describe your initial reasons for being here in India with Dr Singh? Please bear in mind it is in your best interests to cooperate fully with this enquiry."

"Okay, I see. Of course, I will cooperate. Why shouldn't I? It's in everyone's interests to get the fullest possible picture of what happened. I have been painting a picture. It is to be a portrait of the family, or at least it was, until the mother and her boys were suddenly no longer available."

"Your picture is only of the Taj Mahal I believe, but you haven't painted in the family. Why is that?"

"The *family* consists of the doctor's wife, Mahima, and her two boys, none of whom have been here to paint. The doctor's wife is away apparently and as I am sure you are aware, the boys were only found and returned today. I am deeply, deeply hurt by what has happened. I'm traumatised. I want that put on record."

I took time and explained everything that had happened from the day that I arrived until the moment the boys returned, and I wrote down their story.

I told the inspector that I would give him the notebook with the information the boys had provided. He hadn't interrupted until then and I had noticed that neither he nor the uniformed men had written down a single word that I had said. He held up his hand to indicate he wanted me to stop.

"You appear to be quoting from that notebook of yours. Why and when did you decide that you *needed* to write the whole story down?"

"If you'd let me show you the notebook," I said, rather exasperated.

"I will get to that, but if you would just answer the question, thank you very much. I will get to inspecting the notebook when I talk to the boys. You see I want to make sure that what they say is exactly the same as what you have written. Verbatim, Mr Ianson. Everyone can read a story but when asked to recall the events of the past few days without it, can get blindsided, sideswiped, no matter how good they are. That's when I can determine what is and perhaps isn't true. That's what I will be doing and if the news is bad, meaning they come up with a different story, then you might be in a lot of trouble," he clasped his hands behind his back and rocking on his heels, looked at the boys and then at Dr Singh, before returning his weaselly gaze back to me.

"Everything you are saying here will be on the record. Please can we proceed to discuss how you came to write down their story?" the inspector said, waving a hand to indicate I should continue.

"As they had been brutally abducted and nearly burnt alive but then had been miraculously saved, by a passer-by, and then helped to return safely home, I thought that both their father and mother would be grateful for a detailed document while it was fresh in the young boys' minds and useful in finding the perpetrator," I explained. "That's the full reason."

"Mr Ianson, isn't the story of the boys' disappearance a little farfetched, and may I dare say, an idea from way out on the lunatic fringe?" the inspector crowed, circling me now like a black kite would its prey.

"A lot of people, perhaps not knowing what actually went on, would describe your *story* as more of an hallucination or a dream perhaps. Or maybe it is just a complete series of lies that you concocted to hide the real truth that you, yes *you*, abducted the boys and then tried to murder them and when it failed and they escaped, you made up this rambling and ridiculous story."

"That is absurd nonsense," I replied, almost shouting the words.

At that moment, Rakesh broke free from Neelu's grasp and ran forward and stood in front of the inspector.

"He didn't do it, it wasn't him. He told the truth. It was Vijay that took us, then locked us in the boot of mummy's car," he was almost screaming, and his eyes were wide and red with anger.

I suddenly stepped forwards too and stood with Rakesh.

"I think the question you should be asking is, where *is* Vijay? And while we are on that subject of disappearances, perhaps you should also be asking where Mahima, Dr Singh's wife, is?"

The inspector moved his stare from the boy to me.

"Well, perhaps, Mr Ianson, but that was not the question that I was asking you. The question I..."

The inspector stopped suddenly as the lounge doors were smashed open and in the half light of the doorway, a large, silhouetted figure stood tall and defiant, machete in hand.

Inside the lounge, I could sense the host's initial bewilderment, then fear.

"Dr Singh," Vijay choked, eyeing first the doctor and then the inspector.

"Vijay? What are you doing?" The doctor managed to say. Neelu took several steps back and the two policemen a couple forwards.

The inspector saw the shock in the doctor's eyes.

"What on earth are you doing, man?" The doctor continued.

The doctor staggered backwards, shooting a glance at the inspector.

"Put down the machete, sir, if you know what's good for you," the inspector told Vijay in Hindi.

Vijay was silent for a moment and then shook his head.

"This makes no sense, Vijay," the doctor interjected. "This will only end in tears, Vijay, and besides, what is wrong with you? Tell me what the problem is, and I am sure we can resolve it quite easily."

"You have very limited options, sir," the inspector announced, moving a single slow step closer.

"I don't *need* options," Vijay spat the words out, looking venomously at the doctor.

"There is only one way out of this and that is for me to tell you the truth," he said, looking at the inspector and brandishing the machete.

The light glinted off the sharpened edge of his weapon and the boys screamed, moving behind Neelu.

"I presume you have something to offer, something to say about the proceedings here?" the inspector barked, standing his ground as he gained confidence as the two policemen were now standing beside him.

"The doctor's wife is dead. Murdered," Vijay finally said.

My jaw fell open.

"Murdered?" said the inspector who was quite taken aback.

He darted a suspicious look at me, but then having realised my drop jawed expression was perhaps genuine, turned his attention immediately back to Vijay.

"And how would you know that she has been – murdered? It seems inconceivable that you would know that. The doctor knows exactly where she is at this very moment. Isn't that right, Dr Singh?" he said, turning to the doctor for acknowledgement and agreement.

"I also abducted the boys."

"I doubt very much that information is true," the inspector said. "It is fairly clear that Peter Ianson here took the boys. It seems a fairly straightforward case. I am used to fighting crime and determining who are the guilty ones very quickly. I can identify the main culprit quite easily and then move in and take them quickly and suddenly."

Vijay looked at him, as we all did, totally unconvinced. He shook his head and smiled.

"I said that I would never talk. I was sworn to secrecy. Even in the face of death. It was to gain my freedom, but things have changed, have got out of hand."

I gasped, as did Neelu and the doctor.

The boys by this time were totally traumatised and crying behind Neelu's sari.

"Then you are saying that *you* killed the doctor's dear wife?"

"Exactly," Vijay said, "I will show you where I lay her body. I also took the boys and intended to kill them both too."

The doctor's body seemed to sway with the weight of Vijay's words. Then, as if too tired to stand another moment, he fell into a chair and held his head in his hands.

Neelu rushed over, her voice quiet but firm. "Doctor, you must be in a total state of shock, I am sure, but you must understand that this is a desperate situation. I am sure that perhaps Vijay is trying to cover up for Ianson's deeds."

The doctor was pale.

"But why are you, Vijay, standing here admitting these things. There is no reason, no proof and no accusation. Even the inspector is suspecting Ianson here," he paused, radiating a new fear.

"It must be something else that has caused this," he said, glancing up at the inspector.

I suddenly felt very afraid.

"You think I killed your wife?" I almost screamed at the doctor.

The doctor replied: "It would not surprise me at all that you did. You took the boys with the intention of burning them alive in my wife's own car and obviously could have killed my wife too. Did you kill her first and then take her car with the boys in it?" He said, almost hysterical now.

However, even the inspector was now having trouble buying the doctor's premise that I would blatantly murder his wife, as there was no real reason why I should and as Vijay had presented himself and confessed to being the murderer, it seemed even more implausible.

Having also been presented with the boys' version of events, stating that Vijay had taken them, it perhaps was becoming more obvious, even to him, that I was innocent.

"Isn't it possible that Mahima was murdered by Vijay on the instructions of someone else, in order to gain his freedom, as he just said. And who would he want to gain his freedom from, I ask you, Inspector? Hardly from me, I would suggest."

"Did someone promise you your freedom, Vijay, and if so, who was it?" I insisted, turning to him.

"In my experience," the inspector said, "men go to greater lengths to avoid what they fear than to obtain what they desire. I sense a desperation in the assault on the boys and the murder of the doctor's wife."

He had a twisted smile on his face as he spoke the words, suggesting he had been rather pleased with his statement, but as he turned to face the seated doctor, his smile disappeared.

Vijay, as dramatically as he had crashed into the lounge, turned and, running, then jumping clear of the patio, disappeared into the night, machete still firmly in his hand.

The two policemen gave chase, but it was obvious that Vijay knew every inch of the garden and surrounding area and would escape remarkably easily.

Within minutes, Vijay had rushed through the garden and over the wall. He threw the machete into the bushes and ran as fast as his legs would carry him to the road that led to the village and across to the few shops that were still open.

He entered one of the buildings, a hovel just past a bus stop on the outskirts of the village. It was a bar and with a round of drinks for the house, he quickly settled down in a far dark corner with the other dusty and determined drinkers who occupied a long bench. The men he had joined in the bar were field workers, farmers and the usual assortment of lawbreakers. They said little and all wore sullen expressions. The local hooch was probably laced with more methanol than ethanol and certainly enough to make a man go blind. Vijay consumed his drink at a gulp, pinching his nose as he hurled the obnoxious, chemurgical liquid down his throat. He was fiercely determined to keep the foul poison in his stomach, so much was his fear of being caught.

His situation was grim, and the strain showed on his face. He knew he had been defeated and only retribution awaited him, and it wouldn't be long in coming.

Vijay lingered long over his fifth glass of the volatile fluid. He was almost at the point of admitting defeat, but as he gasped and spluttered his way through to empty his glass, he threw it into the corner and moved into the centre of the shabby little room and began to sing, in a loud, off key voice and as everyone else was just as drunk, they all joined him and cheered and clapped their passionate and peremptory approval.

It was the Indian national anthem which was followed by religious devotionals. Some were Hindi love songs and others heart breaking gazals. Everyone began to smile, wagging their heads whilst cradling their cups and glasses. They all clapped and cheered and for a while at least, Vijay was lost in joy.

They were all singing as they left the bar and swayed down the dark stretch of road, leading into the centre of the village.

They were still singing when a police car, siren just about working and blue light flashing, turned in front of them to block their path on the shoulder of the road. Two men got out of the car, and one stayed behind the wheel. The tallest policeman grabbed at Vijay's shirt and barked a command at him in Marathi.

"What is this?" he slurred back at him, in Marathi.

The other man, the inspector, stepped in from the side and hit him with a short right hook that snapped his head back. Two more quick punches crunched into his mouth and nose. He stumbled back and felt one leg go out from under him. Falling, he tried to push them away with his arms wide, trying to hold them back.

The men held him down while they handcuffed him.

Drunk and damaged, he was only dimly aware of the dark shapes that loomed over him. The inspector leaned over him to look into his drunken eyes. His face was hard, impassive. He opened his jacket and shoved his police badge into Vijay's face. They dragged him up and bundled him into the car. Doors slammed and the car sped away, its siren blaring, scattering the other drunk men with dust and small stones.

Vijay sat wretchedly in the back seat. He wasn't badly hurt, but still found time to cry openly. He blamed himself, loudly and often, for what he had done. He said with perfect honesty that he would happily tell them everything. His pride in himself, as Dr Singh's trusted employee, was a tattered banner. And his passionate, unqualified love for his freedom, was about to suffer more than he could imagine.

At the police station he was allowed to wash and as he dried his jaw he leaned on the basin to look at his face. His nose was swollen, but not broken. A black eye was forming but his injuries were not that bad. Both lips were cut and thickened. It could have been worse, and he knew it. He had grown up in a tough neighbourhood as a boy and no police beating was as tough as those.

"You need to tell us all, you know," the inspector told him when he was marched back and into an interview room.

"There is no master who can help, no family, no friends and so it's down to you."

"No freedom?"

"None."

"And you won't get any support, not from any place."

"No?" Vijay answered, as he was forced to sit on the small wooden chair.

"This is a very serious trouble you are in."

"Never mind," Vijay replied. "I will tell you everything I know," he said, as the inspector closed the door to the room for the last time and sat down opposite.

"Abduction and murder are not funny in India, Vijay, I am telling you."

The frown that compressed his lips and consumed his features remained, as the inspector started his interrogation.

chapter 22

It was early when Siddarth awoke. Dawn was just breaking and as he got up he hit his head on a small spinning wheel hanging from the ceiling on which Bhupi had draped a collection of small, brass temple bells.

The most colourful articles in the hut, her clothes, hung from an open rack in one corner of the room as there was no wardrobe. There were loose fitting silk trousers, flowing scarves and long-sleeved cotton blouses. Under the rack of clothes was a row of shoes and next to them, Sid's one pair of rather old sandals. He knelt to pick one up. Her shoes looked so small next to his own.

He slipped a fresh, but crinkled cotton shirt over his head and went outside and poured cold water over his head. His hair was wet as was his shirt that now pressed against his young body, but he pushed his mop of black hair back into its familiar, messy disorder and tried, unsuccessfully, to flatten his shirt.

He felt refreshed and his spirits were raised.

Ducking back inside, he checked on Bhupi. She looked as if she was sleeping contentedly. A diffident smile flickered on her lips. He tucked the sheet over her and watched the rise and fall of her chest in its sleeping rhythm.

Standing in the doorway, he clutched his small shoulder bag. He needed to get some food.

Just as he was about to leave. Bhupi woke up and her sleepy face wore a look of hurt and accusation.

"Are you leaving me?" she asked.

"No," he laughed, "but you might be a lot better off if I did. With all your monies from your client men, you don't have to be staying with me in the slum. This place isn't being very nice for the likes of you."

"I am very happy here," she said, wagging her head from side to side.

He looked at her as the smell of the latrine entered his nose and the lack of water in the slum directed his gaze towards his bucket only half full of water.

"You will have to wash your hands and face in that," he said, pointing to the bucket.

"And the toilet is over there," he said quietly, bowing his head in shame.

"Let me dress and I will come with you."

He gave her a glass of goat's milk before they stepped out into the deserted alley, and pulled the door closed behind them. They fell in step, beside but a little apart from each other. Sid's high spirits had suddenly fallen into the dry dust beneath his feet.

They walked apart as the alleyways were occupied in many places by sleeping street dwellers. Sid told Bhupi to follow his steps precisely, knowing that many used the alley as a latrine after dark because they were afraid of the rats or snakes. On they went avoiding the potholes trying not to trip or stumble as the sun slowly began to rise and the light improved. Bhupi followed him closely, struggling dutifully to step exactly where he'd walked. The stench there, at the edge of the slum, was overpowering and sickening for a stranger. Bhupinder had grown accustomed to it and had even come to think of it with a kind of affection, as the slum dwellers did. The smell meant they were home, safe, protected by their collective wretchedness from the dangers that haunts poor people. The smear of air in the slum, so foul it seems to poison your lungs with every breath and stain the very sweat on your skin.

They could hear the traffic beginning to move and as they reached the road saw a police jeep. The occupants stared suspiciously at them but didn't stop them.

Most of the shops and businesses hadn't yet opened, but there were a few apartments and houses showing lights at their windows. The sun was beginning to rise higher and looked like a blood red orange in the pale blue sky, but obscured from time to time by dense, brooding drifts of cloud. They were harbingers of post monsoon rain. The clouds that gathered and thickened everyday would swell, within the following days, until every part of the sky would be covered by them and then it would rain, again, everywhere and forever.

They came by a little shop whose old owner was just opening up and putting out his wares - sacks of rice and lentils, some green vegetables and onions from the day before.

They weren't far from the slum and Sid turned to see the faint glimmers from a few kerosene lamps just lit, ready to cook the morning meals.

They bought a few groceries and some bottled water before heading back to Sid's hut.

As they entered the slum again, the silence was broken by a burst of ferocious barking from a large black dog. The howls from that one dog, soon stirred barking from several others. Despite the fact that it was only a single but vicious looking hound, Sid new others would come and so they set off and ran through the mass of huts, calculating the distance to Sid's hut and safety.

Just then, as they turned into another alley, several dogs came trotting at them. The danger was extreme as they were a hungry, feral pack. Their aggression and ferocity were legendary in all the slums across the city and attacks on human beings were common.

Sid and Bhupi were suddenly stranded in the alley. The dogs closed to within a few metres as the bravest of them inched a little closer.

Sid picked up a piece of timber that he saw lying next to him and told Bhupi to be prepared to run on his command. When he was sure she understood, he threw his bag of groceries they had just bought, into the midst of the pack.

They fell on it at once, snapping and snarling at one another in their frenzy to rip and tear at it.

"Now, Bhupi! Now!" he shouted, shoving her in front of him.

The dogs were so engrossed in the bag of groceries that they managed to run straight past them and kept running without looking back until they got home.

They slammed shut the door, the smiles shining on their frightened young faces was like moonlight gleaming on the minarets of the Taj Mahal's white marbled monument.

Later, while they drank hot and very sweet Suleiman chai in his hut, with no breakfast to eat, they hugged each other and Bhupi lit some incense to help with the smell from the latrines that were now being used quite frequently as another new day in the slum began.

Vijay's sudden escape and the pursuit that followed, had left me standing, frozen to the spot in the lounge. The two policemen had clumsily followed him through the broken doors, falling over furniture as they stumbled out, leaving me, the inspector, Dr Singh and Neelu with the boys.

It was obvious that I was still a major suspect and so was ordered to my room, escorted by the inspector. He was intent on interrogating the boys, no doubt with their father and Neelu present to add pressure and perhaps suggest that what they had already told me, was not the truth after all.

As I was man handled into the room, the door was slammed behind me and I heard the key turn and I was locked like a prisoner, securely in my new cell.

I sat on the single unmade bed. The numerous thoughts of what had just happened swirling around in my head. Vijay admitting that he had murdered Mahima was unbelievable.

How and why did he become a murderer?

I was searching my mind for a reason as it seemed inconceivable that he would want to kill her and then the boys at the same time, or at least shortly after.

There must have been a clear well-planned reason that turned him into a *decapiter.*

Others were behind all this I was convinced.

It must have been planned for months and no doubt the doctor and perhaps even Neelu, were somehow involved. They must have decided when and identified how long before, and then persuading Vijay to move in and take them all out at the right moment.

Decapitation.

Without a mother and her children, there would be only one member of the family left. And perhaps without the doctor too, if that were the plan, the perpetrators would be free to do whatever they wanted, unless of course the perpetrators were the doctor himself along with Vijay.

If the was the case what had Dr Singh done to persuade Vijay to commit such terrible deeds. What hold did he have over him apart from the the obvious, master versus servant?

There had to be more than that.

I wasn't convinced that Vijay would or even could do these things without someone else's hand guiding him.

The doctor came back into my mind again and again. He had tried to insist that I had abducted the children, with the intention of killing them. He had said it several times and the inspector had agreed with him.

Neelu seemed to agree as well.

How deeply involved with all this was she?

Were they all involved but if so, to what end and worse what was my role in all this, except to be the fall guy?

The inspector was convinced before he even started to question me, disbelieving the boys' story right from the very beginning.

My head suddenly felt heavy and and a dull ache was creeping over the top of it, again. I lay back scared and confused. I was still a suspect or accomplice at least and no doubt more devious plans were being hatched in the lounge below me as I lay imprisoned and with no way of escape.

Down in the lounge, the remaining group seemed very agitated. Vijay's dramatic entrance and exit had stunned everyone, especially Dr Singh and Neelu.

The boys were confused and scared. Their world had been turned upside down once again.

"Peter Ianson is locked securely in his room," the inspector said, bending over with his hands clasped behind his back as he scrutinised Rakesh and Rohit.

"He can't be hurting you anymore, so now you can tell me the truth about what it was he did to you."

The boys said nothing in reply and the inspector sighed and turned to Dr Singh for some sign or direction as to how to get the boys to speak out. Neelu had pushed the boys forward away from her and stood defiantly with her arms folded seemingly unmoved by the series of events.

"You tell this policeman what happened to you. What Mr Ianson did. How he abducted you and how you escaped from the car," Dr Singh shouted at his boys, his eyes red with rage and his hands outstretched towards them, his fingers curled as if he were about to grab both of them by their young and delicate necks.

The boys recoiled in terror at their father's sudden and violent outburst and even the inspector was surprised and grabbed his arms to supress the attack.

"Perhaps we should be letting the boys go to bed and I will talk to them tomorrow," the inspector spoke slowly, letting go of Dr Singh's arms but standing in front of the boys as a shield.

A sudden look of suspicion had furrowed his brow as he sent the boys out of the room.

They took little persuading and hurried out and ran quickly up the stairs to their rooms.

"Maybe it is you that I should be doing the talking to you first, Doctor?"

The doctor's face suddenly changed from one of anger to one of fear and disbelief as his legs gave way from under him and he slumped back down in his chair.

Locked in the room and still lying on my bed, I had had plenty of time to think about the situation that I was in.

I found myself staring at the painting that I was supposed to be creating.

The paint had dried since I last put brush to canvas. The monument itself shone brightly and I was pleased with the effect. I had already pencilled in the outline of Mahima, with the boys on either side of her.

What was I to do now that she wasn't here, now that she had been murdered and by her own servant, Vijay?

What was the point of the painting even?

A sudden upsurge of anger and frustration started to burn in me as I gazed at the unfinished work.

Perhaps I should destroy it, I thought.

I slowly got off the bed and inched over to the canvas, standing proud on its easel. I stared and stared at it, at the detail I had created and the incredible symbolism it had.

A man built it for his beloved wife when she died. Was this some sort of sick joke that Dr Singh had thought up?

My pallet knife lay alongside the easel, on the table with my brushes standing upright in a jar of dirty white spirit, with my tubes of paints scattered about on the table next to my now useless and unnecessary pallet board. Picking up the knife, I ran my thumb along its dull blade, but although it was blunt, I knew I could tear through the thin canvas stretched across its simple frame and it would be ruined, for ever.

I stroked it gently and slowly, assessing where on the canvas to start the destruction. The point of the knife made slight indentations in the dried paint as I dragged it carelessly across the pointless picture.

It only needed a few slashes, and it would be in shreds, for ever destroyed and impossible to put back together.

I let the knife trace the outline I had drawn of Mahima and her adored children, deciding whether I should just cut her out and leave the inevitable hole.

The absent, murdered *model* along with her whole reasons for life, for being, in this world!

What a huge waste and what a terrible situation I was in.

Suddenly I realised that I was *indeed* in a terrible situation.

I was about to be interrogated for a murder I didn't commit and an abduction I didn't commit and an attempted murder that I couldn't possible have conceived, let alone commit.

I needed to get away, not just from the villa and Mumbai, but from India. Get back home, back to England. Forget all this awful tragedy and more so escape a seemingly inevitable death sentence I would undoubtedly receive.

I had been set up.

I had been brought out here, not to paint a family portrait, but to be the fall guy for a family murder.

One thing I still didn't understand, was why me and what for? Perhaps I was in a lottery draw? Name in a hat. Idiot useless painter that would never be missed anyway.

So now was the time to escape. At least I would have a chance to find out more about what had been going on and a chance to exonerate myself.

There was no evidence that anyone had, that showed I had done any of these terrible things unless the police intended or already had planted some at the scene of the fire in the car. The boys could be easily pressurised to change their story and make a statement that would suggest that I took them.

Yes, now was the time to get out, to escape this madness of injustice and horror.

I suddenly realised that although the door was locked, perhaps there was another way out.

Turning from the canvas and putting down the pallet knife, I headed over to the shuttered window.

The single window overlooked the garden, and it wasn't too high to climb down to the veranda roof below. I opened the shutters trying to avoid the hinges from making too much unoiled noise. The window was on a catch but not locked and I eased it open enough for me to climb through.

I picked up my bag and notebook, making sure I had my passport and wallet. I shoved in a spare shirt and other bits of paper along with my return air ticket. Thrusting both arms into my jacket I headed out of the window and eased myself over the ledge, clinging on to the windowsill so that I had as little distance to drop as possible.

It was dark but warm and I heard the waves dashing up against the rocks over the garden wall as I dropped to the lower roof. I hit the tiles harder than I had intended and with difficulty just stopped myself from sliding and hurtling over the edge by grabbing hold of the rusty satellite dish on the side of the building.

I froze, gripping onto the dish with white knuckles, hoping that those in the lounge at the other side of the house hadn't heard my landing.

Listening over the sound of the waves, I could only hear the dull drone of traffic in the distance and an occasional howling dog.

Nothing moved below me, so I breathed again and shimmied to the roof overhang and dropped silently into the Mimosa bushes below. It was a long open road to the gates and beyond to the village where I could maybe pick up a tuk tuk or even a taxi.

I set off running, trying not to stumble over the rough ground in the dark. I looked back once or twice to see the lights in the lounge blazing away and figures moving back and forth as they plotted my downfall.

The inspector stood over the doctor as he remained slumped in his chair.

"The boys I will be talking to tomorrow," he said, "so let's talk about your wife."

"Your servant claimed that he murdered her and although he is on the run, I am sure we will be catching him very soon. Then we can be finding out what he has done."

"She went to somewhere in Pune," the doctor said, suddenly relaxing a little.

"Why did she leave?"

"I don't know."

"She must have said something to you. She was your wife."

"She didn't say anything."

"There must be more to it than that. Was she afraid of Vijay?"

"I doubt that," the doctor said, a little indignant.

"What was Vijay afraid of?" the inspector's question caught the doctor a little off guard.

"Vijay is not afraid of anything either."

"Everyone's afraid of something,"

"What are *you* afraid of, Dr Singh?" The inspector had that same cruel, twisted smile on his face as he spat out the words slowly.

The doctor turned his head slightly to stare up at the inspector, searching in the dim light for some hint of suspicion, some hidden meaning. These were the same damn questions that Ianson had asked him earlier and he didn't like them, then or now.

"What happened the day your wife left and where was Vijay that day as well?"

"I seem to think that Vijay was here at the villa, perhaps gardening or maybe he changed his plans at the last minute, I don't recall."

"But surely, Vijay would have driven you to your surgery, as per any other working day?" the inspector asked, apparently somewhat confused.

"That's true. Well, he would then have come back and got on with his other duties, like tending to jobs in the garden."

"That still doesn't explain why he ended up killing your wife though, unless perhaps there was a problem with your wife leaving, or maybe she was never leaving at all doctor, maybe he came back here with the sole intention of murdering her?" he continued holding the doctor's stare.

"So why did Vijay kill her, I ask myself? He mentioned freedom and promising to keep a secret. Freedom from whom or what? A secret from whom and why, I wonder?"

The inspector was waiting for some sort of answer when his two policemen arrived back, bedraggled, panting, empty handed, and looking wide eyed and nervous.

They spoke in Hindi to the inspector.

Vijay was in a bar in the village.

They had initially lost him as he ran out into the garden. Having realised that he may well have jumped the walls facing the buildings down the road, they had driven down to the village where, on hearing drunken singing and clapping, had espied him in a bar. Being the brave Mumbai policemen that they were but fearing being attacked by the large number of drunken men in the bar and a killer, had rushed back to inform the inspector.

Without a second thought, the inspector jumped up screaming at the policemen to follow him and all three hurried out of the villa and jumped into the car and with sirens blaring and their one blue light flashing, tore off into the night in the direction of the village lights.

chapter 23

Neelu had followed the inspector as he and the policemen charged through the hall and out of the front door, leaving the doctor catatonic in his armchair. Things were not going to plan, and she was determined that she wasn't going to get any of the blame for the disastrous failure.

For several seconds, Neelu stared into the night. She felt as if the floor were tilting under her feet. Her head was spinning as she couldn't fathom out how everything had gone so badly wrong.

She regained her composure and marched back to stand in front of Satwinder, her lover and mentor.

"Now what are we going to do?" Neelu said, her eyes urgent. "We cannot stay here. We have to leave the boys and let the police deal with Vijay and Ianson. They are the primary suspects."

The only thing the doctor realised was going on at that moment was that Vijay had actually admitted to the inspector, that he had killed his wife.

"Why should we do anything?" he said, suddenly looking into the cold hard face above him, his confusion giving way to understanding.

"Why would I want to have my beloved wife killed? Vijay did it, he admitted that and so it would be his word against mine if he says that I instructed him to do it."

"The inspector has to uncover a motive and so far he has not been successful."

Neelu opened her mouth but no words came out.

"I have an alibi. I was with a colleague and down in central Mumbai all the time. The inspector can ask him," the doctor said, almost talking to himself now and half smiling.

"This is insanity! We need to get away," Neelu said through gritted teeth, not believing what she was hearing.

Neelu's eyes widened as if to say how crazy all this was.

"We will have to convince the inspector that Vijay is the one that is insane. He will have more than enough evidence to prosecute Vijay and maybe to take Ianson into custody for questioning too."

The doctor suddenly sensed that he would need a lawyer.

A good one.

Neelu sighed. "This is not a Bollywood movie. Vijay will be under immense pressure to tell the whole truth and then there will be suspicion placed upon your head and possibly mine. Peter Ianson is neither guilty nor stupid and he certainly will be telling his side of the story when they question him."

Dr Singh felt like a caged animal suddenly: "Why are you telling me all this?"

"Because, my darling, we are not innocent and you promised me that our future was going to be perfect and that everything had been arranged and we would soon be together, forever."

Neelu looked away for a moment and then back into his eyes.

"And also, because if you don't fulfil your promise. You are in trouble. With me."

It took Dr Singh a moment to process her threatening words before he felt himself losing touch again. Whether or not Neelu had lost her mind, he wasn't sure, but he suddenly realised she had a point, and realised that perhaps she was right.

Perhaps they should just run for it, disappear. India was a big place and as he had plenty of money banked overseas, they could easily access the cash and live anywhere, unnoticed and happy.

Neelu realised that to threaten him wasn't necessarily the best idea as she needed him more now than ever before.

She bowed her head: "I'm sorry. This is all coming out wrong and I didn't mean to sound threatening..."

Neelu's voice caught, and the doctor heard a sudden melancholy there, a painful past, simmering beneath the surface.

Neelu and the doctor had had a special relationship, at one time. The doctor still saw her as the young and beautiful woman that was so totally desirable, true and honest. Neelu had other ideas about her relationship with him. She knew that aging wealthy men in India often took young mistresses, but she didn't want to be just another kept woman.

She wanted it all.

She looked away and managed a tear.

"Oh, silly Neelu," Dr Singh sighed, taking her hand in his. "You are right, we must leave. Start afresh now. Not wait. Let's pack tonight."

Later that night, they woke Vijay by throwing a bucket of cold water on him.

A thousand shrieking cuts woke with him.

He rubbed the water out of his eyes as they unlocked the handcuffs, lifted him by his stiff muscular arms and led him out of the room. They marched him across an empty courtyard, to a small interrogation room that smelt of sweat and urine.

The inspector sat on a high-backed chair, with elephants carved along its rim.

Two policemen stood behind him.

"This is not exactly how I had planned to spend tonight, but although you said you told me everything, perhaps you should tell me again," he said in Hindi, covering a yawn with his bruised knuckled hand. "Just why the hell can't you just tell me the truth?"

His words were precise and his look menacing.

"Don't want to tell me the truth, eh? What is it? Have my men not beaten you enough?"

Vijay stared at him in silence as he felt every one of the thousand cuts that stretched and cracked dried blood every time he moved.

"I told you the truth. I told you everything," he said finally as he breathed in the stinking air.

He sat still and longed to hear the morning song of the mynah birds, feel the warmth as the sun rose above the horizon and golden light stream through the misty air, scattering the dew of his master's garden as he listened to the sea.

He loved the morning air of the city with all his heart.

"Are you beating him?" the inspector asked one of the policemen, in Marathi.

"Absolutely, sir!" the policeman responded, clearly surprised. "You told us to beat him."

"I didn't tell you to kill him, you idiot! Look at him! He looks like he has been skinned."

"Very well. You will wear chains on your legs until you are willing to tell me the truth and you will receive no food until further notice. Now take him back."

Vijay held his silence, as they led him back to the cells to have the ankle chains fitted.

Compared to the pain from the cuts, his hangover was a mild annoyance.

Out of breath and sweating in the sultry night air, I reached the far side of a small collection of buildings where I saw a group of taxis and tuk tuks.

Although I hadn't many rupees in my wallet, I was hoping I had enough to get me to the city, if not the airport.

Reaching the first taxi I asked if he was available.

He was, but the wad of rupees I thrust into his hand was only sufficient to take me to the outskirts of Mumbai. Being fleeced didn't make me feel good but I knew I hadn't much choice. We set off and the driver did an impressive job of manoeuvring the vehicle along the moonlit track beyond the village.

The headlights weren't particularly useful as we crossed an open knoll and descended down a long slope, moving quickly away from the village and further into the night towards a silhouette of wooded land in the distance, eerily lit by the moon.

I cradled my belongings in my lap and turned to look at the intense frown on the driver's face as he leaned forward over the steering wheel.

His eyes were half closed, and he seemed to be struggling to see the road ahead.

We passed through the wood and as we did the distant lights of Mumbai city came into view.

We lurched on down the dusty overgrown road, the trees overhead occasionally blotting out the moonlight.

I can't see a thing, I thought, straining to distinguish any shapes or, more worryingly, any free roaming on coming cows.

I wondered how much the driver could see as well, even with his nose pressed so up close to the windscreen. It was pitch black. Hundreds of insects splattered, noisily against the windscreen, making it even harder to see out, as the driver rolled the car from side to side to keep it on the track. The road suddenly became solid and metallised so the driver at last could keep the wheel more or less straight now, and we picked up speed.

"You are doing very well," I said, struggling with the lie.

"Thank you, sir, but we will be reaching the end of this, your journey, as we get near to the motorway.

No more rupees means no more driving you, sir," he said, wobbling his head while still peering into the darkness.

"Where will you be able to drop me off then?" I enquired, a little concerned that he would leave me in the middle of some dark and potentially dangerous stretch of road.

"Just before the motorway, there is a slum village and maybe someone there can be helping you," he grinned and squinted at me at the same time.

At that moment we swung off the road. A muted yellow glow fanned out across the dust in front of us as he pulled up outside what I thought looked like a huge shanty town.

As I got out, the taxi lights gave just enough light to indicate the well-trodden path leading to a fence and some huts in front of me.

"Well, thank you, driver," I said between gritted teeth. "There are lights on. My life is in their hands I guess," I hissed, waving a hand at the huts ahead.

"This trail will be continuing through the fence here and into the slum and then arching north. Provided you are not eaten by the rabid dogs or attacked by the drunkards, you shall be emerging unscathed on the shoulder of the motorway."

With that he reversed the car into a dry riverbed, then set off back the way we had come.

I watched the red lights disappear in a cloud of thick, dark dust.

Unscathed.

My head begged to differ as I picked up my belonging.

Several days in India had given me a few simple, everyday phrases. It was a modest achievement I knew, but it might just be enough to help me now.

After a few minutes and slow progress in the dark, I stumbled across an old man squatting by a tree stump and urinating loudly. My greeting in Hindi surprised him and he replied with several phrases that I didn't understand. Realising that I was a white man, he called to a boy who came running. When he heard my few phrase, he seemed delighted and astonished. They had obviously known foreigners who spoke a little Hindi and so they appeared pleased to see me.

The boy could speak English and so asked me why I was in their slum and at night.

They had never seen a white man in amongst their meagre dwellings before.

"Excuse me, please, I am sorry to disturb and ask why you are being here?"

Before I could answer, a voice came out of the dark. It was a young man but even in the dark I could see he had a big smile and big ears.

"I heard you speaking some Hindi and then English to the boy," the young man said as he approached us. "It is obvious and sure that you have been in India for more than a day or two."

His voice and now, as he grew closer, his frame and appearance, even in the dark, suddenly became familiar to me.

He too recognised me.

I had never been so delighted to see anyone in all my life.

"Sid, is that you?" I squealed like a little child.

Before the night was out, I had been fed and given a little money from Siddarth and Bhupinder. We had drunk some local beer that he had acquired on the black market and I had told them the whole story of what had happened since they had brought the boys back home safely.

I spent the next few days with them both. Staying indoors and away from prying eyes and the police, while I tried to figure out what to do. It was a long few days of waiting, with the frustration of false attempts to get me away.

The delay was in trying to find out what the police were doing as well as raise some rupees, enough to get me to the airport.

Although I was restive and agitated with the wait, it seemed interminable. I used the time to learn and practice a few Hindi phrases that they taught me. I would have asked Sid to buy some books but as neither of us had enough ready cash, it never happened. He borrowed a bizarre, eclectic collection from Big Rahul, a friend in the slum. It was a mixture of obscure and fascinating English language books that were an inheritance from the days of the British Raj and then subsequently stolen and somehow ended up in Big Rahul's hut.

"I am thinking you very much are a scholar, Mr Peter," Sid would say on a regular basis when he saw me still reading.

One evening he came back and was standing by the doorway, gazing at me. Bhupi was out, working on her clients. I closed the book I was reading and stood to greet him. He took my hand and enclosed it within both of his own, muttering a whispered prayer of blessing.

He had placed a small parcel on the stool next to me.

"Reading is still something mysterious in this India that I was born in and still the cause of some fear and superstition," Sid said wearily, rubbing a dirty hand over his tired, dark brown face.

"Only for four men in ten can be reading anyways, and half the number again for women and I can't be reading at all, not even a word."

"Where did you learn to speak English so well then?" I asked.

"I was listening always to the tourists and to sell them things you have to be speaking," he laughed softly, brightening with the recollection.

"I am not knowing who my parents were. They had no interest in me. I must have been a bitter disappointment to them. They left me here with an old lady who brought me up until it was she died."

"I think you are much cleverer than you believe and far more deserving. Without your quick thinking, the boys would not have lived. Without your knowledge and skill on the streets, they would not have been returned to their home and family, and without your kindness, I would not be safe and well, and in your home," I could hardly say the last few words before I felt the prickly heat build-up behind my eyes.

Chapter 24

The beatings had stopped after Vijay had confessed all to the police. He admitted taking the boys with the intention of burning them alive in the boot of their mother's car and also of murdering Mahima.

He had willingly agreed to show them where he had buried her body as well, in the garden of her villa. His reasons for doing these things remained locked in his mind.

He had been struck a few times more, but they were habitual gestures, and had not been delivered with full force, but it was a terrible humiliation, albeit perhaps deserving.

The worst thing that people do to others always makes the others feel ashamed.

The worst things that people do always attack the part of us that wants to love the world and a tiny part of the shame we feel when we are violated, is shame at being human.

The hundreds of small cuts Vijay sustained on the night of the first beating, gave him agonising pain. Most of them were infected and some swollen. He was given water to wash them but that was worm-infested and the bites from the kadmal were increasing as he lay on his soiled mattress. There were hundreds of bites, and many of them, too, became infected, weeping sores. Body lice from the mattress swarmed over him at night. His daily slaughter of the filthy, wriggling, crawling pests didn't have much effect as they were drawn to the cuts on his back. He woke with them feeding on him and breeding in the warm, damp sores.

He accepted all this as he knew of his guilt.

He had lost count of the number of days he had been in the cell, but one morning, as he lay on his side, conserving energy and watching the lice, two men burst into his cell and he was dragged out by two powerful policemen, who seized him by his throat and grabbed both his hands behind his back.

"Time to go," one growled at him in Hindi.

The chains were released from his ankles, but handcuffs were clamped around his wrists. Rough hands tore his thin, dirty shirt. They hit him several times, pulling him from one to the other until he felt his collar bone wrench and tear away in the socket as he felt his strength oozing from him, with his blood.

Then the bamboo sticks rose and fell with aggression.

Vijay thought they were going to beat him senseless, maybe even kill him and save the effort of a trial.

At the end of it, they dragged him to the inspector's office. Inside he saw three men – the inspector and two plain clothed police officers – sitting at a metal table.

The three exchanged neutral glances at the sight of Vijay and his terrible state.

"Sit down," the inspector commanded. He remained standing, on weakening legs.

"Sit down, now."

He sat and stared at the wall of blank faces in front of him.

"We are going to the villa and you will show me where you have buried the body. So far we have not been able to locate it. Dr Singh is not there, and we are unable to contact him," the inspector said, seeming rather agitated.

He listened, his ears full of blood.

"I brought… I brought you a clean shirt..." he said, falteringly.

The shirt was to make him appear a little more presentable on the visit to the villa, but the inspector hadn't expected to see Vijay looking in such poor condition, and it had certainly surprised and upset him.

He told the two police officers to wash and dress him in the clean shirt and return him – safely – in fifteen minutes.

"Have you broken his shoulder?" the inspector enquired just as they tried to pick him off the chair.

The policeman turned to the inspector, hunched his shoulders and raised the palms of his hands in a question.

"He refused to cooperate," he mumbled as he hid his eyes from the inspector's gaze.

There was a little silence before the inspector waved his hand to dismiss them.

As Vijay was being marched into the courtyard, the few words the inspector had said kept ringing in his blood-filled ears.

Dr Singh wasn't there... unable to contact him.

A bucket of water was thrown over him and his hand cuffs removed. He was helped with the clean shirt as his collar bone hurt as much as the sores on his back.

It was nearly midday by the time the inspector and his forensic police team screeched to a dust halt outside the villa.

A team with spades followed and finally a dark blue prison van holding Vijay.

They assumed that the site was now a crime scene and so the teams followed the usual protocol, planting canes everywhere and draping tape round the whole of the villa and its gardens.

Immediately on arriving, the inspector instructed his men to surround the building. It seemed rather pointless as there were only four excluding the two men with spades.

Local grave diggers, he was informed.

As no one answered the door even after several fruitless minutes battering it angrily with his fists, the two largest policemen broke the lock to allow the inspector access, who marched in shouting for attention. There was nobody home.

The boys weren't in their rooms and it was assumed, Peter Ianson had obviously escaped from his, as the window was open, and the shutters swung gently backwards and forwards in the sea breeze.

It was hot in the villa as the inspector searched every room, before finally arriving at the doctor's bedroom, where there were obvious signs that the good doctor had packed and left in some hurry. Discarded clothes and personal items covered the bedroom. An empty but broken suitcase sat on the bed.

He realised that the doctor had done a runner and probably with his personal secretary, Neelu.

Vijay had already explained to the inspector that he thought they were lovers but hadn't elaborated further.

The inspector's men then took up positions around the garden to sweep the area in case any other intruder or accomplice was hiding there.

Peter Ianson had obviously escaped from the villa, but the inspector thought he might possibly be still be hiding somewhere close by, perhaps in an out-house or the garages. After fifteen minutes of searching the garages and various sheds, including Vijay's living quarters, they had found nothing.

"And?"

"We found no one, sir, but there are signs of disturbed soils and an open window and damaged tiles at the back. Someone looks to have escaped from upstairs," one of the burley policemen explained to the inspector in Hindi, as he pointed to the villa.

"Yes, I am aware that both the children and Mr Ianson are no longer inside. Ianson must have climbed out through the window and then damaged the tiles on the veranda roof as he jumped down. Where are the boys?"

The inspector signalled to the prison officers, who bundled Vijay out of the back of the prison van and dragged him over to where the inspector stood at the entrance to the garden.

"So where did you bury the body?" the inspector whispered into Vijay's ear.

It was hot and Vijay was sweating profusely.

Vijay pointed down the garden at the sundial by the rose beds.

The inspector lifted his gaze and followed Vijay's outstretched finger. He thought he was pointing to the sea beyond the walls and started walking towards the end end of the path, but then he realised, when Vijay stopped by the sundial and its stepped surrounds, that it was the place.

It was tilting a little and the soil around it looked disturbed.

Immediately he set the men with the spades, to work. It didn't take them long to dismantle the sundial and find the shallow grave beneath.

In the centre of the round plot, like a mummified butterfly pupae, the corpse of a person lay wrapped and bound.

The inspector felt a deep chill as he approached the soiled cloth and unwrapped the top by the head.

Before him was indeed the decaying face of Mahima, the doctor's wife.

The pallid corpse of Mahima was laid out on the grass. Vijay hung his head and tears of pain rolled easily down his unshaven, sweating face. As the inspector stood over the body and squinted in the harsh midday sunlight, he reminded himself to his amazement that perhaps Dr Singh, in some way was responsible for the woman's death after all.

"Vijay?" The inspector's dark eyes settled on him again.

"I killed her and initially buried her behind the garages before moving the body here. I thought it would be less likely found," Vijay offered quietly, his voice disappearing easily in the sea breeze.

The body had not been stripped of clothing and she had been carefully lain down on her back in the centre, under where the sundial had been. Her arms and legs were gently bound with white cotton cloth to keep them together, like those of a child tucked up in bed.

Just her neck and chest showed the signs of the wounds and the measures taken that had killed her.

"I don't believe that you killed this fine woman and mother without reason," the inspector said, turning his steely gaze back at Vijay once more.

"Did the good doctor have anything to do with this, I am wondering?" he suggested as Vijay suddenly raised his head.

"Why would he want his lady wife killed?"

Vijay turned his gaze to the sea as the inspector eyed him with a hooded expression and a determination to find the truth.

Dr Singh and Neelu were sitting on the veranda of an exclusive Yacht Club in the Seychelles. The cocktails, elegantly served on the simple but sturdy stainless-steel table before them, sat warming in the glorious island sunshine, the ice having long since melted, while Dr Singh mooned lovingly over Neelu as she gazed serenely across the waves.

They had been there a couple of days having taken the boys to the airport, initially promising them a holiday and then callously leaving them stranded there.

For several hours, the boys had waited and wondered, but then afraid as well as upset and with no financial means of getting home, had finally decided on finding and telling two soldiers who were on duty at the airport. They told the soldiers, that they didn't know where their father was and were afraid they had been left or lost. The two infantry men had taken them back to their barracks and reported the finding to the police.

As in many situations in India, the administration and total lack of communication meant that the information was yet to reach the office of the inspector.

It was early morning when Sid came running into his hut having found a discarded Mumbai daily newspaper and handed it to me. It wasn't the headline that had caught his eye. I knew he couldn't read Hindi let alone English, but he had recognised the photograph on the front page of yesterday's *Mumbai Times* was of Dr Singh's valet and confessed murderer, Vijay.

I speed read the article, catching the key words.

Vijay had shown them where the doctor's wife's body was, and the inspector's forensic team had exhuming it. It also mentioned that both the doctor and his boys had vanished and a suspicion that they had all run away, fearing that their own lives might be in danger from the vicious, murdering servant, who had initially escaped from the clutches of the police.

I sighed a sigh of relief, as perhaps I might not be a suspect anymore, but then I was puzzled by the disappearance of both the doctor and his sons, and neither did I understand the reasons for their disappearance. There was no mention of Neelu in the article, which I couldn't get my mind round either. Where was *she* then, I wondered?

Sid suddenly said he had to do a few things but would be back very soon and with that he disappeared out of the open door.

I lay back on my make-shift camp bed, four wooden crates and a smelly mattress and weighed up the options I now had. I was a little concerned about getting through the airport. I also had another pressing problem which was my tourist visa. It had almost run out and I knew I would have to make a move soon. Every hotel in Mumbai had to provide a register of foreign guests, with a valid visa entry for every foreign name and a passport number and the police were vigilant in its supervision. Overstaying on a visa is a serious offence in India. I knew that and if the police were still after me, a hotel would be the last place I could stay, but I was living off Sid's hospitality and had no money left.

Sid was capable of earning money as a middleman, a go-between, a thief and helping foreigners deal with black marketeers. It provided him with enough rupees to feed us all. Bhupi was paid for her work as a prostitute but after paying her pimp, usually had little left.

So, I was about to become an overstayer on my visa and would soon technically be guilty of a criminal offence.

Sid assured me that the police would see the lapsed visa as an oversight, and extend it without an enquiry, but I couldn't risk my freedom on that chance. I couldn't visit a police station without possibly being arrested anyway, so I couldn't alter my visa status.

I needed to get out of the country.

I remained on the bed, listening to the sounds of the slum that buzzed like the flies through the open door. The paanwalla, calling customers to taste his spicy products, the watermelon man, piercing the hot, humid morning with his plangent cry and music, always music. Did ever a people love music, I wondered more than the Indian?

I could hear both radio and live music and suddenly the sound of a group of men picking up the rhythm and starting to dance.

So many people had come from their villages to try and make money in the city.

A man can make his way in Mumbai with his heart and his soul crushed within a clenched fist, but to live in the slum he has to unfurl both his heart and soul, and try and see with his eyes, the life he has as if he were still in his village. Life is much harder here, in the stinking, ghetto like slums around Mumbai. Life in the slum puts a lie in the echo of every laugh, and at least a little larceny in every act of love.

Suddenly, Sid stepped through the door and behind him, Bhupi. I was so glad to see her and I clapped Sid on the back, smiling as I did, at Bhupinder, and we all walked out into the hot sun.

"Oh, Mr Peter!" Sid beamed, when our eyes met. "I am having some very good news for you! It is very important that we now are getting you out of the slum. We can be doing this as you are no longer a suspiciously person," he said as his huge smile got even bigger.

I was so pleased and shook hands with them both.

Just as quickly though, his smile evaporated. His gentle face was stamped with a sadness that invited sympathy. It was the kind of sadness that's a companion to uncompromising honesty. He suddenly realised that I would have to be leaving, both him and Bhupi and would no longer be part of his life. Thick brows hooded his intelligent, dark eyes. They stared at me, those knowing, mindful eyes.

I liked Sid very much and knew that I would miss him.

We talked for a while and we discussed ways of getting me to the airport, but before that, to the villa to pick up the remainder of my belongings and decide what had to be done with the painting.

We laughed together and I was inspired by their optimism and enthusiasm to help me. The slum was filthy and crowded beyond imagination, but for them it was freedom and there were no visas required to live there.

I now had to think and plan.

"I... well... thank you both. I accept your kind offer to help me get my things and then get on a plane back to England. I am very grateful, and I will repay you for your kindness and generosity."

"Not being a problem," Sid replied, shaking his head and my hand, and meeting my eye with a determined and penetrating stare, trying to remain unemotional.

I didn't know then that Sid and Bhupi had spent all their time scrapping together enough money for taxis to get us to the villa and to the airport. Nor did I know that they had been talking to the head man of the slum, to ensure I was protected.

In my ignorance and self-centredness, I'd initially recoiled at the thought of the terrible conditions of the slum, and had at first accepted their offer to stay, reluctantly.

"Okay, Mr Peter," Sid grinned, "day after tomorrow, we are to be taking a taxi and picking up your goodness self and then your many things from the doctor's villa."

"Thanks, Sid. Okay. But wait! Day after tomorrow – won't that be a little late? Can't we go tomorrow morning?" I said, a little lamely.

"My visa is only going to be valid for a few days more and I really need to try and arrange a flight as soon as possible. I have a return ticket, but I need to book a seat."

Sid dropped his gaze as Bhupi gently grasped my arm and nodded.

"We will go tomorrow, Mr Ianson."

I now realised that I was able to escape while they would remain as slum dwellers, still living in these squalid, squirming acres, where they could easily just – disappear. I knew that I could not let that happen. They had fallen far enough, as I saw it then, and my shame would keep me from them as completely and mercilessly as a prison wall.

chapter 25

The military police driver pulled up outside the villa. The shutters were closed, and the place was deserted.

He switched off the engine and watched the boys in his rear-view mirror take their cases out of the boot. Rohit tried to wrestle open the door. He was crying. In his agitation, he couldn't turn the door handle, and the door wouldn't open.

"Take it easy," Rakesh said, prizing his hands gently from the handle and holding them in his own.

"It's okay. Take it easy."

"Nothing's okay," he sobbed. "I don't know how we got into this mess. Daddy left us at the airport and mummy has left us for ever. Daddy cheated us, you know, and he and Neelu have got away with it. Now we are alone, and I am scared. I don't know what we are going to do Rakesh. They are going to kill us, both of us. I think the police are on their side too. Are we such bad boys?"

Rohit reached across to open the door. They stepped in and turned to wave at the driver. He waved back and started the car. They watched the glow of the rear lights disappear back down the driveway.

Rohit was trembling and sobbing on the doorstep and Rakesh held him in his little arms until he cried it out. He looked up into his brother's face. He couldn't see much as it was dark, but he saw that his brother's mouth was slack with exhaustion and fear, but his eyes were drawn to the distant moonlit horizon somewhere out to sea.

"We have each other, don't we?"

"Yes."

"That's good," he said dreamily, wistfully, looking away. His hands suddenly gripped his brother's arm as he held him.

"We'll start again. Starting tonight. We will stay here a little while and then we will go to Goa and find aunty Rupali. She sent a letter to us once, remember. She lives somewhere near the beach. In her letter she said she could see the ocean from her front door, like here."

"Okay, we will go there then and find her. Look for her and find her. That is our only hope, in the whole world and she will look after us and she will love us."

Pushing open the door, they entered hallway, switched on the lights, Rohit's tears, swarming with light, until they dissolved in the glittering, shining brightness from the chandelier.

His brother's words, *and she will love us,* passed like prayer-bead wishes on a thread of possibility as the happiness of being back home crashed around them.

When the light on that long night became the dawn, and the boys woke up from where they had collapsed, together on the sofa, Rakesh was the first to seek out some food in the kitchen and started boiling up some rice and lentils.

They talked about how to get to Goa and how they would cruise the beaches, from Calangute to Chapora. They would check every street, avoiding the local thugs and drug dealers, like Sid had taught them in the streets of Mumbai.

They knew there would be thieves and child snatchers, but they would just have to trust their luck. They would stop for tea or juice or a snack at the main beach restaurants, asking waiters and managers. As long as they spoke Marathi and Hindi, they would be sure to help.

They continued chatting easily as Rakesh found some cabbage leaves stuffed with potatoes, green beans and sliced up with ginger and aubergines. They found a jar of sour green chutney and crisp fried okra.

He brewed some coconut feni.

"Very Indian," said his brother. "Mummy would have been very proud."

Later that morning, before the sun got high and the heat built up, they took their bikes out beyond the villa walls and onto the road by the sea. Paddling, with their legs outstretched from their bikes, along the soft, sandy avenue between tall palms, they came to a small, empty house made from bamboo, coconut poles and palm leaves. It stood with a wide view of the dark blue sea. The floor was sand, and the boys pulled in and dropped their bikes. Rohit wanted the toilet and disappeared to the back of the hut. Like many toilets, it was nothing more than a smooth, steep slope behind the squatting keyhole. Waste matter rolled down the slope to the lane beyond for the wild pigs to eat.

Rakesh meanwhile walked down the beach, only a few paces from the hut, and sat on the dunes.

The sun was white hot and pinned like a medal to the chest of the sky. The heat rushed at him with every rolling wave to the shore, as if the bright light itself was pulling the waves one after another, relentlessly.

Rohit suddenly approached him, carrying two mangos.

Rakesh turned from the sea towards him as his brother dropped a mango into his lap, squatting to look into his eyes. He told him that they couldn't go to Goa.

Rakesh reacted with startled surprise as he bit into the delicious flesh, spitting out the skin onto the sand.

Rohit watched his brother eat and tried to resist, as his brother held him with his free hand when he attempted to stand.

Rakesh started to sing an old sad, and much-loved song from a Hindi movie.

Ye doonia, ye mehfil
Mere kam, ki nahi….

All the world, all its people
Mean nothing to me…

"Why can't we go to Goa, Rohit?" he then asked his little brother.

"We don't have any money, Rakesh, and I don't think I can cycle *that* far," he said, as the tears spilled out of his big brown eyes to wet the sand beneath his bowed and saddened head.

Being in India is like being in a land of myths and magic and miracles.

I needed a small miracle now as I climbed into the taxi with Sid and Bhupi as we headed off back to the villa the following morning.

As the taxi struggled through the usual madness that is Mumbai's traffic, I gazed out and thought about what had happened.

I have just a few more days here before I have to get back. I will have to arrange a flight before the week is out, I know.

My time in Mumbai was nearly over, although the reason for coming in the first place had been more than just a disaster. I still had to plan and possibly negotiate my exit from India and decide on the future of the painting.

The administration and accounting of the whole project was in tatters and I had no idea whether I would be ever likely to get paid any amount of money at all for what I had done so far, or whether the opposite, that I would end up having to pay for something I hadn't completed !

Although all my expenses had been settled for the feasibility studies, the planning and trip to Agra, I hadn't actually been paid a single rupee. Now all I had to do was to finish this final stage and get out.

I certainly didn't want to be here still, with the dry winter season approaching.

I had been worried absolutely sick; there had been no news of the whereabouts of Dr Singh and Neelu, only rumours and I didn't really know if the inspector and the police where still wanting to interview me, even as a formality.

Some of the rumours I heard, a few days ago, had made it worse. How is it possible that so much time can go by, so many questions asked about where they are, where the boys are and what is going to happen to Vijay, and yet still there are no answers.

How can people have been so cruel to have been part of a plan to take the lives of two innocent boys, let alone the murder of their mother.

I sat in the taxi, dreading the moment we arrived back at the villa. I was just as fearful for the health of the boys.

What had happened to them? Even if the news about them was the worst possible, the news that I have feared I would receive almost hourly since all this happened, would not that be better than this endless not knowing?.

I had lost weight. No bad thing, you might say. But I had looked at myself in a small mirror that Bhupinder had in the hut, and some of me had gone.

I seemed to have been evaporating with worry.

Today, for the first time, I feel a profound sense of relief. Or perhaps it's just a sense of release.

Finally, I can perhaps stop all this. I am hoping that I am out of danger now. I also hope that the boys are indeed safe. I don't know where they are but, but I feel sure they have reached somewhere where no one can harm them. I hope it's true. I believe it's true. I feel sure that when I return to the UK in a few days' time I will already know that the news will be good.

I closed my eyes and dreamed that I was back home, but as dreams never make sense, everything got mixed up in my mind and I opened my eyes with a start as the villa came into sight.

The brilliant morning sun was climbing over the hills and the sea. I opened the window to smell the ocean and inhale air rich with the aroma of spices, and the scent of flowers and fruits. It felt strange to be back and yet everything seemed calm and natural.

The despair I had sometimes felt over the last few days had, for the moment, quite gone from me.

Down in the village beyond the villa walls, I heard the familiar market noises. A distant busy hum, as I opened the taxi door and stepped out.

The front entrance of the villa was closed but unlocked and some windows and shutters were open. The three of us had climbed the steps and I entered the hallway slowly. I turned to see Sid and Bhupi staring at me impatiently in the doorway. As they followed me along the corridors of the villa, I grew sullener and more fearful with every step.

I led them to a room at the very end of a corridor.

The door was open.

The room was strewn with clothes, empty pots and pans and some recently used plates. The tangy smell of ginger filled the room.

Sid picked up a couple of items of clothing.

"These are belonging to the boys, I am thinking," he said, puzzled.

Bhupi was standing behind me, very still. I didn't understand any of it. I had no idea what was going on or why Sid had mentioned the boys' clothes. She reached out with one hand to touch me. The hand rested on my shoulder and pressed down with a little pressure. It was the tender, reassuring gesture she might have used to calm a frightened animal. She was staring into my eyes, but I wasn't sure if she was asking me or telling me something. She breathed deeply, quickly. Her brown eyes were almost black in the shadow of the room.

I put my hand on top of hers.

"I think the boys are here," she whispered gently and smiled.

"Come on," she said, "let's go find them."

I climbed the two flights of stairs to "my" room. There was still my suitcase and my few clothes and belongings and of course all my paints and brushes.

I stared at the half-finished canvas. The Taj Mahal without its family portrait added was, for me, unfinished business!!

I took the painting and carefully managed to carry it down the stairs to the hall and stood it up in one corner. Sid and Bhupi had been waiting there for me.

"It is a very handsome painting of our most sacred of monuments, Mr Peter, sir. You have been capturing its beauty most perfectly," Sid smiled and waggled his head.

He was such a wonderful and gentle soul and his kind words, I knew, were what he totally believed and truly felt.

"And I have to do something with it," I replied, trying to prompt a possible suggestion.

"Yes, you will," Bhupinder said, with a little laugh.

Her very dark beauty and her flashing smile made me laugh with her.

It was very obvious why Bhupi was one of the most popular girls in Mumbai's night scene and had many clients. She had an easy way with men and Sid was certainly crazy in love with her.

"I am sure that you could be leaving the picture here with the boys perhaps," she continued, still smiling.

"Or maybe with some other people who would appreciate it more," I ventured, staring at the pair of them, who were still grinning at me.

We were all still gazing at each other and the painting, when the front door suddenly swung open, letting the light and heat pour into the hall.

Standing staring at us were two little silhouettes. Their shadows twice as long as their bodies. Two bikes had been dropped and left where they had fallen, out on the driveway.

I clamped my open jaw shut, listening to the ruffle of air breathing in and out of my nose, until the patterns of breath matched those around me in the rhythmic rise and fall.

"And where is it that you have been?" Sid asked, like a scolding schoolteacher, his eyes wide open in disbelief.

"We are very sorry," a voice said from one of the silhouettes. "We will tell you everything."

Rohit started to cry again.

"Have you been out and misbehaving? Is that why you are crying?" he continued but with a twinkle in his eyes, as he furrowed his brow in pretend disapproval.

"If you must know," Rakesh said softly, his voice emptied of all its music and emotion, "we were on the beach talking about going to Goa to find our aunt, but we don't have any money for the bus or train and Rohit can't cycle that far."

I let the raining silence remain as Bhupi put her arms round both the boys and hugged them close.

I knew we would be able to listen to their story later, although I also knew the small daubs of colour that would be excluded from their sad and traumatic summary would be at least as important as the broad strokes they would include.

The devil they say, is in the details, and I knew well the devils that lurked and skulked in the details of their most terrible story.

Later, after some lunch, the boys gave us a hoard of new treasures.

I'd learned more about them and their family in that exhausted, murmuring hour than in all the many days before it. Brothers, sons and mothers find their way by such insights and confidences.

They are the stars used to navigate the oceans of family love. And the brightest of those stars are the heart breaks and sorrows.

They brought me their precious gift of their suffering. So, I took each moment of their sadness they confessed to us and pinned it to the sky.

They wept openly for their mother as Bhupi mopped at their tears with her scarf. They talked of the sickness they felt for their father. They talked a lot about hope and death and defiance. They had no idea what was going to happen to them, but they were determined that they would succeed in life and believed in their future. Rohit had stopped crying and fell asleep on Bhupinder's lap. I touched the soft surrendered curl of Rohit's tiny fingers to my lips while he slept, and I pledged my heart for ever.

chapter 26

Sid and Bhupi were both native to Mumbai and simply had no homes of their own, which is why they inhabited the slum. Many of the tradesmen were itinerant workers who followed where their skills were needed, and whose homes were hundreds of miles away in other states. The kinship fostered in workers' slums guaranteed a sense of unity, familial solidarity and loyalty to both the community and the companies they worked for at the time.

Sid had started like that. When he signed up he received one of the plots and a sum of money with which to buy bamboo poles, reed matting, hemp rope and maybe some scrap timber or a wooden pallet or two. Sid had built his own house. The sprawl of fragile huts spread across an area like a shallow, tender root system. Vast underground wells were sunk to provide water for the community. Rudimentary lanes and pathways were scraped flat and finally a tall, barbed wire fence erected around the perimeter to keep out squatters, but it didn't last long. Sid had built on the edge of the slum which had both benefits but also dangers.

Bhupi was initially one of the squatters, squeezing through the new holes that appeared in the fence on a daily basis. She used the slum dwellers, as her clients initially, one of them being Sid. The companies tried to discourage contact between the workers and squatters, but the people thought of themselves as one group; their days and dreams and hopes were entangled in the ravel of ghetto life.

To workers and squatters alike, the company fence was like all fences; arbitrary and irrelevant.

The friendship between Sid and Bhupi flourished and an arrangement of love, and freedom to work developed.

"This is a special day," Sid said, smiling at Bhupi and me, with the boys asleep between us.

"To be seeing the boys safe and well and at home, it is indeed a special day."

He looked at Bhupi again and then dropped his gaze.

"It would be so good if we could be looking after these children," he continued, "but we are not people and we don't have a house, where we are not living."

"The slum doesn't have a schooling place, not even a temporary one, so the boys won't be learning."

"One day the slum will be cleared, then all will be gone," Bhupinder added, turning to sweep the room we were all sitting in, with her sad gaze.

"But today's a big day for the boys, no?" Sid sat up with a coat hanger smile on his young dirty face.

Then suddenly, I had a brain wave.

Suddenly it came to me. Everything seemed so easy now.

I knew what I had to do. The thunderbolt had struck !

"You can have the painting," I cried out as the boys stirred.

"I will give you and Bhupi the painting. We can sell it here in Mumbai and you can have the money and maybe with the profit, buy a house, or at least rent a decent place and..."

Sid's smile disappeared quickly. I wasn't sure what had upset him, but his frown appeared, and he didn't look at all happy.

"What's the matter?"

Sid waggled his head, but not with agreement.

"I can't be taking this picture, Mr Peter. It is not for the likes of me to be making benefits for something that is so beautiful but is not mine."

"Rubbish," I exclaimed. "It is my painting. Dr Singh isn't going to want it and besides, it's not what I was commissioned to paint.

The boys sat up and rubbed their eyes as I sat in the middle of them all, not really knowing what I was or should say.

I looked at both the children and saw their sadness and despair.

"I just want to say how dreadfully, dreadfully sorry I am for you when I heard the news about your mother. I must thank you, Sid and Bhupi, for saving and looking after them so well. You didn't have to do that. I also know that you both have been worried for your own safety and wellbeing, living in the slum.

"When I was accused of kidnapping them, I realised how terrifying it must have been for the boys. When Sid brought you back here that somehow you knew something terrible might have happened to your mother, I was very upset," I took a breath and pressed on.

"What a bitter blow for you then to receive the news that you did. It must be awful that you know for certain what has happened. You all must be brave and not hesitate to turn to friends and family for whatever comfort and succour they can give. Perhaps you can all rest, while I try and sort out what to do, because I am going to try and help you, all of you," I said, realising now what needed to be done. I looked at the boys' faces and then at Sid's.

"I will try and get you to your family in Goa and I want to help you, Sid and Bhupi, to get out of the slum."

I hadn't finished when Rakesh interrupted me.

"Maybe Sid and Bhupi could live here, with us," he said, his eyes as wide as his smile. "We can look after them and we can grow vegetables in the garden," he continued with amazing enthusiasm.

"And grow goats too?" Rohit interjected, grabbing hold of Sid's arm.

"You don't grow goats, stupid," was his brother's reply, and we all laughed.

"All I want you to know is that I will do as much as I can to help, now and in the future. Sid, I think a great deal of you. You are not only a life saver but now a dear friend to me and I think the boys too."

Rakesh stood at my side, but the smile had gone.

"I can't sleep. I can hardly eat. We both cry all the time. I know we are being pathetic, and daddy would be angry, but we can't help it. We know thousands of children are going through, or have gone through, what we are now experiencing. It doesn't make much difference to us loosing mummy," he dropped his head and sat beside me and then hugged his brother.

Later on, as the dusk was falling and the walls of the prison turned violet, Vijay was taken from his cell. In the endless chill of stone and bars, of vertical cliff like expanses and holes for windows, they brought him, chained. He was bruised and battered as the inspector greeted him at the big oak doors. His face was pale, his eyes red, and his mouth set in a bitter, miserable twist.

He said, "I hope you will be more compliant now."

"I have been," he said, "in every way I have told you that I killed the lady, and I am sorry, but that man is as guilty as me. He promised me my freedom."

"Let's be objective about this, Vijay. You have confessed to everything. The doctor and his friend are nowhere to be found. From a police investigation point of view, the big question is what will happen to you, now that you are a confessed murderer, and on top all this, you still haven't helped me find the doctor and his friend."

Vijay stared at him for a long time without speaking. Behind the inspector, he saw the security guards brandishing their long batons.

"I'll tell you what will happen," the inspector said. "You are finished. You are dead. You should have known this would happen. You should have known that you would take the blame, if what you say is true of course."

Vijay began to sob. The inspector reached out to touch his arm to comfort him but retracted it almost as quickly.

"You've killed an innocent woman and you've ruined the lives of two boys at the same time, having nearly killed them too. And all you can think of is blaming your bloody master."

He turned away and Vijay was dragged behind him into the interrogation room through a side entrance by the prison gates.

A terrible silence hung over the room. Vijay stared straight ahead at the floor where it met the bare stone wall.

"You are going to die," the inspector repeated over and over into a silence that was thickening around Vijay and seeming to press in upon his burning eyes.

"Tell me everything, again."

He waded through the past events, his eyes blazing recollections, and then he shook himself back into the moment once he had finished.

"It is late. Here, I want to give you a chance. A chance at having your freedom, the freedom that you say you were promised. Well this time, I am going to offer you that same promise of freedom."

He opened the desk drawer to reveal a pistol, a single magazine and a box of ammunition.

"This is a Stechkin APS pistol," he said, taking up the weapon. He took out a single bullet from the box and put it in the magazine, which he inserted into the pistol. He checked to make sure that there was nothing in the chamber and placed it on the desk far enough away, out of Vijay's reach.

"You can fire it as a single shot and do the honourable thing. It is not the best gun in the world, but it will do the job if you aim it right."

With that, the inspector stood up and left the room, taking the guards with him before closing and locking the door. Vijay leant across the table and slowly lifted the heavy piece of metal, feeling its coldness in his grip, he slipped his finger against the trigger.

He stared at the gun in his hand and raised it to his temple.

Chapter 27

On that same night, the swollen, flattened, yellow moon, known in the slum as the grieving moon, hovered hypnotically full, above the villa. There was a breeze from the sea, but the air was warm and humid... Swarms of bats were flying overhead, along the line of the electrical wires leading from the villa to the village - thousands of them, like notes on a sheet of music.

The brothers, awake past their bedtime and threading jasmine flowers with Bhupi as presents, came up to me and gave me a garland that they had just finished tying up. I slipped it over my head and they both laughed and ran back to Bhupi, singing the chorus of a song from a popular Hindi movie. Sid and Bhupi both joined in. I watched them and smiled, happy to see them all together.

There is no act of faith more beautiful than the generosity of the young and the poor. Both those sets of people were sitting, in the evening warmth, opposite me tonight.

Sid was quietly talking to them. I had the impression just then that he probably never raised his voice above that softness when talking to the boys.

"You talk very gently to the boys," I said when Sid looked across at me. I was genuinely impressed by his engagement with them and the way he was expressing himself. The response from the brothers was one of smiling agreement with whatever it was he had been discussing with them.

"No, not always with them, especially if they are misbehaving, just like the naughtiest of young boys," he said, wobbling his head and trying to look serious. The light in his big brown eyes told a different story though.

I waited for more, and he hesitated, looking out over the sea, but when he spoke again it was to change the subject.

"Tell me, Mr Peter, did you have a good father when you were growing up?"

"I did, Sid, yes," I said, a little surprised at the question. "Every child should have a good father, don't you agree, Sid?" I waited a second and continued only when he dropped his head.

"Even if a person didn't have a good father himself, it doesn't mean that he can't be one for some other child," I said deliberately quietly and slowly, hoping that he would understand my meaning.

"I am thinking…" he turned to stare into my eyes, and I felt my scalp tightening with an uncomfortable dread. "I am thinking I could be a good enough father, if I am being given the chance, maybe?"

My heart suddenly jumped, and I sighed noticeably as I heard his words.

The two boys smiled up at him and Bhupinder slipped the remaining garland of jasmine flowers the boys had made, over each of their heads.

Sid had saved the life of the two boys.

It had had a profound effect on them and suddenly I realised perhaps more so on him.

I smiled and put my hand on his shoulder and told him just how much that had meant to everyone concerned.

"You will have to be paying me and Bhupi lots of rupees to be looking after these two tigers," he said, loudly and they all laughed again.

I remembered the first time I heard him laugh out loud, in the alley way in Mumbai and often after that in the hut in the slum.

It was a good laugh, guileless and completely unselfconscious, and I knew why I liked him so much.

"We are having a saying in India. *Sometimes the tigers must roar, just to remind the oxen of their fear.*"

I wasn't sure whether that was indeed an old Indian saying, but it certainly fitted the situation tonight. The message was very clear. He was the oxen, but the boys were the tigers and perhaps they had had a little roar in the past, but I think the oxen didn't really mind.

The following morning, I rose early and spent an hour or so as the light broke through the shutters, preparing the painting. Although it wasn't complete as initially intended, I had painted in the rill as foreground and so it was finished as far as possible to enable it to be sold. I made it ready to be moved, although I still needed to varnish it.

Sid found me and came to stand alongside me to look at the canvas. I put my arm around his shoulder, and he grinned and wobbled his head.

"It is indeed very fine, Mr Peter, but looking rather strange without the including of the family," he mused. "You are going to be making a friendship with Shafiq?" Sid said as he stood back and folded his slender arms, still admiring the painting. "This is a good thing. He will be able and very much willing to purchase such a fine piece."

Sid said this with seeming knowledge and yet we hadn't even met the chap having just called him on the phone the night before, let alone got to the point of any agreement regarding its purchase.

The taxi we had booked arrived late, as expected.

We both carried the painting towards the car as the driver popped the boot open. I had wrapped it in an old camel hair blanket, and we placed it sideways in the boot. It only just fitted the meagre space.

We set off and as the taxi reached the Mumbai City highway, I thought about what Sid had said.

I found myself thinking that, for all the differences between us, there just might be some perceptive truth in the young man's observations.

The taxi drove on for almost a couple of hours.

It slowed, at last, on the outskirts of Mumbai, in a street of shops and warehouses, and then bumped into the entrance to a narrow lane.

The street was deserted, as was the lane. When the car door opened, I could hear music and singing.

"Come, Mr Peter, we are going," Sid said, feeling no compulsion to tell me where we were going.

The taxi driver remained with the car, leaning against the bonnet and finally allowing himself the luxury of unwrapping the garlic nan that had been sitting *warming* on the front seat.

As I walked with Sid, down the lane, I realised that he hadn't spoken a single word, and I wondered at the long silences so many Indian people practiced in this crowded, noisy city.

We passed through a wide stone arch, along a corridor and after climbing a flight of stairs, we entered a vast room filled with paintings, smoke, and clamorous music. It was a long room, hung with faded purple silks and aging carpets. At the far end there was a small, raised stage where a large, dark figure sat on silk cushions. A pale pink, bell-shaped lantern was suspended from the wooden ceiling which cast trembling hoops of golden light.

We stopped and stood still, both looking at a grey-haired man sitting very upright in the back of that darkened room.

Shafiq and I looked at one another as I presented the painting, slipping off the blanket.

At first glance, he didn't seem to be at all impressed. Sid stared from one to the other of us with a puzzled frown, and was genuinely bewildered by our lack of acknowledgment, that we both said hello at the same time.

A small servant in Afghan pants came in and moved round us and served Shafiq with black tea in a long glass. A table next to Shafiq had some books on it and a hookah pipe, pearling the air with a thin blue line of smoke and the perfume of charras.

He didn't rise to greet us, but acknowledged Sid with a nod but said, not a word. Shafiq was a short man, plumply buttoned into a Kashmiri vest that was too long for him. The white lace cap of a hajji, one who'd made the pilgrimage to Mecca, covered his grey head. He shouted instructions, and at once the servant came back in and brought an extra table and some cushions, setting them up below the stage at Shafiq's feet.

Sid and I sat cross legged. The servant brought us a bowl of popped rice, sharply spiced with chilli powder, and a platter of mixed nuts and dried fruits. He then poured black tea from a narrow-spouted kettle through a metre of air without spilling a drop, placing the tea before us and then offered us warm sweet milk. I was about to accept some, but Shafiq stopped me.

"Come, Mr Ianson," he smiled, "we are drinking real north west country tea, isn't it?"

He sipped the tea, endowing his little custom with a peculiar dignity and solemnity, as in fact he did with every expression. He appeared to be quite imperial sitting on his throne of cushions, although deep down he wasn't a man I was so willing to admire or trust.

Suddenly Shafiq stood up and crossed the room to the painting.

You could hardly see it in the poorly lit space. He stared at it, looking closely at every inch.

"How do you like the painting, Shafiq?" I asked him.

"I am liking it very much. It's incredible. Amazing. I have never seen anything like it. There is so much beauty in it and so much power as well. Was it difficult to paint?"

"Yes, it was, under the circumstances."

"What circumstances are those?" he enquired and smiled.

The smile was both knowing and unnerving. I wasn't sure how much Sid had already told him, but his plump twisted lips told me more than was wise.

He leaned across to rest his hand on my forearm. It was damp and cold.

Throughout the city, people touched one another often during their conversations, emphasising the points they made with a gentle squeeze of pressure. I knew and liked the gesture well from daily contact with people in the slum, but on this occasion, I didn't.

"I didn't have time to complete the original brief and so it is something that I would like to sell while here in India, as I am sure the image of the mausoleum, India's greatest marble monument, would be much sort after and fetch an excellent price."

He nodded, saying nothing, but his silence prompted me to speak again.

"You are a man of good taste?" I asked, not sure how convincing I was.

"I believe that I am being so," he replied.

"I believe that you are too," I declared, smiling now. "I think you either *have* good taste or you do not."

"Well," he laughed, "I certainly know a good painting when I see one, and frankly I am inclined to think this is one of the most excellent paintings of the Taj Mahal that I have come across."

"Oh, of course, naturally, I will be needing to find the right customer and that person might not be in Mumbai, so the costs for me might be considerable. I am sure you will be understanding these things."

He was staring at me intently, his sweaty hand still resting coldly on my arm.

Be careful, I thought. *You are falling into a dangerous bargaining discussion with a man who's used to making good deals - for himself. He's testing you. It's a test and the water's deep.*

"Let me get this straight - you're saying that the painting is excellent, will sell well, but you will have some expenses. Well of course," I said, pushing a canoe of thought out into the uncharted water of his devious thinking.

"That is absolutely, correctly right."

"So, will you be offering me a price then, Shafiq, that is good for us both?"

"Precisely, I will!" he said, smiling more widely. "I am delighted that you understand."

"I can *say* those words," I answered, laughing to match his smile, "but that doesn't mean I *understand* them."

"Let me be putting it another way. There may be agents involved and much travelling and perhaps gallery fees. Then there will be multiple phone calls and paper workings and inviting prospective buyers and maybe more. Now do you understand?"

"Not really. It seems to me that you are suggesting that what I will receive will be very little in comparison to what the painting will be sold for."

"Are you suggesting I am making the lie and trying to give you a poor deal?" He said with a flash of real hatred in the gold-flecked amber of his eyes. His hand finally left my arm.

"Yes, I am, exactly," I said, looking deep into the gold-flecked amber.

"I have not said," he recoiled with a sudden look of uncertainty.

"What I am saying is that there has to be reality - and I indeed see it. I am now feeling that reality with all my heart. There is a way of reducing those costs I am being sure," he said without the smile.

"Let's start again. You know the real costs, you know the truth, all you have to do is tell me what it is," I said with a determination I never knew I had. "It's that easy!" I laughed.

My canoe of thought was floating still, and I wasn't ready to bail out, not ever.

"Perhaps," he replied, accepting my push back with tolerant equanimity. "I can offer you a much more reasonable price, than I first thought. A very real and true price, I am sure of it."

While Sid and I were driving back to the villa in the taxi, I was thinking about the money that Shafiq had agreed to pay me for the painting. I turned to Sid, who was dozing next to me.

"I was just thinking, it was a good price, wasn't it, Sid?" I said, waking him.

"That's funny, I was thinking this very same thing," he said quietly. "I was thinking too, about how pleased the brothers will be. Not having their mother, they will be needing the money that you said will be for them," he said and paused for a while. "I have no brother. I am only one person. One person is a sadness, isn't it?"

I couldn't answer him directly, but he needed a response.

"I was also thinking that perhaps you would look after the brothers for me. You could be a brother to them then or even perhaps a *father* maybe. Perhaps with Bhupi, you could all be one family and you would all share the money."

"Maybe we can," he said quietly and smiled.

"I have decided to be liking you very much, Mr Peter."

He said all this with such solemnity, despite the smile, that I had to laugh.

"So that's a yes then?" I said, and he wobbled his head in agreement.

"Well, I guess in that case you'd better stop calling me *Mr Peter*. It gives me the heebie-jeebies, anyway."

"Jeebies?" he asked, earnestly. "It is belonging to an Indian word?"

"Don't worry about it. Just call me Peter."

"Okay, I will call you Peter. I will call you Peter *brother*. And you will keep calling me Sid, isn't it so?"

"I guess it is, yes," I said, closed my eyes and rested my head on the back of the car seat.

Chapter 28

When I got back to the UK, I seemed to have become a non-person, like Sid had, at one time. I found myself in a cold and wet Sussex with no one to discuss the ongoing events in India. The painting had been sold before I reached England and I was so glad that the benefits of the sale would now help Sid and Bhupinder stay at the villa and look after the boys.

Dr Singh and Neelu, I learnt later, had been arrested in the Seychelles, but I had found out little more than that.

I knew that my involvement there was over. I believed that they would all have a better life.

I received a letter from Rakesh, with a little addition at the bottom from Rohit and a few strange and badly spelt, but heart felt words from Sid. The boys had obviously been trying to teach him to write - English. The letter thanked me for all I had done for them. A small water mark had blurred a word or two and my sentimental side hoped it might have been a tear, but I think actually, it was only a spilt drop of water maybe.

I wanted to pick up the threads and start painting again and decided I needed to move on from what had happened in India, but I did read the letter again, several times.

"So that's it, then?" I spoke out loud to myself.

I shrugged my shoulders and realised that my life certainly did need to move forwards again.

I looked out over the shingle beaches from the study in my small cottage, the wind rattling the old wooden frames and wondered.

I was grateful for the experience in India, while it lasted, of course I was, but I knew it couldn't have gone on for ever. What I hadn't bargained for was what had happened to me and those who I had spent some frightening and yet exhilarating times with.

I phoned Elizabeth. She was resigned to our new "partnership" and it was obvious our separation was probably going to be permanent. She was staying with friends in Surrey and vague about her plans.

"I'm so glad you had a good time, if only for a few weeks. You must never let anyone take that away from you. You must treasure that. But I am afraid that we are not destined to be together, Peter."

"Are you going to come and see me?" I asked.

"I haven't any particular plans. I'm not spending much time socialising up here, but my work is going really well up in London, and my friends seem happy for me to stay as long as I want. Although I don't mind the commute, I'm getting my own flat on a road around the corner from them. You know, the sun shines most of the time and the woodlands and walks here are so wonderful, and no one bothers me. It's what I need. For now, I just want to be quiet and get on with my career."

"Will I see you in your new flat?" I asked. I hadn't meant to ask any such thing. I had no right to.

"I don't know, Peter. I don't know. We'll just have to see what happens, but I doubt it."

I heard some weeks later that she had moved into a brand new, expensive apartment in Esher and was seeing a local property developer.

The following day I picked up a voicemail from the police inspector in India, saying "You are no longer a suspect in the murder of the doctor's wife", or something along those lines, but then I heard him mention something about her children before the line broke up and he hung up so I didn't think about it any further. But maybe he would have tried to stop me from leaving Mumbai and also have still tried to implicate me in some way. I don't know that I would have gone back there anyway.

I also heard from an old friend that day, a teacher and in the end I did find a job.

It's not really a teaching job. It's painting work, and the pay is what you might call minimal and I didn't get any more commissions.

The good times that I thought I was entering never materialised, after all.

I am working with terminal cancer patients in a hospice in Chichester. My job is to help those who have had treatment to come to terms with their situation, by teaching them to draw and paint water colours. The idea is to ensure that they can see some future in their lives ahead, for whatever time they have remaining, even if they don't have much of that time left.

I like the work. It's very interesting and often quite hard, emotionally.

It leaves me with plenty of time to think. Thinking is what I do most days now.

I never talk to anyone about the painting of the Taj Mahal commission.

The painting acquired a degree of notoriety in the press after its sale. It was linked to the both the death of Dr Singh's wife and the strange disappearance of the prime suspect. There had been little appreciation in the art world in India, but in the villa by the sea in Mumbai, they bizarrely remained very proud of their connection with it.

It was announced in the Mumbai newspapers, that perhaps one day the artist would return to finish it, but that it hadn't happened yet.

Looking back to the days when Mahima died and the boys were saved, I know now that I was in shock, and those terrible events had not hit me.

There was just too much happening. I couldn't take it all in at the time.

Since then I have both grieved for her and also celebrated for the boys and their new "parents" and now as I sit and silently draw, with a patient at the hospice, I have conversations with the boys, which are more than imaginary.

I hear them say to me, from somewhere behind my right shoulder, "Yes, Mr Peter, you did it for us. We thank you for the painting and we thank you for our new lives."

I hear the smile in Sid's voice and laughter from the children, although I cannot see it. "I am thanking you for helping us out of the slum, for making me a father, for giving us a family life."

I put down the pencil as my pupil continues her drawing, and say, "I am glad."

And fainter than the smothered laughter of the boys in the distant rose garden, comes the reply: "Thanking you so very much, that we are having so much happiness."

So, I teach at the hospice, and at night I sit in my studio near Elmer Sands, looking at the sea.

I sit and I think.

I don't know what it is that I think about although I still think about the painting of the Taj Mahal.

I try not to do that too often. That awakens memories I would rather not have.

Sometimes I think about Sid and wish I could speak to him. There is no point trying to email him, although perhaps I could through Rakesh. They are part of another life now.

I have spoken to Elizabeth once or twice. She is working hard and spending time with her new man. I'm not sure it's the relationship that she was expecting. I think it has been more of a sideways relationship move.

We all have our disappointments in life.

I also, often paint in the evenings. I can't get a decent television signal where I live, and I don't want to pay for satellite TV. I don't miss it. I never watched it much anyway.

So, I paint. I paint anything and everything, and at weekends I walk the streets of Arundel and Chichester, my nearest towns and sketch what I see. In the centre of these places I find the great monuments and the stone statues, the wonderful houses and little streets. The places and things that I rather like. I sketch and paint them. They are sacred places, but I always make sure that in front of them is a family or mother with her children, and so I paint them in too.

I like that. Don't you?

about the author

David I Brown was born in 1953 and was educated in Harrogate, Yorkshire and then London. He spent his early career working for large global manufacturing businesses, which took him to many places around the world. Later, he started his own consultancy in risk management, continuing to travel widely.

His business and travel helped him keep focused when, in middle age, he discovered he had a life-threatening cancer, which drove him to write his first ever book, a memoir. He then wrote his first short novel, which is much lighter and amusing. It was such a joy writing it, he explained, as it enabled him to express his earlier adventures and embellish his thoughts about some of the characters he met whilst travelling.

He has been married to Grace since 1981, has three grown-up daughters and is now a retired grandfather, with three adorable grandchildren He and his wife live in Buckinghamshire, England, spending time at their seaside retreat on the West Sussex coast and travelling further afield whenever possible.

cover image

The cover of this book was developed from one of the author's own photographs, taken on one of his many trips to India and the Taj Mahal, a place that he loves and one that is very dear to his heart. His passion for oil painting, that he also spends many hours trying to perfect, provided the ideal work environment for his main character.

Printed in Great Britain
by Amazon